THREE SILVER RINGS

To those who keep everything in mind... it's not
wrong to feel with your heart sometimes, for you are human.

THREE SILVER RINGS

SPIN-OFF OF THE ILLUMIVERSE SERIES

GUADALUPE GONZALEZ

SIGN UP FOR MY AUTHOR NEWSLETTER
AND VISIT THE ILLUMINATED WORLD

Be the first to learn about Guadalupe Gonzalez's new releases
and receive exclusive content for both readers and writers!

For bonus content, merch, and a golden ticket to the worlds
of the Illuminators visit:

WWW.ILLUMIVERSE.STORE

Illuminators

Powerchart

EARTHKALAIS (ORDER OF ELEMENTS)

FIRE (Flamers) = Mercury
Manipulates fire
ICE (Flakers) = Venus
Manipulates ice
WATER (Liquis) = Earth
Manipulates water
AIR (Aires) = Mars
Manipulates air

JOVIANKALAIS (ORDER OF SCIENCE)

BIOLOGY (Bios) = Jupiter
Controls and manipulates biological matter
PHYSICS (Physicists) = Saturn
Controls and alters metal-related matter
CHEMISTRY (Chems) = Neptune
Controls and creates chemical matter
ARCHITECTURE (Archs) = Uranus
Controls and creates architecture techniques

CELESTIALKALAIS (ORDER OF THE MIND)

MEMORY (Eidetics) = Pluto
MIND HEALING (Menders) = Ceres
ILLUSIONS (Illusionaries) = Eris
PROTECTING (Protectors) = Make Make
INVISIBILITY (Invisibles) = Haumea

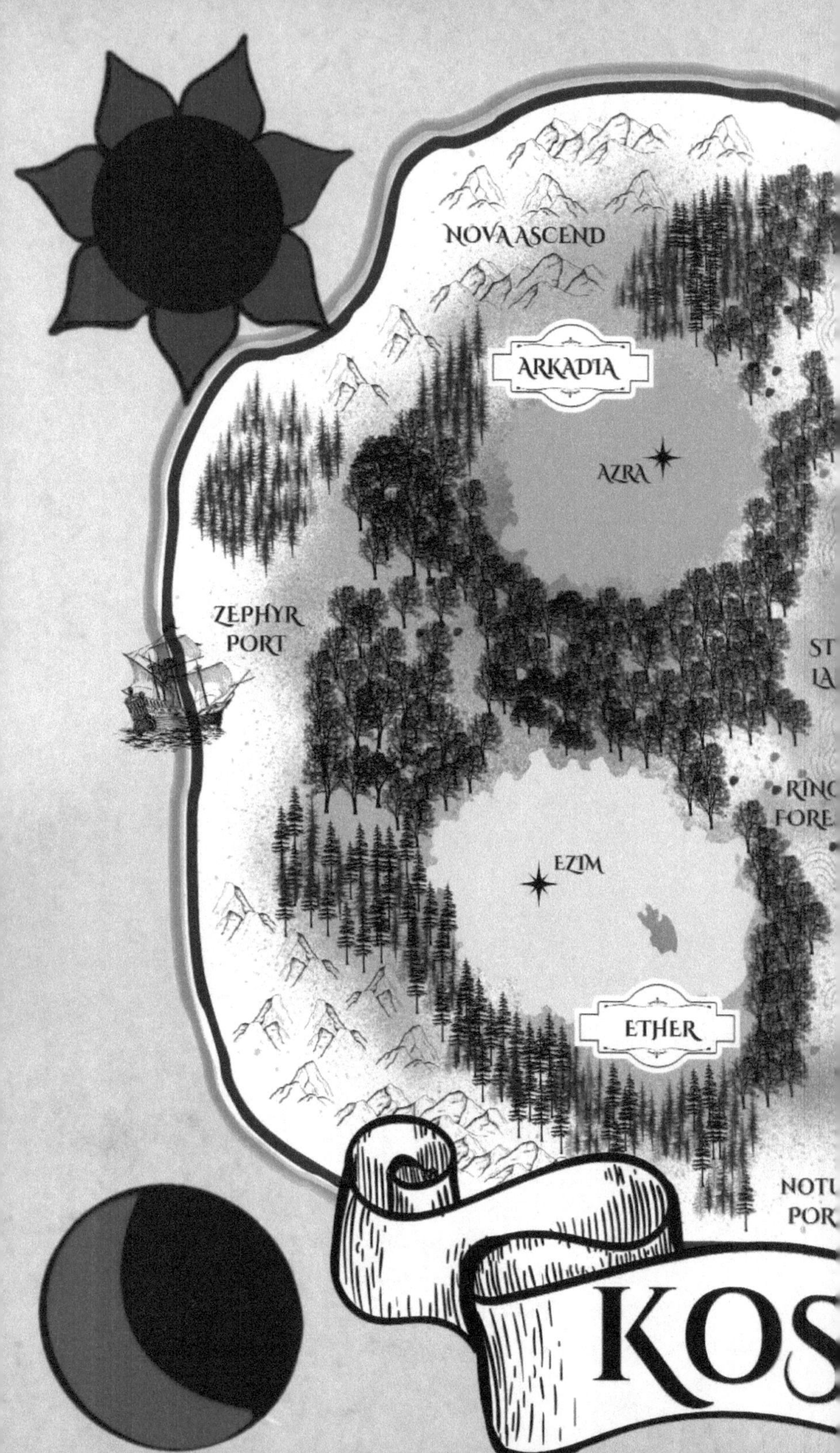

NOVA ASCEND
ARKADIA
AZRA
ZEPHYR PORT
ST
LA
RING
FORE
EZIM
ETHER
NOTU
POR
KOS

REAS
ORT
SOLAR CASTLE
STELLAR CASTLE
LUNAR CASTLE
PLANETARIUM
CONSERVATORY
OBSERVATORY
N
W
S
E
MOS

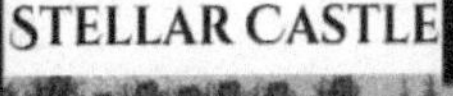

PART ONE

ENEMY

CHAPTER I
CITY OF ARGENTI

K*EEP YOUR FRIENDS CLOSE, but your enemies closer* was Adrik Montova's motto. Except he had no friends, but a long list of enemies and cowards who were of no account. There was no witch, Illuminator, or light-blood in the city of Arkadia, Kosmos, that did not know his name. Running around, doing errands, or heists for his benefit. Or that's what everyone believed.

His partner and only one-hundredth of a friend, Franko Sezin, called him an outlaw for his heinous strategies. *If misery were a person, that would be you, Adrik.* He told him after Adrik had come back once again with blood in his hands. Blood that was not his. But Adrik paid him well, and he managed Adrik's barbaric and mysterious plans.

Adrik disliked, to an extent, every single day of his old life. Almost hated it because he remembered it so well. But today was different, and he felt it the moment he looked in the mirror, ignoring the barely visible scar under his left eye, with his new, clean black clothes. He neatly placed his brown caramel hair back into place and buttoned up the silver buttons of his long coat. Anyone could have mistaken him for a high official of Kosmos, except that the back of his coat was empty, with no Sun or Moon design. Before he walked out of the messy wooden room, he looked at his right hand, making sure that over his black gloves stood three silver rings. When he looked twice, he headed out, closing the brown, creaky, and almost fallen door behind him.

He passed Franko's partially organized room in the hallway and almost frowned at the open box stashed with empty sandwich bags in the doorway. The double doors past the room were closed. Noises of metal clashing into each other had resonated around the small residence last night. At least Franko was keeping himself busy creating science experiments and making tech. The wooden stairs creaked with each step Adrik took towards the dull light of the dark first floor.

"Yes, every bomb here is very well handmade by me, it—" Franko stood over the counter, talking to a customer. The man stood in front of him, inspecting a grenade until he turned and saw the silhouette of Adrik appearing in the shadows. He shook his head frantically.

"You work with..."

"It's *not* what it looks like," Franko said immediately, but the customer was already out of the store in a second.

"If you could only listen to what I say, I would've been rich already," Franko said, shaking his head at Adrik. Indeed, he was right, after seeing Adrik inside Franko's tech store, most customers would run away, afraid to be inside the room of a merciless person. Adrik didn't say anything, not because he felt bad, but because he truly didn't care what people thought of him, as long as it meant that nothing would be in his way. And to be known as a bad guy deleted all potential distractions that could hurt his overall plan.

"I thought you would be in Ether by now," Adrik said, walking towards Franko, who shook his head, looking at his bronze pocket watch.

"No, I've decided to stay and go the day after tomorrow. I have customers to find. Are you going out again?" Franko frowned. "It's been three days since you've been free from the bloody job, and your plan is to walk around the city?" Adrik didn't answer and instead continued his way towards the exit of the store and into the bright light. Franko followed behind him, locking the door of the store before Adrik could take another step without him.

The streets of Arkadia filled immensely as the seconds passed by. Not even the Moon itself could silence the chaotic city. Whether day or night, hot or cold, people would be inside and outside their homes. Some were barely able to stand the resources of life, while others had given up and walked the streets like daily tourists. Not that there were many tourists anyway.

Adrik saw most people and recognized most, especially the ones who named the streets their home. But he didn't look at them, and they didn't either as he walked through the crowded street. Franko walked next to him at once, watching people struggling and hurrying to their excruciating jobs.

"There's nothing in Arkadia to do but to watch, learn, and scheme," Adrik replied a few seconds later, analyzing the people around him.

"This is you watching?" Franko said. "For three days..."

"No. This is me calculating."

Franko frowned, wondering what in the universe Adrik meant.

"Certainly, no surprise," he answered anyway.

Since he met him, he knew how bonkers Adrik was. He was incredibly smart, but he was a little twisted. Yet he never knew the whole story about him, so he never judged. He knew of the rumors. What people said about him being a heartless person. At first, he didn't believe them. However, after living with him for almost a year and probably being the only person in the whole world to somewhat know Adrik, now he wasn't entirely sure. Yet, he wasn't scared of him. Instead, he was inspired.

They walked through the busy streets, taking a left turn onto the main street towards the center of the city. People quickly got out of the way at the sight of Adrik. He could easily pass up for one of the youngest and most respected kings, if Kosmos were structured as a monarchy. An abundance of stares followed him. His black coat swung behind him so gracefully. But the moment Adrik glanced their way, they would look away faster than the speed of light as if Adrik's hazel-gray eyes could kill in a millisecond. As if they hadn't heard about the most fearful person in the whole country of Kosmos—Kaan Kostov from Stellar Court.

"Montova!" Someone screamed from within the crowds of people and appeared in front of Adrik. "I know you heard me, Adrik," the man standing in front of him said. Adrik recognized him in a second. He had met the man before while he worked for Craven. Franko had only heard of him.

"And you are?" Franko, being naturally friendly and trying to make a quick conversation, asked.

"Carlos. Partner of Craven, who you must know..." Carlos held out his hand for a handshake. Looking at Adrik, Franko ignored him. He could tell Adrik was dying of annoyance, which he was at the sight of Craven's new and shiny pet.

"What do you want?" Adrik asked at once. Carlos's hand dropped back beside him.

"Alright. I'll get to the point," Carlos said. "I'm interested in your work... You know..."

"Torturing people? For money?" Adrik said, glaring at Carlos. "I just got freedom from Craven. I won't work for anyone but myself."

Adrik continued walking ahead. Not giving up, Carlos took a step slowly towards him.

"I'm not your enemy, Adrik," he affirmed.

"If you are not my enemy, then who are you?"

Carlos was taken aback for one second. "*I*... could be your ally."

"You work for Craven. You will never be my ally. Even if you didn't, that will not happen." With that, Adrik walked away, leaving Carlos with no other words or plans that could help him get someone who would do his dirty work.

"By the way, mate... just because we have ears doesn't mean we want to hear you," Franko said, turning around for two seconds to look at Carlos' crooked silhouette. If it wasn't for Franko, Adrik thought, his days would have been extremely boring. However, he just turned to look at him, shook his head, and kept walking. And he *never* smiled.

That was the only thing Franko couldn't understand. *How does someone spend one year or more without fully smiling?* Even Adrik himself wondered if he had forgotten to laugh or if he ever would.

But Franko had one future goal and one goal only. He knew and hoped that one day Adrik would show any emotion of good faith and that he'll be there to see it... *Well, that would be the goal besides becoming rich, making bombs, eating thousands of sandwiches, and owning a zoo.* Franko thought. Unlike Adrik, Franko's head was filled with wild, rich dreams.

Getting to Azra, the capital of Arkadia, was a piece of cake for Adrik (not that he even liked cake or any sweet dessert). There was not an inch of the city that he did not know, just like the city knew him so well. No hidden place that he could not find after he had been ordered to go around doing work for Craven for years since he was young.

It was the famous city of Ether that he did not know at all. Only by Franko's mere visits to the City of Aurum and hazy memories had he heard stories about how beautiful the city was. Completely the opposite of Arkadia. Ether was filled with gold, both modern and vintage resources, and *peace*... things that were certainly not in Arkadia.

Chaos stood before Adrik and Franko. Downtown was filled with groups of people screaming from the bottom of the black, almost broken stage.

"What is a high official doing in Arkadia?" Franko asked, seeing the high official witch slowly getting up onto the stage. His face frowned here and there as he looked down at the cracked wood and up at the defeated, angry faces.

"Must be extremely important. They can barely step three feet into the city," Adrik responded, examining the high official, whose face was filled with confusion and disgust.

The high official was indeed disgusted and annoyed. He couldn't believe he had been sent to give a message to the lost city by Stellar Court. Worse, he couldn't believe the Court hadn't done anything about the place yet. He looked at the time on his shiny gold watch and up at most of the people who wore only jewelry made from strings. For a second, he felt sympathy for the people screaming and protesting, but only being a high official, he didn't know what answer to give them.

"Hello, everyone!" the high official tried to speak over the loud voices. "Excuse me! I have a message from Stellar Court!"

Only some voices calmed down, while others continued to scream.

Will we have a reconstruction?

Where's the money? The country is run by Witches! For the universe's sake!

Why is Ether getting everything? Why not us?

And many more questions with only one answer that nobody except those in Stellar Court knew.

The high official remained silent, waiting until the crowd quieted down. Two guards stood behind him, analyzing every single move.

"I have a message from Stellar Court," the official repeated as the voices lowered. "I have been informed that they are in need of an... assistant."

"An assistant?" someone spoke from the front of the crowd over the non-stop whispers.

"Yes," the high official responded. "It is just stated that they require assistance. The chosen one will have the opportunity to live in the castle and will be given food and clothing. Most importantly, a sum of money in exchange for their work."

The whispers started to increase again. Franko raised his eyebrows at Adrik, who had a look he had seen many times before.

The high official continued, "Those who want to sign up can come in an hour and fill out a form with your name and a few questions. That is all."

Some hands started to rise, while others asked the same questions they had asked at the beginning, but the high official had already turned his back on the crowd. His red coat moving in the wind.

Suddenly, two men from the front of the chaos got onto the rough stage, trying to get to the official. The guards reacted quickly, holding the men away as the dumbfounded man ran to the safety of his carriage. The two men, however, were thrown back into the crowd by the guards, once again failing to obtain the riches they always wanted.

"They will never get tired," Franko whispered, turning around to look at Adrik, who turned to walk away from the crowd. He walked next to him, quickly noticing Adrik's expression.

"Oh no," Franko said. "You have *that* face."

Adrik made a very slight frown, looking at Franko.

"What do you need, boss..." Franko half-smiled. "A bomb? A sandwich?"

Adrik stayed quiet for a second, glanced at the silver rings in his hand, then looked at Franko with all seriousness. "You are going to sign up for that list."

"What?"

"Under my name."

"What?" Franko looked at him, confused about the task. "The list..."

"Yes, that is the job," Adrik demanded, walking away, leaving Franko confused.

For Adrik, it was like the universe was finally on his side. Everything he had planned his entire life for slowly came to him so easily. And it had indeed. Even if it hadn't, he would have found a way to make it so. A way to fulfill his purpose. A way to get his revenge.

And the only way to do so was to get into one of the castles of Kosmos.

Adrik couldn't tell what he hated more: the smell of fire and blood he knew so well or the smell of cigarettes that had started to follow him once again.

"Craven," he said, turning around to look at the toad-faced

person standing a few feet away from him with a cigarette in his hand.

Craven smiled, his short mustache making him appear much older, not that he already wasn't anyway. He believed it made him superior, but after years of doing his dirty work, Adrik certainly knew otherwise.

"Enjoying your freedom, are we? I would have thought you to be in Ether or out of Kosmos." Craven smiled.

"I have matters at hand," Adrik responded. "To which are none of your concern," he added, feeling a question from Craven coming ahead.

"Matters at hand, ah? Montova is always busy. You must have spare time, don't you?" Craven walked closer to him, but Adrik stood his ground. Not long ago, in his first encounters, he was afraid of Craven. Now, ten years later, he saw him as a little mouse running away from a cat.

"The deal is closed. I have no intention of going back."

"Not even for a billion *Kosniz*?"

Adrik looked straight into Craven's eyes. "I think I've made that clear." He walked back to Franko's half-home and half-tech store, his footsteps echoing in Craven's ears, reminding him of younger Adrik. Craven had never felt any kind of affection for anyone he took under his wing, especially since it was rare for him to aid someone. But for only one second, the emotionless man was proud of how far Adrik had come. Leaving the other seconds with rage, knowing very well that it wasn't he anymore who held the power in Arkadia. And people had started to notice, leaving Craven business on the verge of bankruptcy.

Craven had gotten weaker; he had become powerless, and now Adrik knew all his dirty secrets. The underground Casino was half-empty, its customers couldn't even manage to stay for more than four hours like they used to. Only a few guys still under Craven's 'debt' remained with him, mostly out of fear. But since Adrik's leaving, he had started to notice a change, a change of betrayal and power.

"I have other better ways to spend my money, Craven," one of Craven's common customers said as they left the Casino.

"I'd rather do the job myself if Adrik is gone," another one added.

Franko followed Adrik's orders to stay in Azra and waited for an hour to sign the papers for the so-called assistant job. He was never sure of what Adrik's plans were, but he did know that everything Adrik did was calculated and filled with abundant evidence. He liked to help Adrik, not only because he did get paid by him but because even if Adrik didn't want to admit it, they were the only people in the entire Kosmos who could understand and respect each other's actions. For Franko, they were like adopted brothers, even though Adrik never seemed to feel anything.

"Here," the guard said, pointing down at the 19th drawn line. Franko nodded and signed *Adrik Montova* in neatly cursive handwriting. His writing would have matched Adrik's if the businessman hadn't switched between different creative fonts at the contract deals he made.

"Neat and perfect. Way better than Adrik," he whispered as he put down the pen and moved out of the line.

"Franko?" a voice said, coming from the line, only a few feet ahead.

"Liam? Merhaba." Franko greeted in Turkish and looked up at the semi-tall boy standing in the line. He was just a year older than Franko but could easily pass as younger. "What are you doing here?"

"Hey, I would ask the same question. How is *Metal Tech* going? I didn't know you needed a job?"

"It's going great, and extra work doesn't hurt," Franko responded. "They might have sandwiches... You know, their riches and all."

Liam snickered, uncaringly. "Are you going to the protests tomorrow? Unless, of course, you must be very busy with that store of yours," Liam said, his mind still curious about Franko's sudden want to work for Stellar Court.

"I don't mean to be rude, but you seem suddenly interested in my life," Franko responded calmly. He had known Liam since he arrived in Kosmos as a young and lonely child. One more thing he had in common with Adrik, or he could guess they had. Both of their families had disappeared and were taken under the care of others. As far as he knew, Craven had 'saved' Adrik from being taken away by witches; what happened to his family, he didn't know. While Franko had been passed down to an Uncle from his adoptive family in Arkadia. Both were given the resources needed to stay alive until they were grown enough to go on their own. However, Adrik owed Craven his life, which he had already paid, and Franko used up all the money his family had kept safe for him to survive in Arkadia for more.

Liam had everything handed to him from his not-so-wealthy-anymore family. Franko thought him to be spoiled, but he was never jealous of him. Ironically, it was the other way around. Franko was proud of who he was, and Liam always kept tabs on his life by asking more questions at each meeting. Or by watching him, when he thought Franko wouldn't notice.

"It feels like I haven't seen you in years, Franko," Liam responded quickly.

"I saw you just two days ago, Liam. Coming out of the Casino to be in fact..."

"I wasn't at the Casino. I was home with my father..." Liam shook his head in denial.

"Is that so? You must have a twin then or be barbaric enough to make a deal with Craven." Franko smiled.

"I assure you it is neither."

"Great for you, Liam. See you soon," said Franko. "*Or never actually.*" He whispered, walking away from a confused Liam.

The fresh breeze and warmth of the Sun made Franko happy, even though he enjoyed rainy days the best, while he walked back to Metal Tech. Adrik was already inside the gloomy store, sitting on the mini bar in the back left corner, staring at the wall.

"Anyone dropped by?" Franko asked as he put his burgundy coat in the brown coat rack next to Adrik's black one. Adrik didn't respond to the obvious question.

"I didn't think so either," Franko half-smiled, walking behind the counter to get the keys and close the store. He opened the door ajar, seeing the sunlight still shining and for a second wishing the store didn't look as gloomy as it was. But he liked the mystery of it all and decided that it was better as it is.

"What are you doing?" he asked Adrik as he walked back to get a glass of club soda from the bar. He had won a box of a variety of alcoholic and non-alcoholic drinks in the famous *House of Cards* bar, just a few days ago, playing cards and making bets. Anyone could say he was one of the best at any card game in Arkadia. Franko knew it well, and sometimes avoided bragging about it, of course, but he took great pride when he always won many shiny and costly things.

Adrik didn't respond after two seconds. "Waiting."

"For what?... If you don't mind me asking."

Adrik looked at him expressionlessly, not because he didn't want to tell him what he was waiting for, but because he was waiting for the right time to tell him. Right on cue, there was a slight knock on the door.

Franko frowned at Adrik and proceeded to go back to the entrance door he had just closed. He took a look outside to see a beige folded paper hanging from the edge of the dark window next to the wooden door.

"I'm guessing this is for you," Franko said, noticing Adrik already walking towards him. He took the piece of paper, opening it without concern.

It is Done. The messy written words on the paper said. A *triquela*, three overlapping circles, of silver rings was drawn at the bottom edge of the paper.

"Important message?" Franko said, noticing the drawing that

Adrik always used in his secret messages and parcels.

"Extremely," Adrik said, going back to his seat at the bar.

Franko furrowed his brows but decided not to ask questions; he knew he probably wasn't going to receive answers for them yet. Instead, he went upstairs to make himself a sandwich in the small green kitchen. He passed by his and Adrik's room, noticing the big box of sandwich plastic bags. Feeling a bit disgusted and anxious, he went ahead to tidy up his dark brown room before heading to the kitchen for the 'sandwich reward'. He glanced at the double doors, deciding to stay up late again and organize some of the boxes with metal scraps.

Adrik sat in the bar for at least an hour, until Franko came to sit next to him and offered him the second sandwich he held in his hands. Preoccupied with his own burning thoughts, Adrik looked at him and shook his head, taking another sip of his black coffee.

A second later, a small swoosh sound was heard from the door, followed by a hollow knock. The low moonlight hit Franko's face as he opened the door and looked down at where a vintage envelope stood on the dry, dirty floor. He could easily recognize the witches' message based on the dark and burnt edges of the envelope. The effects of transporting messages through fire and air.

"Another," he said, closing the door and handing the envelope to Adrik, who had stood up after Franko. He opened the Eclipse sealed envelope, knowing very well what the message read in golden letters.

Adrik Montova, you have been selected for the position. Report to Stellar Court tomorrow at dawn.

"You were selected... out of all the applicants..." Franko said, re-reading the message again until he realized. "Why do you have that look?"

Adrik slightly smirked; it was the closest expression he could make to a smile. "I was getting that position one way or another."

"Are you stating you orchestrated a scheme... *without me?*"

"You think that fight downtown was a coincidence? I knew Stellar Court was looking for someone, and I knew when they were going to announce it. The men who initiated the fight are acquaintances with a Stellar Court guard, those same men have been reporting to me for three days about any important news in exchange for *Kosniz.*" Adrik looked back at the envelope. "It seems to me that they managed."

They indeed had. The hired men had been hungry for money. Adrik was aware of that. He could see it in the faces of most people in Arkadia. So, he offered them an easy job and a very well-made payment to change the draw. After the scare, the high official wrote all the names on pieces of paper at the edge of Ring Forest, before entering his carriage and having a dilemma whether to go back to Stellar Castle without an official winner announcement. One of the men created a distraction, allowing the other to swap the name on the piece of paper the official had chosen before he opened it. Franko raised his brows in amazement, part of him bothered at the lack of reliance from Adrik, and the other part wondering how an official could be so mindless.

Adrik continued, "You were part of the scheme, all you had to do was…"

"Sign your name." Franko nodded, adding the pieces together. "*Of course*, nothing a load of *Kosniz* can't do."

Adrik looked back at the piece of paper, his mind already circling the next plans ahead.

"Will you head to Ether tomorrow morning?" he asked, still looking at the piece of paper.

"Yes, chief." Franko nodded. "I will look for the *additional* archives and supplies."

"Going to Stellar and getting those archives are the proof I need," Adrik responded, his eyes losing reality once again. Then there was a small look of anger Franko hadn't noticed in a very long time. A look he always wondered about but never asked. After a while, curiosity got the best of him, and he couldn't help it.

"Pardon my intrusion, boss, but what do you need proof for?" Franko asked with furrowing brows. "Justice?"

"No." Adrik shook his head slightly, looking at Franko's curious eyes. "For *death*."

PART TWO

GONE WITH THE FIRE

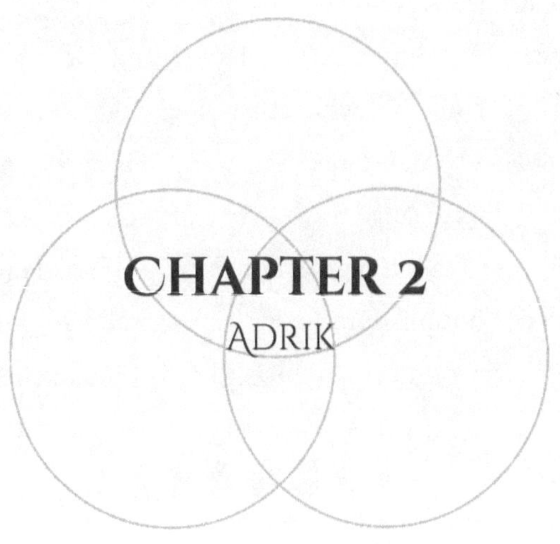

CHAPTER 2
ADRIK

To say that Adrik Montova hated every single day of his old life was an understatement. He didn't hate it because he ran cruel errands for Craven and did horrible things to horrible people but he did because he couldn't wait for the day his actual plan would come into action. His old life made him stronger, made him prepared for what was coming next. And as he stood up early in the morning with tired but concentrated eyes, he knew he didn't regret any part of it.

Franko was his normal content self as he walked downstairs to open the tech shop. Adrik could hear his quick footsteps, reminding him of the time they met at a bar close to Craven's tavern two years ago. That day, Adrik was following one of the new recruiters from Craven's gang. Being the most discreet and experienced under Craven for almost ten years, his job was to torture and spy on those in debt or against Craven.

Craven, of course, had a lot of enemies for all his dirty businesses of tampering with other gangs for assets and money laundering. He was absolutely arrogant. There was nothing he wouldn't do in exchange for power and money in Arkadia. But most of it was all talk and no action. Yes, people had died because of his orders, but unlike Adrik, his 'right-hand man' as he used to say, he didn't have more than three gallons of blood on his hands.

The new recruiter had about four minutes and thirty seconds to live after he entered the busy bar where Franko had worked two years ago. Adrik followed the recruiter inside, watching as he sat down at a table in the corner. He waited for someone, checking his watch every five minutes. It wasn't until another man in a dark hat sat in front of him, looking around the bar suspiciously, when Adrik turned away to look at the silver watch on his wrist. Then, he watched Franko approach them to ask the recruiter for drink preferences. Both men shook their heads at him, wanting him to leave. But as per the rules of the bar, which Franko must have known well, anyone who sat down was expected to buy a drink or leave at once. Franko had gone back to the counter, looking at the clock behind him. He glanced back, probably deciding to go back and ask about the drinks again. Before he could, Adrik was already in front of him, asking for a drink and explaining his deal.

"Four hundred *Kosniz* for you to tell me what they are talking about," he said, staring at Franko's energetic brown eyes.

"Six hundred, and I won't ask any questions either," Franko replied, to which Adrik nodded once.

Following Adrik's deal, Franko headed to the table with two drinks in his hands, concentrating on any words that came out of the men's mouths.

After watching Franko leave the drinks on the table, both men looked up at him in rage.

"I said leave us alone." Adrik could hear the man who was talking to the recruiter say in loud annoyance, and saw Franko move away as they got out of the bar by the back door that led to a deserted alley. But Franko could never be at peace with an unfinished job, so he went quietly behind both men, glancing at Adrik only once and following out the door.

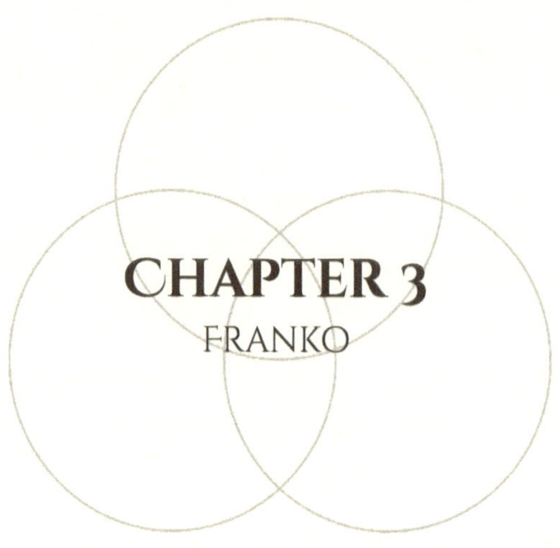

CHAPTER 3
FRANKO

A DOG'S BARKING and the muffled voices of people in the main streets filled the alley. Franko didn't know what was worse, the deserted alley or the fact that he was actually following two men for six hundred *Kosniz*. He liked the physical adrenaline, either way, a feeling he rarely got as a bartender, and a reason why he felt he should quit and become the owner of his own tech store. His footsteps squelched above the puddles of dirty water, imitating the men's footsteps. Ten seconds after following had the two men heard Franko's steps.

"What are you doing? Who are you?" one of the men asked, looking somewhat more startled than the man wearing the hat. "Why are you following us?" *Alexei* was the name he had overheard the other hatted man next to him say when he tried to calm him down.

"Me? Following you?" Franko shook his head. "Hayir, of course not. Why would I?"

The man frowned, not believing Franko's words. He proceeded towards him as Franko took a small step backward.

"He is not following you," Adrik appeared from the darkness, to which Franko frowned. "I am." He looked back and forth between Adrik, who stood five feet away, and the men ahead of them, who took a step backward in slow motion.

"Mister... I assure you that this is not what it seems," Alexie said.

"It seems what it is." Franko shrugged, receiving a side look from Adrik.

"Craven has a lot of enemies. Your boss included." Adrik looked at the man standing next to Alexei, stepping forward until he was five feet away from the frozen statues. "And I can't let you tell him anything at all."

Alexei didn't have time to flinch before Adrik stabbed him with one-fourth of his silver sword and fell to the ground, shaking in pain. Franko flinched and turned around, shocked to see what Adrik had done. *That was indeed unexpected*. He thought horrifically.

"Now, I suggest you take your friend and hope that I'll never find you around again," Adrik said towards the hatted man, his voice calm as the wind.

"Yes, Montova." The man quickly bent down to get Alexei and hurried out of the alley as fast as he could.

Franko cleared his throat, still slightly shaken. "Montova? As in *Adrik* Montova."

Adrik glared at him. "Is there another I should be aware of?"

He started walking out of the alley as well. Franko looked at the building next to him. His thoughts were shaken at the actual thought of wasting time inside the noisy and filthy bar.

"Wait. There is something I would like to discuss," Franko started, making Adrik turn around. "It is a convenient matter..."

"Go ahead then. Make it quick."

"I would like to work with..."

"No."

"I didn't even finish my sentence..." Franko frowned.

"No," Adrik responded. "I'm not looking for anyone to work with."

"Listen, not right now, of course. *But* I have a plan, and there are rumors you won't stay long with the 'big bad gangster of Arkadia'. Some people, including myself, if I may add, actually think that... you have surpassed."

"Is that so?"

"*Evet*," Franko said slowly. *Yes*, in Turkish, hoping he had convinced Adrik to hear his plan.

To some extent, Franko was right. Adrik's contract with Craven was going to end after one year and a few months. And with eighty percent of Arkadia knowing Adrik's reputation, his chances of finding allies were less than zero. Franko was one of the only people who didn't seem afraid of being around him for too long, not that that was not true because Franko was at least terrified.

"What is the deal?" Adrik walked towards Franko.

"A drink first? Coffee?" Franko nodded, continuing backwards to open the back door and go inside the bar for a talk.

)) ◗ ●● ◖ ((

"Günayden. Coffee?" Franko said, watching Adrik's eyes adjust back from whatever idea he had in mind as he walked towards the mini bar and grabbed a large cup. Adrik's no response made him look back. "Did you see yourself in the mirror?" Franko continued. "You look like a ghost."

Adrik glared at him, making Franko glad that his boss was at least alive.

Typical Adrik. Franko thought.

"Today's the day," Franko added, finishing his cup of coffee and placing it in the small sink behind him.

"It's time," Adrik responded, checking the silver pocket watch Franko had given him for communication. It was one of Franko's best handmade devices with a dash of magic. The pocket watch worked as a normal watch. Without modern technology in Kosmos, he made two watches, one bronze and one silver. With the help of a witch, paper notes could be passed through the mini-portal inside the watch with a third click of the crown.

"You know the plan."

"Like a bomb, chief." Franko responded with a smile. "I will go to Ether in a few hours."

Adrik looked him seriously in the eyes. "No diversion, Franko, and stay focused."

"Of course, boss, I know. When have I ever detoured? I will get the supplies, the information, and be back as soon as I can."

Adrik frowned, giving Franko a bag loaded with coins and a few blue, purple, and red *Kosni* bills.

"When have I done the job wrong?" Franko took the bag and shook his hands in the air. He indeed never did a bad job. The ultimate goal was always achieved in the end, but the road there was always chaotic. *To problems and chaos, there are always solutions.* Franko used to say after every wrong turn in his hands.

Adrik shook his head slightly and turned away towards the exit of the tech store.

"You are not taking your sword?" Franko asked before Adrik opened the door.

"If I find the witch, my sword won't take his blood. My hands will." And just like every day, Franko once again saw the face of a shattered boy full of vengeance and malice. He did not know why or how to understand Adrik, but he was glad to be part of a team towards a common goal and, hopefully, a bright future of happiness *and* wealth.

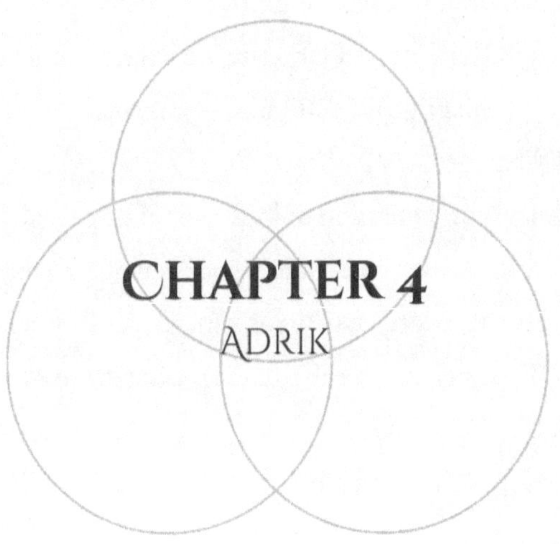

CHAPTER 4
ADRIK

I T WASN'T LONG BEFORE the streets of Arkadia filled up again in the early afternoon. People ran and hurried to their destinations.

"Newspaper, Sir?" A young boy slightly touched Adrik's elbow, to which he ignored and continued walking. The young boy blinked; his face filled with disappointment once again.

"One," Adrik said, hazel-gray eyes turning to the boy. The weary boy walked back towards him with a smile, giving him a newspaper as Adrik handed him a few *Kosni* coins from his coat.

"Thank you!" the boy exclaimed and hurried away into more crowd.

For a second, Adrik remembered the last time he was free like a child. He pushed away the thought, letting it fill with rage at loss time. For him, memories were a weakness. A nonstop cycle holding him back from the future. So, he pushed away any old memory he had of his childhood. Every single one of them, including the one that started his vengeance. Of course, he did remember it once in a while, but his main goal overlooked the memory, making it all a blur. A hidden memory in the depths of his bitter heart.

There was no hesitation to look back as he passed downtown. A black carriage with a golden Eclipse design of the Sun and Moon colliding on the doors waited for him, parked by the southeast outskirts of the city. Before the guard protested Adrik's approach, Adrik got out the envelope, showing and handing him the eclipsed wax-sealed letter that stated his name. The guard nodded, inspecting the envelope before opening the door to the inside of the small lit carriage. Adrik caught a glimpse of the guard's black uniform, an Eclipse pin attached to his coat chest pocket. The Stellar Court sign. To show ranking and leadership, a pin was always given to Kosmos guards and a special-colored coat for high officials.

"To Stellar Castle," the guard said seconds after Adrik entered the carriage. A slight grin appeared over Adrik's face. *A plan well-made and a plan to accomplish.*

Isolation was a word so used in Adrik's life. He didn't fully mind the darkness inside the carriage. He didn't mind the limited Sun or the small amounts of words he spoke throughout the day. Most of which contained orders to Franko or others for whom he temporarily paid *Kosniz* for Court information. He focused on the next actions, remembering to breathe in the air that came from outside.

His mind was filled with thoughts that always contained plans. A list of an infinite number of crossed-out finished tasks and only one marked in fiery red ink that for years could not be unscathed. And it would never be unless he found the person to blame. Break them until they no longer exist and make them pay with their own blood the time he lost for himself and the only people he had ever loved. Forgetting wasn't simple at all. Even for a ten-year-old. A scarred memory could remain forever. Adrik was living proof of that, and his past verified it.

It was a great day, just like every other day. Better for young Adrik to be exact, because it was the day he was able to spend it with his father in the secret room.

"I believe *Mom* is done with the pastries. It smells great," Adrik's father said, looking at his son over the boat model on the wooden table. The words *Silver Rings* carved in small letters at the front of the boat. They shimmered under the bright light of the flashlight that Adrik held next to his father's concentrated eyes.

The entire room smelled of wood mixed with the sweet odor of the cupcakes and cookies being made in the kitchen. For everyone else beyond the village in Venice, Italy, it must have been early in the morning. But for the Montova family and the residents, time was as valuable as money.

As every Wednesday morning, a knock was heard. *The Bread Lady.* Adrik thought as he headed out of the craft room, knowing that she never missed a day to knock at the door to give bread samples from downtown.

"Hello, Flora!" the bread lady said the moment Adrik's mom opened the door.

"Hello, good morning," Flora answered with a smile on her face, shaking flour out of her flower-designed apron.

"Making pastries, are you dear? I can smell the sugar miles away."

"Yes, we are. It is a beautiful day to do so, in fact."

"Yes, it is indeed," the lady said, handing her the bag of bread bites. "Here you go, as every Wednesday!"

"Thank you, I will see you in the afternoon at the bakery. The kids want to walk by the river downtown, so I might as well pass by."

"Certainly, see you then," the lady said, walking onto the next house on the street.

"Adrik, you can come out now." Adrik, who stood behind the sky-blue doorway, appeared with a frown on his face. Flora smiled at him, walking back into the kitchen.

"I don't know why you hide. Ms. Lucia is a nice lady." She set the bread bag on the counter of the lively lime green kitchen. Flowers and plants filled twenty-five percent of the house, especially the kitchen, where the Sun was visible and the waves of the sea were heard the most.

"She always touches my hair and ruffles it up," Adrik responded, glancing at his dad entering the kitchen behind him.

"What's wrong with that?" he said, ruffling Adrik's hair on purpose.

"Dad!" He moved away and sat on the green bench to look at a raw batch of cookies on the table. "Where's..."

"Surprise!" Adrik's sister appeared from the open balcony with flowers in her hand and handed them to Adrik.

"You know I don't like flowers..."

"I don't like you, but that's unchangeable," his sister responded. She was only one year younger than Adrik, but smart and brave enough as him. Adrik smiled anyway, held the flowers, and handed them to his mom instead.

"Don't be mean to each other," Adrik's dad said, opening the oven.

"Hey! They aren't ready yet..." Flora frowned and then smiled as she held the flowers.

"I know, but it smells great," he responded, looking at Flora. "Just like you, of course." He approached her and hugged her.

"Aww," the Montova siblings smiled, looking at each other mischievously. His parents' silver rings shining on their left index finger, just like Adrik and her sister's rings. Except, the siblings' rings were too oversized for their small hands. Their dad wanted them to be wearable when they were older, without any change to the designs. So, her sister would sometimes wear it around her neck with a silver chain. Adrik made sure his ring never fell out of his finger or his pocket when he was out for adventures.

"Ready?" Adrik whispered to his sister with a grin on his face.

"Are you?" she responded. They both headed towards their parents, throwing flour at them and running around the kitchen before they got hold of them. They jumped, joked, and laughed that morning. Adrik had put that day as one of the best days of his life on his list. One of the best mornings, along with others.

Inside the confined carriage, he felt a sense of home. Not the way he had felt that great morning, but the way everything had changed in the afternoon. He wasn't scared, not like his ten-year-old self was ten years ago. But the dark memory was there, and the hiding spot materialized before him. Yet instead of feeling slightly anxious, this time he only felt anger and spite.

"Don't be scared," Adrik said to his sister as they hid inside the closet of the secret room. Far away from the chaos and the sounds of people screaming, just like their parents had said to do before they closed every door and window. The room filled with smoke and fire every second that passed.

"I'm trying not to be," his sister responded in a soft voice, holding her parents' silver rings in her hands tightly along with hers. "But—" She coughed, the effects of smoke filling her lungs. Adrik could already feel it, the small amount of oxygen he could barely breathe. *Stay calm. Stay calm. Breathe.* He said over and over again. Telling himself to stay awake for his sister.

"Stay awake, ok," he whispered as his sister nodded. "And stay quiet. Mom and Dad will come back soon." The fire burned through the wood as fast as the creaking sounds of the room door opening. The Montova siblings drew in their last breath, trying not to cough in the darkness. But the smoke was too much for them to take.

"Who is there?" a voice said, footsteps approaching the hidden door. Adrik shuffled around, getting his silver blade from his shoe before the hidden door opened. A man in a red coat grabbed him first. "You are coming with me, kid."

For Adrik, the memory was like a blur. Another man grabbed his sister; he could barely see her through the smoke but could hear her low coughs.

"Let her go!" Adrik cried. "Let her go!" He fought the man holding him hostage, stabbing him with the silver blade and running to his sister. But he couldn't hear her coughs anymore. Becoming replaced with the clash of silver rings hitting the floor, three beats one by one.

ONE DOWN, MORE TO GO

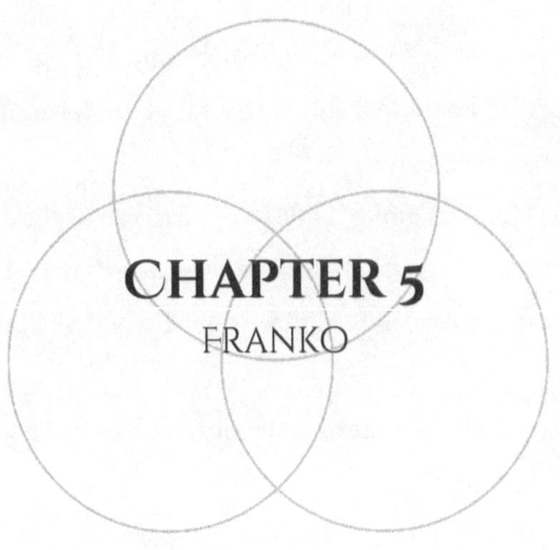

CHAPTER 5
FRANKO

F RANKO WAS HAVING THE DAY of his business life as people entered Metal Tech. He shook his head as three people entered at once, wondering if there was a sign outside that said *Adrik Montova (former gangster of Craven's gang and many more!) is not here. You are safe!* Yet there was no sign and no halt for the people entering the store. It wasn't till Liam entered that Franko knew how the rumors of Adrik's leave were heard.

"Liam, what are you doing here?" Franko said, his smile mismatching the tone of his voice. Liam looked around the store and inspected the gadgets placed on the wooden counter.

"Did you do a magic spell to attract all these customers?" Liam half-smiled, grabbing one of the metal lighters on the table next to him.

"Hayir, Liam. I'm not a witch... are you?" Franko spoke loudly, making sure that people heard him. Some customers turned to look at Liam, waiting for an answer.

"Of course not." Liam laughed, shaking his head.

"Good to know. Arkadia is the last place in Kosmos a witch might live in, as you know."

"Yes, I know, Franko. I know…" Liam placed the lighter back on the counter. "What I also happen to know is that Adrik Montova has left the city. Where did he go, I wonder? Stellar Castle, maybe?"

"That would be none of your concern. Really, I don't see how that helps you in any way."

Liam shook his head. "Oh, but it does for me and others."

"What? You work for the big bad *supposed* gangster now… that is barbaric," Franko said, putting his hands on his hips. "And not surprising really."

A customer approached Franko, just as Liam was about to respond.

"Pardon. *I* have a tech store to run." Franko smiled before Liam's words left his mouth and ran away to attend to his frenzied customers.

CHAPTER 6
ADRIK

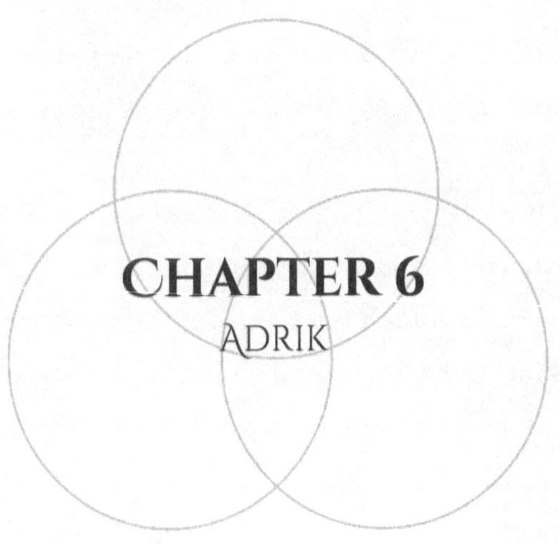

T HE MORNING HUMID SMELL of the forest took Adrik's fiery memories away. He kept them deeply inside for years, and he would keep them inside for as long as he sought and fulfilled revenge. It took hours and Adrik's alternative mind plans until the carriage had reached one of the ends of Ring Forest and proceeded towards the castle.

Out of the three castles in Kosmos, Stellar Castle thrived on architecture and design. Not only because it was the main capital of Kosmos, but because the white castle inhabited Stellar Court, the six main leaders of Kosmos. As far as Adrik had immensely researched, the white castle was built of high-quality materials of bricks, wood, and especially glass. Most of the fanciest and modern but vintage designs. He only realized the words he read in *History of Kosmos: The Courts in their Castles*, stolen from a thief by him when he was young, were only half-truth. The castle was pleasing indeed, yet from the outside, he saw it just as a normal castle with exaggeration. Or maybe he just got used to the fact that inside the castle, most likely, inhabited the person he had been looking for ten years.

The black carriage had finally entered the land of Stellar Castle. Green terrain surrounded the entire area. It was the maze on the right that caught Adrik's eyes first, then the lake to the left in the middle of the garden that was only visible by the black lit posts. The observatory, planetarium, and conservatory buildings stood out of the castle, encircling it. Out of the carriage, he smelled the sweet odor of the garden mixed in with the humidity of the drizzling rain. He tilted his head slightly as he got out of the carriage to shake away the smell. *Everything here is sugar-coated.* He thought for a second, missing the dampness of Arkadia. For most of his life, the city had been a home to him. A reminder of who he had become and how much more he could be.

Up close, he had to admit that the castle looked at least much better. From the smallest patterns on each wall to the stamped floor. He walked down the path to the entrance of the castle. Guards stood on each door or window visible to their post, each with golden and silver Eclipse pins attached to the left side of their gray uniform. There was no entry to the castle that wasn't heavily guarded, at least not for normal people.

"State your name and business," one of the four guards at the entrance said. His eyes inspecting every inch of Adrik.

"I have business with Stellar Court." He didn't inspect any of the guards' movements, he analyzed them. What their eyes followed, how they stood, whether they seemed to actually guard the castle or just daydream of the life they wished to have. Anything that could give him a pass on deals and offers. He handed him the envelope that Stellar Court had sent him. The guard shuffled, his hand towards his belt and the end of his sword. He inspected the letter. Adrik glanced at the firearm on the other side of his belt. *Right-handed and better with swords.* Now, he knew Stellar Court had at least picked guards that seemed most intimidating. Maybe not all were the best at fighting. Not that there were any civil battles or wars in Kosmos since the Supernatural War. Everything was usually under control by witches except Arkadia.

"He does look like a businessman," the guard next to him whispered, looking at Adrik's black coat. *That is the point.*

"Alright. *Adrik Montova.* Come on in," the guard in front of him said, giving back the envelope. "Open the gates!"

With pleasure, Adrik thought. The guards on the other side opened the wide gate that revealed a path towards the large white-black doors of the castle. Two other guards stood by, opening both doors as Adrik approached. Even he had to admit that he couldn't exactly believe the indoor architecture that he was seeing. The first floor of the castle looked like a palace. Grand stairs turned into infinite halls and rounded around to different floors. All the walls were mostly gold, silver, black, and white. The white rugs in the staircases were designed with golden drawings of planets, stars, and constellations on the edges. Adrik had studied the layout of all castles for years, especially Stellar, getting the different versions of blueprints each year he heard even the smallest of things were replaced or changed around in the castle. He knew most of what each hallway led to and what each door revealed. But standing at the exact entrance of the castle was much different, expected, and completely planned. He had waited for this day, now it was time for action. Nothing was more satisfying than a plan gone right.

"Sir, do you need help finding your way?" A man to his right had spoken, gold stitching on the collar. A high official from Solar Castle. *A witch.*

"No need," Adrik responded, his voice firm and steady. The high official only frowned at his attire, passing Adrik towards the hallway on the other side. He turned to see the high official's red coat, a Sun design on its back. Making a mental note to later go to the fabric room where Kosmos uniforms and coats were made by Joviankalais.

Adrik started to walk up the grand stairs in front of him, turning left to go up to the next floor. The meeting room was on the second floor of the castle. Stellar Court usually spent their time there deciding and planning for the country. The first floor was merely the visitors' floor, a sugar-coated floor with a ballroom, museum, theater, an aquarium, meeting rooms, libraries with worldwide information (except Kosmos' important texts). He held his posture high, ascending the steps and looking around, taking in every detail and the people around him.

It was easy to identify the most important floor of the castle, with less gold or white, the second floor gave a more serious and gloomy dark mood of red and blue. High officials from both Solar and Lunar Castles walked around the floor, entering different rooms. As part of Solar Castle, some high officials wore their golden-Sun designs on their red coats and collars. Lunar Castle high officials, however, wore their silver-Moon designs on their blue coats. These were the selected witches and Illuminators trusted by their Court to keep general tasks and assignments around the castles. Everyone at least had some kind of material that identified them. Other witches and Illuminators that didn't have coats had a *visitors* pass or a colored Illuminator uniform based on their power. They either had gone to make a deal with Stellar Court or were employed.

"Good morning," a man dressed in a business suit greeted Adrik with a smile. He nodded back, approaching the door at the end of the main hall that the dressed man had just left.

The meeting room was nothing like its own definition. The ballroom-sized room contained no windows, but the ceiling and walls filled themselves with projections of the solar system, unknown galaxies, and constellations. They floated on every golden and white wall, around the chandeliers that made the room a bit brighter than the rest of the second floor. Adrik took notice of the mix of candle lights and modern light bulbs that hung around the room and the castle.

"The meeting with the Ether council will be in four hours." Adrik heard the voice of a woman. He walked forward towards the dais, passing tables with articles, books, bookshelves, and museum displays.

"We will take care of it," a man in a gray coat spoke. "As part of Lunar Court, you three should be leaving tonight."

"We are aware, Terrance. The other three members are at Lunar Castle, they are taking care of the preparations for the new Illuminators," a blond-haired lady in a green coat explained. "We will leave before dusk."

It wasn't until she got up and saw Adrik walking towards the dais that Stellar Court noticed his presence. The members sitting on the right, two women and a man at the table, wore their colored uniforms. Green, orange, and purple colors of Illuminators. At the left, three men sat in their gray and black coats. *Witches.* In Adrik's eyes, the court shifted in their chairs. Only one sitting at the foot of the table half-smiled.

"State your business," Terrance spoke firmly. Adrik walked up the dais, showing the envelope in his hands. Up close, he could see the modern wooden table displaying the map of Kosmos in the middle with a glass covering it on top. It matched the projected map on the left wall.

"*I am* the business. You have an assignment and I'm here to do it... for the right price."

"Who sent for an assistant?" the other man in gray asked.

"I did." The man in black, who had smiled earlier, spoke in a less rough voice than the other two men. Only then did Adrik look at all the members' features. Every single one of them was no older than forty, especially not witches. Most powerful witches didn't age and had many more years to live. Adrik knew for a fact that the witch members in court must have been around beyond the origin of Kosmos. After all, the newspapers always gave news when Illuminator members were appointed or removed, but not of witches. The man in black seemed a bit younger than most of them, maybe Adrik's age but not much older. The court members turned to him.

"Why? For what reason?" Terrance sat up in his chair.

"Private matters."

"What happens in court concerns me, Kaan."

"Everything concerns you." Kaan smirked slightly. "You are forgetting there is no leader of the Court. There's only us, and that's it. I would have thought you knew that after years of being alive."

Everybody at the table nodded in agreement. Terrance only crossed his arms. But Adrik could see the angry glance he gave Kaan. He could tell Kaan enjoyed being right.

"Very well then, I will be heading to lunch now," the lady in an orange coat said, followed by the other two Illuminators.

"Keep us updated," the green-coated man in glasses said to Kaan. They walked past Adrik, giving him another look. Now he stayed alone with the Court witches. *Any of them could be my enemy. I will find out who.* Adrik stayed unmoving like a statue. Terrence still had annoyance on his face. The other man in gray examined the open files on the desk, which were filled with scientific symbols Adrik barely recognized. He didn't exactly expect any of them to recognize him. There was never a watchdog in Arkadia, hence the rise of gangs and thieves. Yet, Kaan stood up at once. "Mister Montova," he started. "Follow me."

"How is it that you know of me?" Adrik started the second they were out of the grand meeting room.

"I've heard of you, Montova. Stories and rumors. Member of five gangs. Right hand of that man... Craven Barnes, is it?" Kaan started walking forward. Adrik followed next to him, listening intently. "Always up to the job for the right price." Kaan shook his head. "Other than that, you are a mystery. I don't care about your methods. I care about the job."

Adrik wasn't sure whether to believe him. After years, that wasn't even a statement in question anymore. The answer was always the same. As it should be. *Of course not.*

"What is the job exactly?"

"Espionage."

"On whom?"

Kaan turned to him, looking around slightly to make sure that no one was around. "The new Illuminators." *Illuminators? Now, why would a Stellar Court member, especially a witch, want to deal with Illuminators? What is the largest price Kaan would go for to have the job done?*

"What is your deal?" Adrik looked at Kaan, his voice firm.

Kaan smiled. "Six hundred fifty thousand *Kosniz.*"

"Do I have to assume you have that amount of money?" Adrik asked, knowing well it was possible for any Solar Court witch member to have much more.

"I've been alive far before Kosmos existed, Montova. I may have way more than anyone in the world, not that I would use any of it."

Alive far before Kosmos existed. That's all he needed to know for suspect number one.

Six hundred fifty thousand Kosniz. And revenge. Adrik thought, his hand out for a handshake. "The deal is accepted."

PART FOUR

IN PLAIN SIGHT

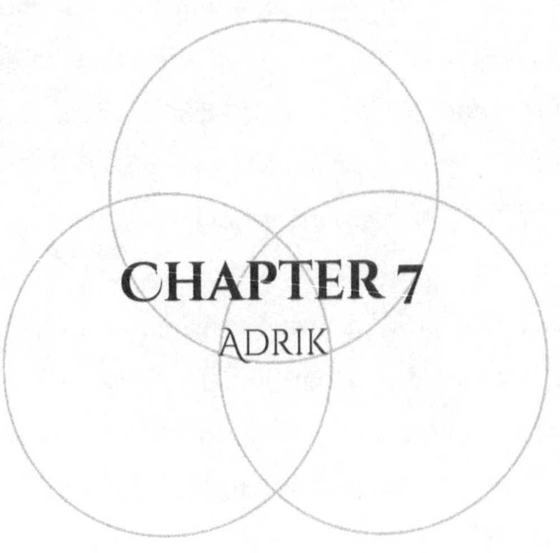

CHAPTER 7
ADRIK

I LLUMINATORS. Maintainers of balance between the super-natural. Adrik had only seen a few of them running around Arkadia. Rare kids born from the bloodlines of light-bloods were later chosen to go to Lunar Castle to learn how to fight and control their powers. Only a small percentage of Illuminators resided in Kosmos. Their families, usually their light-blooded parents, either lived in the cities or worked in the Courts.

Why would Kaan want to deal with the Illuminators? Adrik thought as he walked upstairs to the fifth floor, following a high Solar official, whom Kaan had ordered to take him to a suite. Kaan wanted information regarding the new Illuminators. The only way, however, to be that close was to be in Lunar Castle. Either Kaan would leave, or he would send Adrik to the castle, far away from Stellar Castle and the rest of the Court. *New plan.*

Adrik didn't exactly know much about who he was working

for. There was a fifty-fifty chance for him to go to either Court.

Now, he needed to find a way to gain information about any witch court member before leaving, including Kaan. Being close to him would be easy. One down and two to go.

"This is it," the high official said, standing a few feet away from the suite door. Adrik made a slight nod and headed inside the room. Whatever Kaan knew about Adrik, he knew to a certain extent. The classic dark room brought Adrik back to his room above the tech store. An inch of home, where his sword stood in a safe place. The suite was spacious, large enough to pace around and think, just as he was doing now. He examined the room for a while. There were a few modern and new designs around the room, different decorations, an eclipsed wooden table in the middle, and a window that gave him a convenient view of the front of the castle.

Adrik stood on the balcony, solving the maze from above like a puzzle. The middle of the maze shone brightly as the water flowed through the glass fountain. He watched the guards move every thirty minutes. Two shifts had passed when, finally, a knock was heard. Adrik straightened himself and went ahead to open the door, shaking his head against a small headache.

"Pardon, Sir," a young lady in an apron said. "I was told to bring a few coats and to get your measurements for clothing."

"That will not be necessary," Adrik responded, moving aside when the girl entered the room. She placed the coats she held on the foot of the bed.

"I was told—"

"It is already handled." Adrik stayed by the door, waiting for the lady to leave. She didn't insist further and headed out of the room quickly. Her presence was replaced by Orson, who watched the hall back and forth.

"You are on time," Adrik said to the young man holding a black traveling suitcase in his hand.

"I'm not Franko. I should be your partner instead. What is *he* doing anyway?" Orson asked, holding out the case towards Adrik, who walked to the table to open it. The bag was filled with his dark trousers and coats, white and black shirts, and silk vests. He had the case sent hours earlier with Orson to make it easier for him not to get checked at the gate and hide the maps.

"He is attending to different matters," Adrik responded, placing the clothes on the brown bed end chest and taking out the large sheets of paper from under the bag. Orson closed the door behind him at once and approached the table to look at the plans better.

Adrik neatly unfolded the prints. "Are these all the new layouts for the three castles?"

"All the same. Except for Solar Castle. They seemed to expand the Armory." Orson pointed at the print, where a room was built next to Solar Castle.

"I've heard of the trade from Bore Port," Adrik nodded. Solar Court was making space for the stock of armor and weapons they were bringing in.

"Witches' problems. I'm glad to not be one of them." Orson was a light-blood, brother to an Illuminated sister. At first, he was jealous of her. Talking badly about how she handled her powers. But after a while of watching the people of Kosmos deal with their magical problems, he said otherwise.

"What else?"

"Regarding the Court," Orson started. "The three Illuminators of Stellar Court are already heading to Lunar Castle to meet up with the rest of Lunar Court. Apparently, the new Illuminators arrived."

James, Davina, and Ingi. Adrik remembered the Stellar Court Illuminators, whom Orson had mentioned a few months ago on his trip to Arkadia. They were part of Lunar Court just as Kaan, Isaiah, and Terrance were part of Solar Court. A total of twelve leaders within all Courts. Only in important matters did the main Illuminators and witches he'd seen earlier meet up in Castle, becoming Stellar Court all together.

"Where is your Illuminator friend? He works with you, doesn't he?" Adrik folded up the plans.

"Down on the second floor. They had him switch shifts this morning to the Armory for inventory count."

"Send him a message. Tell him to meet me in an hour at the bar on the third-floor balcony and to be on time."

Orson nodded, leaving the suite room.

Two other shifts had passed. Adrik had just been reviewing the dimensions and architectural drawings, now he headed down the never-ending stairs to the third floor. Some high officials passed by, glancing at Adrik and the coat he wore. He was used to it, stares that meant nothing but fear, envy, or curiosity. Sounds and voices increased. Adrik stepped into the main hall of the third floor. Workers walked around the large dining room, crossing the hall to the left and right. Further ahead, the outside bar overlooked part of the left side of the castle and the conservatory, on the balcony where more dining tables stood.

"Coffee. Black." Adrik spoke to the man in a red apron at the counter. *Will.* The name tag read. Will nodded and turned around to serve the coffee as Adrik walked to the railing, looking right at the path to the greenhouse.

"Here it is, Sir." Will placed the coffee on the table next to Adrik. He nodded, picking up the cup and continuing to slowly watch around the bar. Finally, the Illuminator appeared. He looked around at first, then continued walking to Adrik.

"Mister Montova?" he whispered.

Adrik nodded. "Sit. I have a well-paid job for you."

"Yes, Orson told me about it," the Illuminator smiled. "I'm up for any job that will get me out of working double shifts here."

"Tell me, what is your name and Illuminator order?"

"Jack O'Rendell. I'm a Joviankalai. A physicist, to be specific. I can move metal with my mind, hence why I'm working at the Armory. Or alternate it to make weapons too, even though that is not my best suit."

"What are your other tasks?"

"Taking materials from the storage room to the labs, down by the conservatory."

"The Illuminator biologists and chemists work there," Adrik added.

"Yes, some of them," Jack said firmly. "There are a lot of rooms in the castle, but you get used to it all."

"Indeed."

Jack nodded, his face awakened as the late afternoon Sun hit his face.

"I need you to get a few things out of the fabric room," Adrik said at once, looking around.

"Fabric room? Things? Do you mean uniforms?"

"Yes, all of them, of all kinds. The Courts' coats, guards, and high official uniforms, including the gold and silver pins. By tonight."

"Tonight?" Jack frowned, his face now filled with shock and curiosity. For a second, he thought Adrik was joking.

"Yes, tonight."

But he wasn't. "Ok... it will be done. I will get them to your room before midnight," Jack responded.

Adrik held out his hand for a handshake. "Make sure no one sees you, especially not the Court members." Jack nodded as if saying *Of course* and stood up to leave. Time was still ticking, and Adrik didn't waste any time. He checked his silver pocket watch and got up at once, leaving the cup on the table. *Time for action.*

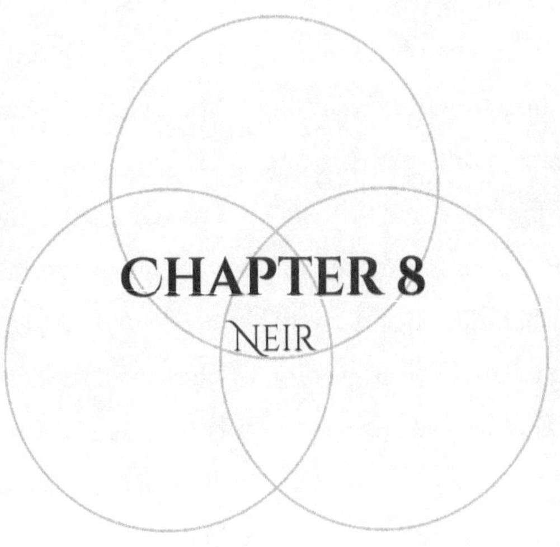

CHAPTER 8
NEIR

"Neir, we need another batch of sugar cookies!" Briz screamed from the counter.

"Ils arrivent!" Neir hurried, taking out another batch of cookies from the top oven. With the cold weather increasing in Paris, France, more people entered the bakery during the holidays. Later in the day, it would get fuller, especially at night. It was good for the business, but Neir could barely handle the somewhat angry, frustrating stares of customers waiting.

"What else do we need?" Neir said, looking at the line of customers, mentally preparing herself for the next hours... not for baking but for complete self-control.

"C'est tout... for now," Briz responded, taking the batch of sugar cookies and placing them on the rack under the glass counter. A light on the ceiling corner of the store started flickering again.

Neir had called the technician this morning, but the light was starting to bother her.

"I'll be at the back, checking on the loaves of bread," Neir said to Briz, who had started attending to another customer.

"Merci," Briz thanked the customers and nodded. "You know—" she whispered to Neir, "—if you could just tell the recipes for all the pastries you make, we can work much faster."

Neir half-smiled and shook her head. "No matter how many times you tell me. The answer is no." She passed the brown curtain into the kitchen and headed towards the back, where the ingredients were stored in the fridge or the storage room. A clashing sound came from the back of the bakery. *What the hell?* Neir turned around, opening the back door, revealing the dark, lonely alley and other shops' back doors. The sound came again from the right, where a few boxes stood. It wasn't hard for Neir to see in the dark or move as fast as the wind. She quickly grabbed hold of someone's hand and pushed it towards the light of the shop to see their face.

"Hey! Chill, Neir! It's just me!" a voice she recognized said. Neir rolled her eyes at the sight of the 13-year-old kid with a short haircut and let go of him.

"Erin, really?" Neir crossed her arms.

"What?" Erin started, fixing his shirt. "You know I always come through the back door. It's not like I'm going to steal anything."

"There is a reason for the existence of an *entrance*. Did you know?" Neir mocked, walking inside the bakery kitchen with Erin behind her.

"Yeah, yeah, whatever..." Erin closed the door behind him, rolling his eyes.

"Briz! Your *annoying* kid is here, by the way... again," Neir exclaimed.

Erin sighed, annoyed. "Oh, shut up, *grandma*. At least I help you too, *and* without getting paid by the way."

"*That* is why I don't," Neir said quickly before Erin disappeared behind the brown curtain. She liked annoying Erin, he reminded her of his younger brother, only back when they were young and actually happy. The memory of them playing as kids was a complete blur that seemed like it never really happened. But she didn't have time to ponder about old times, she always moved on with life, and that is what she continued doing. The bakery was the only thing that kept her composed, distracted from the urge of going out into the darkness, no matter how much she longed to return to her true self.

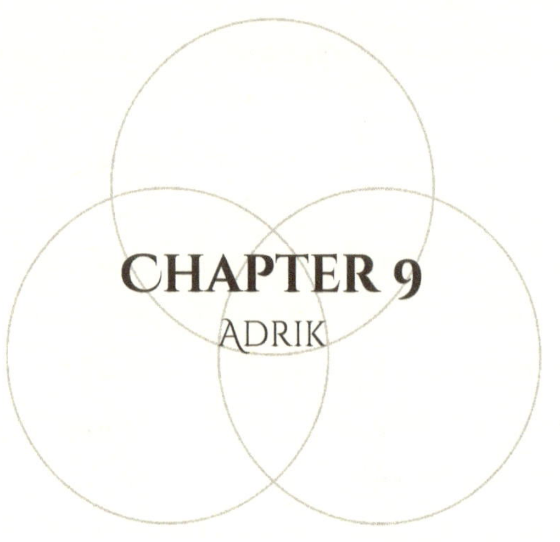

CHAPTER 9
ADRIK

THE ETHER COUNCIL meeting, Adrik had heard earlier, was happening in ten minutes. *Other than business? What did the Court want with Ether Council? Must be important for them to come a long way.* He walked through the greenhouse path, taking a turn at the stairs to the isolated second floor. The grand meeting room was connected to two other rooms on each side; their visible entrance was directly inside the large room. *In every place, there's always a secret.* Adrik walked back and forth, pacing each hallway of the second floor and looking closely at the walls, paintings, and tapestries hanging. A clue. Something that would help him know what was going on inside that he didn't know.

"Mister Montova, correct?" a man's voice he recognized said. Terrance appeared from the main hallway, crossing the grand room door to the right just where Adrik was standing.

"*Adrik* Montova," Adrik responded.

"Terrance Deakins." Terrance half-smiled, holding out his hand for a handshake. His bad posture reminded him of Craven. Between Terrance and Isaiah, it was clear who was more intellectual. Each witch showed it in their appearance. Kaan wore the dominance of all wearing black. Then, there was Isaiah's red streaked hair and glasses. And Terrance with short, almost bald hair and a crooked smile. Adrik looked at Terrance's right-hand palm. *A bullseye tattoo.* A memory sparked. He glared at him without shaking his hand.

"You are not taking my assistant, are you, Terrance?" Kaan appeared from the main hallway as well, walking towards them. He stood beside them, and that's when Terrance finally lowered his arm. "No, not at all." He smiled.

"I hope not. Mister Montova is a trusted ally." Kaan looked at Adrik. He nodded back at his statement.

"I'm sure of that." Terrance smiled back and forth. "I hope you accept me for a drink someday, Mister Montova."

"To hoping, Mister Deakins," Adrik responded. *Sometime very soon.* Terrace started walking away, entering the grand room. Once he was out of sight, Kaan started speaking.

"What did he want?" He turned to Adrik.

"Not exactly sure. I would have known if you hadn't shown up," Adrik said, trying to keep his voice calm and composed. He had to figure out how to keep his deal with Kaan while completing his plan, too. The freedom of just being close by was helpful, but with Court members and judging high officials always around, he had to keep hidden and careful. After all, being part of five gangs and somewhat a partner to Craven hadn't been all that bad. Adrik had grown up to be a thief, a criminal, a spy, a businessman, a murderer, and any other word that meant 'bad' in the world's thesaurus.

Kaan smirked. "I'm putting my wealth in you, Adrik. I assure you that siding with someone else or betraying me will gladly put you in my book of death." He was about to turn but paused. "By the way, Mister Montova. There are a few things I have to discuss with you. Let us meet in the dining room after the meeting in two hours."

Adrik made a slight nod, watching Kaan walk into the grand room. The same memory sparked again, and now he couldn't avoid it.

Smoke and people's screams filled the village. "Walk!" the masked man said, pushing ten-year-old Adrik forward. Behind them, the village burned, and ahead they walked to the edge of the Adriatic Sea. Adrik clasped the silver rings in his hand. The man behind him held a sword, blood dripping from both the sword and his dark coat. With anger, Adrik turned and, without luck, tried to push the knife into the man's hand, the one with the bullseye tattoo in the palm. The man screamed, "You piece of shit." Adrik started to run but didn't get far, stopping in his tracks when the silhouette of a horse approached him. The masked man was quickly behind him again, wincing in pain but grabbing hold of Adrik once again with his other hand. He looked at the hooded man who got off the horse, hiding his bloody hand with his coat sleeve.

"Sir—" the masked man started, looking at Adrik back and forth. Adrik winced quietly at the tight hand holding him.

"Any vampires?" the hooded masked man asked, his voice cold as ice.

"None," the masked man replied, his eyes glaring deeply at the angry boy. "Three dead from his house. A man, his wife…"

"And my sister," Adrik spoke furiously. He had never felt hate in his entire life, but now he was pretty sure he knew of it.

The masked man mocked. "Calm down, boy. You won't remember any of this in the next few hours."

"Are you going to kill me?" Adrik spat out.

"Something worse," the hooded man spoke. "A mind spell won't hurt." The masked man pushed him forward, passing the hooded man, closer to the coastline where a medium cruise ship stood. An eclipse design on its dark surface. Adrik turned around, and even though he couldn't completely see or hear from the smoke and screams of people, he managed to speak as loudly and coldly as he could.

"Go to hell, witch!"

The hooded man laughed, speaking in a raspy voice. "Been there. Done that. I can't die."

Adrik smirked. "Not yet." And continued walking to the boat with the masked man following behind. He didn't try to fight afterward or cry a single tear. From that moment as he sat on the edge of the cruise, watching the moonlight hit the three silver rings in his hand, he promised himself one thing and one thing only. He wasn't going to die, not until he sought revenge for his entire family.

Adrik waited until the three witch members from Stellar Court entered the grand room to continue walking around the hall. Ether Council hadn't arrived yet. *Time is ticking.* He watched each wall like it would give him the answer on how to dissolve through, then he walked into the hallway next to the grand room. The bottom half of the walls were designed like rectangles. *Small doors.* About four entryway tables stood in the entire hall as decorations, but only one stood against the wall at the end of the hall, closer to the grand room. Adrik headed to the end quickly, watching around for any sudden person who could be circulating on the restricted floor.

With the eyesight of an owl, the secret passages beyond the door were exactly how Adrik had imagined them, similar to the underground Casino alleyways. He walked down the tunnel, turning right with a silver lighter in his hands. A few spiderwebs, candle lights, and lightbulbs hung from the corner of some hidden passageways, showing the desertedness of them. Paths that the blueprints hadn't shown.

He avoided turning on the light switch on the wall, in case it triggered some alarm. There had to be at least someone from Stellar Court who knew of them or someone that used them from time to time. Just ahead, he could see steel stairs and a formless shape in the broken ceiling. *Another entrance.* He headed towards it, grasping the lighter in his hands to see clearly. Dust came off the ceiling as he opened the small door.

The bright fluorescent light from the room made him blink twice. Wooden cold floor greeted him as he stood around the messy room. Half of it was storage with piles of books on the floor and closed barrels. The other half, where the bright light came from, looked like a lab. Two tables stood in the middle with lab equipment, while all around them stood glass shelves. Adrik closed the wooden door, fitting exactly like a puzzle. He headed towards the shelves on the walls first. Glass cylinders with a clear liquid stood on every open space. There was no name or sign determining what chemicals they held, but Adrik could tell that everything in the hidden room was deeply important. Next, he checked the tables. They were all filled with equipment, except for a folder and a book that stood on the edge of one of the stainless steel tables. He opened the folder first. Yellow pages fell to the side. Drawings and writings on each of them. Adrik hadn't really gone to school for education, Kosmos didn't afford that. He was homeschooled at his young age, nothing much to remember either. But based on the books he read from Craven's compact library, he had learned enough to understand. *Chemical structures and equations. For what?* Then there was one page that was different from the others. This one was filled with words. *A witch spell.* Though he didn't understand much of the language, he recognized the Latin writings. And at the bottom the word *Volka* was written. *Volka.* He checked the book again, but there was no sign as to what *Volka* was, only more chemical and scientific equations written on its pages.

Sound emerged from outside the room. A door closing and chairs sliding across the floor. *They are here.* Adrik put everything back in its original place, taking another look around the table before opening the door by a crack. From where he stood, he could see Stellar Court witches and members of Ether Council sitting down at the large table on the dais. Slowly he got out of the room, trying to hear clearer. The bookshelves and museum displays helped him cover himself. He made a mental note of the people in the room. *Six Ether Council members, Kaan, Terrance, Isaiah, and a young man with blue-streaked hair, standing by the witches.*

"Now, let's get down to business," a voice started. Adrik recognized it as *Terrance's*. He peeked from the shelves every second he could.

"We will gladly elaborate. But first, coffee or a drink, anyone?" Kaan said, nodding at Terrance and turning to the Council.

"Sure," a woman answered. "Coffee, it's fine."

"Axel, please, if you could be so generous as to give our guests a drink," Kaan turned to the young man next to him, Axel. He walked down the dais, heading right. Without hesitation, Adrik went back inside the room, hiding in the shadows of the barrels. Axel entered the room and quickly opened a box that stood at the edge, placed nine cups on the table, and grabbed one of the glass tube cylinders from the shelf. He carefully poured the clear liquid into only six of the cups, then added a dark food coloring to them. From where Adrik could see, they were almost full. Then, Axel continued to pour a brown liquid from a thermo flask onto the three remaining cups.

"Just like coffee," Axel whispered, putting the coffee cups with sugar cubes on a wooden tray. He headed quickly out of the room, holding the tray in his hands. Adrik waited for a few seconds before heading quietly back out of the room and hiding between the displays.

"This coffee is imported from France." Terrance laughed, taking a sip from the cup. "Best coffee I ever drank." Isaiah nodded, doing the same, followed by Kaan and everyone else.

"Mmh, you're right," a man from Ether Council responded.

Terrance smiled. "All right, let's get down to business then."

"Yes, we only know the basics that you all stated last meeting. Nothing regarding the actual plan. We are all curious." The man that spoke looked at the rest of Ether Council. "How exactly will you help us have more power than we already do?"

"The plan takes time... *but* the plan is perfect indeed," Terrance responded.

"It will take a lot of effort from everyone in Kosmos. Witches and Illuminators alike, including our new ones," Isaiah resumed.

"How so?" A Council woman coughed, looking back and forth at the three witches.

Kaan shuffled in his chair, sitting up. "Fairly simple really," he smirked. "All you have to do is drink the cup and do as I say."

That's when everything seemed to shift. Ether Council had come to a realization, their shaking bodies and coughs becoming more uncontrollable.

"What did you—" a woman was trying to speak, interrupted by a cough.

"Bastards—" one of the old men exclaimed, his voice quivering slightly.

"Now." Kaan stood up, followed by his companions. "What is coursing through your veins right now is called *volka*." He looked at the man, who had started to get up slowly. "No. No, don't fight it, old man. It won't work." The three Solar Court members stood upon Ether Council, waiting and looking at them without sympathy.

"In a matter of seconds, you will do as we say," Terrance said. "One."

"Two," Isaiah continued, his face showing no emotion.

Kaan grinned, looking down at the frozen bodies on their chairs. "Three."

PART FIVE

VOLKA

CHAPTER 10
ADRIK

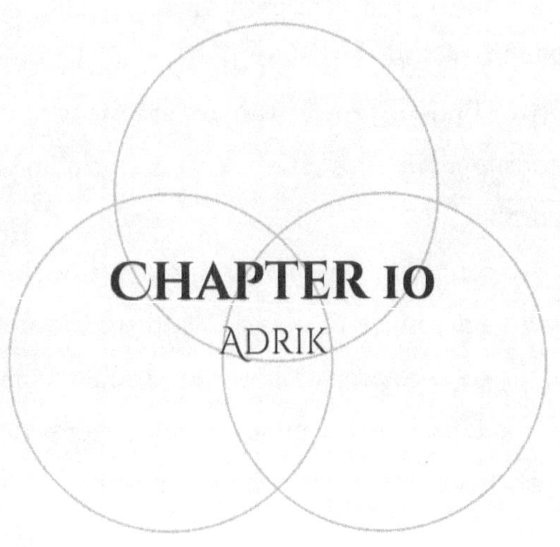

*V*OLKA WAS A DRUG. A controlling one. A magical poison made by Stellar Court for power and control.

Ether Council sat on their chairs like rag dolls. Puppets waiting for their masters to control them, to tell them what to do next. Soldiers with loyalty on their sleeves.

"What is our job, Sir?" the old man had started to speak, his voice firm and sure.

"That's more like it," Kaan responded. "From now on, you will do as we say."

"Yes, Sir," the council said in unison.

"Perfect," continued Kaan, nodding at Terrance.

"This is the plan. Listen carefully," Terrance spoke. "You will head back to Ether in the next hours and act accordingly. Like your usual selves. Except it isn't only you all who will head to Ether alone. *Volka* will go with you."

"I don't understand," one of the members said.

"We will send *volka* to Ether," Kaan clarified. "Your job as the Council is to find all people who are against witches, traitors, Illuminator supporters, protesters... anyone, including Arkadians, if that's possible."

They responded in unison once again. "Yes, Sir."

"I will send you all a message. Till then, you must wait to distribute the *volka* to people's houses, restaurants, and cafes. Say it's a gift from the Council, a miracle medicine, or better yet... We will send officials and guards to make sure everyone takes it. *Understood*?"

"Yes, Sir."

"Very well then. You will hear from us soon."

"Yes, Sir." Ether Council stood up from their chairs and just like that, they left the grand room with glazed eyes, acting as if everything was normal. Adrik hid back into the dark, still listening closely. Then, looked through the small crack between two bookshelves.

"It worked, Sir." Axel turned to Kaan.

"Of course it did." Terrance faltered. "I—I mean, *we* are powerful witches, and we never fail."

Kaan laughed. "Sure, Terrance, maybe exclude yourself."

Isaiah smiled. "Terrace, what were you doing the past few years we were working on the chemical? Being lazy, drinking *sulya*, and eating *sulya* cakes."

"Be quiet, Isaiah." Terrance rolled his eyes.

"You just know I'm right."

"Wrong."

"You are both *idiots*." Kaan shook his head and looked at Axel. "Make sure to bring all high officials from the castle here at midnight. We will start with them and then the guards. We will need everything in control to expand the *volka* to Ether and the other Castles."

"Right away, Sir," Axel responded, starting to walk down the dais.

"And Axel," Kaan said. "Make sure the truth about *volka* doesn't spread."

"It is clear, Sir."

Kaan grinned. "The Supernatural War isn't over."

It was never really over to begin with. Adrik thought.

CHAPTER II
NEIR

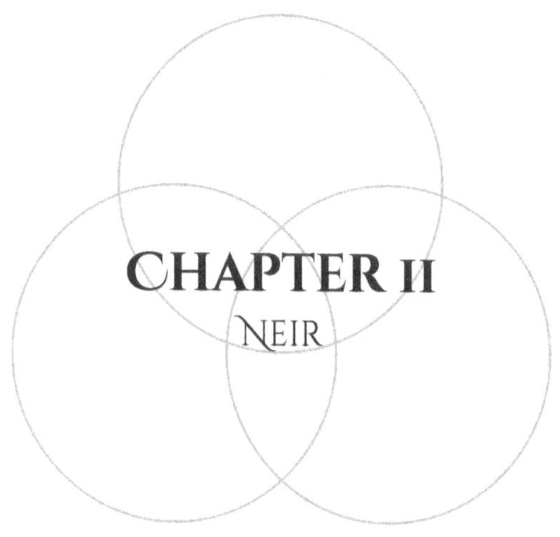

IT WASN'T THAT NEIR wasn't used to it. She liked the adrenaline that came with baking and having a lot of customers coming through the doors of her bakery. But it wasn't the same as running above buildings or fighting against the monsters in the dark. The thought sometimes came to her every night she stayed in the bakery cleaning, but she'd push it away again, knowing well that those times were over. Her old self was gone and needed to be gone.

"See you tomorrow!" Briz exclaimed, grabbing her purse from the counter. "Come on, Erin, let's go!"

"You're not my mom," Erin said. Briz looked at him as if to say, *You better be joking.* "I'm just kidding, Mom. It was just a joke."

Neir smiled and waved goodbye. "I think you should ground him."

"I think you should not listen to her." Erin rolled his eyes, following Briz to the exit.

"Night, Neir," Briz said.

"Night, Briz... and annoying kid," Neir responded.

"Bonne Nuit, Neir *annoying* De Van." Erin smiled.

Neir rolled her eyes at him but smiled back. "Shut up, Erin," she said before the kid closed the door. Joking around with Erin was one of her favorite times, even though she didn't want to admit it. She admired Briz for her hard work in trying to take care of him during her current circumstances. Erin always used humor to brighten the day, and Neir had gotten used to being around them. She finished cleaning the last few tables of the bakery. The broken light mocked her and reminded her to make more adjustments. She always changed the interior setting and the outside clean, to attract new customers, and it worked. Right now, it was a cozy, winter weather atmosphere with holiday decorations and yellow lights hanging from the ceiling. She had placed bookshelves on the walls, a coffee station at the right of the shop, and candles on each rustic beige table.

The bakery was clean once again, ready for tomorrow. Neir put all the cleaning supplies away in the storage room and headed out of the shop, turning out the lights and locking the doors. She let her blonde, wavy hair down from her ponytail. A simple night routine for a simple day. Yet as she walked down the next street, where her apartment was located, she could feel an instinct, one that she hadn't felt for a long time. Tingling in her wrist and ankles. The feeling that she wasn't alone in the absence of the light. She turned into a dark alley and stopped. The weight of eyes on her shoulder. Someone was already in front of her in a matter of seconds. Neir took a knife from inside her jacket, hitting the man on his left leg and putting the knife to his neck. *A supernatural.*

"Who the hell are you?" she said, tightening her grip on the man's neck. *Either a hunter or a vampire.* She couldn't tell. "Speak now, or I won't hesitate to cut your neck. I guarantee you won't be able to speak afterward."

The man didn't speak, but a mocking laugh emerged from the dark alley beside her. "Nice, sister! I see you haven't lost your hunter instincts after three years."

Carden. Neir let go of the man she held. *A vampire.* She realized, knowing the proximity of a hunter and a deathly monster messed up her sense of recognition. He walked away from her, watching her closely, and disappeared down the street. Carden smiled, the same old, cold, and annoying grin on his face. A part of her wished she could punch him. She was certainly a better fighter than him, way better when she felt angry.

"Oh, come on, sister. No huge greeting for your little brother? After three years?" Carden crossed his arms.

"You stopped being my brother three years ago, so of course not. We both know I'm still a better hunter than you, Carden." Pride certainly felt good.

Carden smirked. "And yet sister... I'm the vice-director of the HSS." *The Hunter Supernatural Society.* Hunters maintained the balance between humans and the supernatural. Hunters with a vengeance against vampires. Their main enemy for years. *Haven't heard of that in a while.*

"Only because you made our parents believe you were that *good.* How many vampires did you kill that day? One," Neir half-laughed, trying not to let anger control her. "No more than me, of course. Mr. I-Killed-About-Fifteenth-Vampires-In-Less-Than-Five-Minutes. Six of which were light vampires."

"I lied. Get over it." Carden shook his head, and Neir almost lost it.

"No. You betrayed me. Stabbed me in the back... literally." She remembered it all like it was yesterday. The emotional and physical pain that she went through that day. A mission the siblings have been tasked to take for their father, the former vice-president of HSS. Their dad had told Atticus, his best friend and director at that time, that they were one of the best hunters. The siblings were practically well-known in the HSS, children of the beloved vice-director. Everyone liked her father, he was kind and respectful. Still, there was one thing about him that bothered Neir and mostly the women in the HSS: Mr. De Van was just not up-to-date. In his eyes, there could never be a woman leader. Sure, there were a few exceptions, thanks to Atticus, but other than that, Mr. De Van would never agree to have a director, vice-director, or even HSS council member as a woman. Even Neir's mom seemed to go with the flow. She didn't fight or protest, she just stood there in silence. And that bothered Neir the most. Standing there, not moving forward.

"I've heard rumors that someone has been killing vampires all around Paris. Four, to be exact, in the past two weeks. Three night vampires and one light, which *I* found with wooden stakes in their hearts before they dissipated into air." Carden continued to smirk. He always wanted everything to be about him. Neir couldn't decide if that was pathetic or embarrassing.

"How is this my problem exactly?" Neir crossed her arms, knowing well Carden had a plan up his sleeve.

"You've become a vampire vigilante now?"

"If I'm no longer a vampire *hunter*, then what else should I be?"

"A normal human being, who doesn't get people's way." Carden took a step forward, but Neir stood her ground.

"What? Scared I will take your spotlight… again." Neir smiled. "What are you going to do this time? Lie. Cry to daddy. Increase your rank as a hypocrite? Maybe all?"

"Neither," Carden responded. "I can just kill you in your sleep." *Now, this is something unexpected.* Neir wasn't sure how far his brother would go for power. Betraying the closest family member was already beyond the line.

She smiled. "I can kill you when you are wide awake and with my eyes closed."

Carden walked closer until he was about three feet away. "Listen closely, Neir," he said slowly. "If I happen to cross myself with another dead vampire of yours. I will make sure you get back inside the HSS—as a *prisoner*. Not only are you banned as a hunter, but you are messing with supernatural business. I suggest going back to your pretty little bakery human life."

"The wooden stake doesn't leave hunter DNA marks. You don't and won't have proof about who did the killings."

"I don't need proof." Carden shrugged, walking backward.

"No," Neir said. "But soon you will. The vampire killings won't stop, and whatever business the HSS has with them will go down." She walked closer to Carden, finally seeing him slightly shiver in the dark. "I suggest starting to take notes, little brother. It has been three years. I'm coming back. And this time, I will not only come back as a hunter. I will also go back to take the spot as the director."

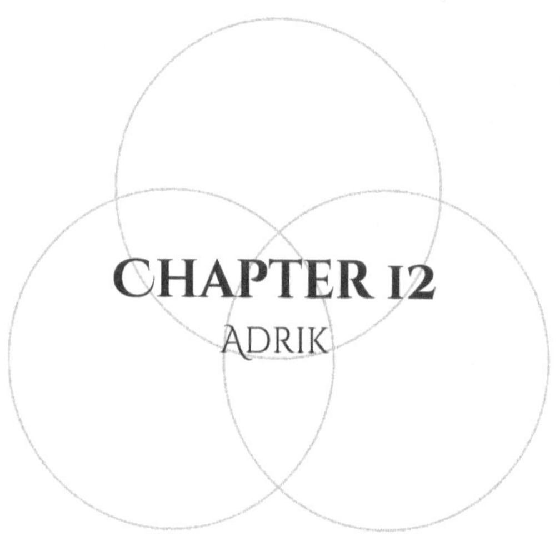

CHAPTER 12
ADRIK

K AAN'S EYES LANDED on Adrik the second he entered the dining area on the third floor. He sat at the table at the edge of the room. Nobody dared to sit close to him. One of the waiters, Adrik heard, was avoiding going over to his table. "Go. For me. Please." He heard the waiter say to his friend, who then shook his head. Adrik couldn't understand what exactly was frightening about Kaan. His words. The way he walked. *All words and no action... yet*. Based on what Adrik saw, that is what Kaan missed. *Action*. But then again. He always knew not to underestimate people. Especially if they seem to have something up their sleeves. Like controlling people with a drug. *That fits my book.*

"Mister Adrik Montova. Sit," Kaan started once Adrik approached the table. "What I have to say is interesting and brief."

Adrik looked at Kaan, knowing well what he had to say before he even entered the room and sat down. "We are heading to Lunar

Castle, aren't we? Illuminators can't be watched this far."

Kaan tilted his head. "I knew you were right for the job the second I saw you come into the grand room. Believe me, it will all be paid well."

"As it should," Adrik replied, the feeling of fortune and revenge crawling in his mind. He got up from the table, hearing the clock ticking every second that passed. Time was the only thing that was never in his favor. It was manageable, but with any distraction, he would lose himself out of the pattern.

An hour before midnight, the traveling bag filled with Jovian-kalai-made coats and uniforms stood on the table inside his suite.

"Everything you need is here, Mister Montova," Jack said. Adrik opened the bag and checked each item. "Most coats are made by Archs or others who specialize in creativity and design. The pins are handmade by witches," Jack added while Adrik inspected.

"No one saw you."

"No. I made sure to get there before they guarded the second floor." Jack smiled, as if proud. "Orson will be walking around the halls as instructed. I will also be around if needed."

Adrik held out a pack of *Kosni* bills. "Your part of the deal."

Jack bowed his head. "Thank you, Mister. If there's anything else I can do for you in the future, please don't hesitate to ask."

Adrik nodded, watching Jack get out of the room quietly, putting the purple-blue bills in his pocket.

There is nothing that money can't do. Adrik remembered Franko's quote as he walked through the fourth floor. Five minutes before midnight and everyone—high officials, guards, and other guests residing in the castle, were in the grand room already. Stellar Court had a big, suspicious, and messy plan. *One that can hurt mine.*

The fourth floor was isolated. Half of the castle's residents were gone. He suspected Kaan was already in the grand room, and he had just seen Isaiah walking down the stairs to the third floor eight minutes ago. Jack had made sure to re-check that they were down on the second floor, pretending he had forgotten his coat in the greenhouse. The fourth floor was the level filled with only chambers and resting rooms. Each room looked the same, with only different types of decorations. Adrik noticed the walls, he now recognized some of them to be secret door rooms behind tapestries or tables. They were nicely hidden, but looking closely from different angles, the slight discoloration gave it away.

"Jack made it to the greenhouse, Adrik. Everyone is down there," Orson said after finding Adrik on the third floor. Then he nodded down to the fourth floor. "Maybe third hall, second to last room. They all switch rooms once in a while, but like you ordered, I investigated this morning."

Adrik now stood in front of the door that Orson indicated. He looked around one more time before he entered, his muscles tensed. His hazel-gray eyes concentrated on every small detail he could absorb from the room: book pages on the floor, self-portraits on the walls, bright red everywhere, tiger monuments, and the balcony windows were open. The cold air hit Adrik's face as he walked further inside the chamber. Light entered the room from the open door beside the nightstand. The water running in the sink stopped, and lights in the chamber turned on from the other side.

He could see the person he was looking for standing at the foot of the bed.

"Mister Montova?" Terrance stood, startled.

Adrik raised his eyebrows. "No trust issues, I see. You are a Stellar Court member, and your room wasn't even locked. You must feel really comfortable."

Terrance stood in his place, a confused expression at the sight of Adrik. "I was heading out—"

"To the grand meeting room?"

"Yes, I forgot something. Thus, I didn't lock it," he rambled and stopped. "How did you know where I was?"

"I know a lot of things, Terrance. A great deal. Even the future and what is going to happen in a few minutes."

Terrance fixed his black hair, his hand shaking through the gray strands. "Adrik, are you alright? Have you been drinking? You shouldn't even be here. Have you forgotten your manners?"

"I'm perfectly awake, Terrance." Adrik walked closer. "There are absolutely no manners to show to murderers."

"Don't move closer, Montova. What the hell is wrong with you? I won't hesitate to—"

Like a flash, Adrik was already in front of Terrance. Before he could even mumble a spell in the air, Adrik injected a syringe with a clear liquid into Terrance's neck. In a matter of seconds, *volka* was running through his veins. "I suggest taking a seat."

Terrance did as he was told, watching Adrik with glaring and somewhat cold eyes. The *volka* was working, but not the way he had seen with the Council members.

"What do you want?" Terrance croaked. Adrik started pacing

around the chair, deciding on where exactly to start.

"I can recognize that bullseye tattoo anywhere, Terrance. How many people have you killed? One person, a group, maybe a few villages?"

"What? I have not killed anyone?" Terrance shook his head.

"Really? Not throughout *all* these years." Adrik looked at him. "Do a little remembering, Terrance?"

Terrance shook his head again.

"Or do you need help remembering?" Adrik got a knife from his coat. "Speak." He saw Terrance's eyes widen at the knife. *Fear.* He sat frozen. The *volka* weakened him and stopped him from hurting those he was following orders from.

"Villages. A lot of people died."

"You mean you killed them... You are a murderer." Adrik shook the knife in front of the witch's eyes.

"For good cause."

"Nothing is for 'good cause'. Innocent people dying is no *good* cause," Adrik spat in anger. "You killed a family in Venice, Italy. A small, quiet village by the coast was burnt under witches' orders."

"I don't remember. Too many killings," Terrance choked, his face now filled with sweat.

Adrik shook his head. "That scar on your hand. A kid made it right after you killed his family, didn't he?"

Terrance nodded slowly. "Yes. That stupid kid—" Realization came upon his face, making Adrik smirk.

"Remember anything yet?"

His brown eyes looked up at Adrik. "*You.*"

"It has been a while, *witch*." The young boy enjoyed the look on Terrance's face.

"What do you want?" Terrance said at once. "Revenge?"

"The truth. You will tell me the truth." Adrik wasted no time.

"You can't make me."

"Yes, I can. *Volka* is already running through your system. Or I can go to old methods instead." He shook the knife in front of Terrance again, who just sat back quietly in his chair like a puppet. "Now, tell me who was involved? Who was in the plan? Who sent the order? *Who killed them?*"

Terrance shook his head, keeping silent. Adrik drew the knife closer to his hand and pressed it hard against the tattoo. He watched Terrance wince.

"Were they in it?" Adrik grunted. "Kaan? Isaiah?"

"No..."

"No, what?" Adrik gritted his teeth.

"They weren't in it. Neither of them was there at the time..."

"Kaan said otherwise."

Terrance rolled his eyes. "He was just showing off. He is like that. For the universe's sake, he is the youngest of us all. He has been part of the court for five years, right after Isaiah got in."

"What about Solar Court members from years ago? *Who* gave the order?"

Terrance shook his head weakly, sweating. "I don't know."

"Tell me." Adrik pressed the knife again.

"I don't know," Terrance winced, blood dripping from his hand. "I swear I can't say. I can't. I won't!" Adrik slightly frowned as he realized that Terrance was fighting the *volka*.

"How is it that you are fighting the drug?" he asked, still pressing the knife.

"I'm slightly immune to it. I've experimented on myself for years," Terrance grunted, his voice becoming lower each second.

"Answer my questions, Terrance. *Who* gave the order?"

"I *can't* say."

"Then tell me the *volka* plan. What is Stellar Court planning?"

"I can't say that either."

As Adrik had suspected, there was something else that forbade Terrance to speak, something like a blood pact. Witches happened to be known for that. "That's a pity," Adrik said, grabbing Terrance by the neck and dragging him away from the chair. He placed the knife in Terrance's clean hand.

"What are you doing?" Terrance looked at the knife.

"Keep the knife," Adrik said, his voice distant.

"You can't kill me. They will come to look for me if I don't go to the grand room. I'm already expected to be there."

"Really?" Adrik tilted his head. "In that case, you can head out through the window." He shoved Terrance out the balcony without care, hearing his body hit the floor of someone else's balcony downstairs. Terrance's glazed eyes looked up into the night sky. *Say hello to Hell for me.* Adrik thought, glancing at the lifeless body.

PART SIX

CITY OF AURUM

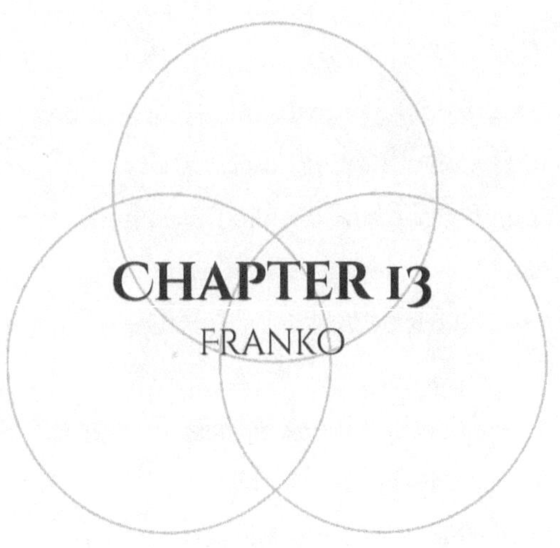

CHAPTER 13
FRANKO

*S*ANDWICHES? YES. "What else am I missing?" Franko whispered to himself, smiling at his leather bag, one-fourth of it filled with Kosni bills and coins. He couldn't sleep the entire night. It had all felt like a dream. *I wouldn't be surprised if bombs started to go off these few days.* Most people didn't buy bombs for personal use, though. Most Arkadians have learned to trade and make deals. The only ones best at it were Craven and Adrik. Now, Adrik was gone, and Franko had accomplished to sell more than he ever had. Yet he couldn't decide if his absence was good or bad. He had gotten used to him. His only friend... at least in his mind. *He is my friend, but he doesn't know it yet. Or won't admit it.*

Franko counted the money again, re-checking his bag for all his necessary items, which mostly included bags with sandwiches cut in half horizontally. He closed all the blinds of the store before he headed out into the light rain.

"Where are you going so fast, Franko?" a voice behind him started. *There goes my happy morning.* Franko almost glared at Liam, then realized as he turned around that he wasn't going to give him the satisfaction of ruining his perfect day.

"My number one fan," Franko fixed a smile, hanging the bag over his chest. "Do you want an autograph?"

Liam smiled back. "You will want mine whenever I have my riches."

Franko laughed and shook his head in disbelief. "Sure, Liam, *kill* me when that happens."

"You can laugh all you want, Franko, but you know what I see in my future? Fortune. Never-ending money and gold," Liam said, looking behind Franko as two of Liam's friends appeared behind him. Franko shrugged like it was nothing. No fear ran through his bones; another lesson Adrik had taught him. *Fear. Never reveal it. Not an inch of it.*

Franko stood his ground, his left hand gripping the suitcase and the other inside his coat pocket. "Really?" he started. "Because all I see is the word *coward* in big, bold, capital letters."

Liam walked towards him. "Are you scared, Sezin? Now that your boss isn't around?"

"Scared?" Franko frowned. "I'm not the one sending his sidekicks to fight me because you can't do it yourself." A cloud of smoke surrounded them in seconds. Sighs and grunts surfaced from the gray cloud. But far away, Franko screamed, "You aren't rich yet by the way!" running into the crowds of the streets without looking back.

Running was not exactly his best hobby. He panted as he walked into Ark Station.

"I'm going to *die*," he whispered, gasping for air.

"Me too, man," an old man who sat on the street replied. He held a cup with Kosni coins in his dirty hands. Franko checked for spare change in his coat pocket, twenty *Kosniz*, and gave it to the man. "Thank you." He smiled, fixing his brown hat.

"Never mind, I can't die," Franko said to himself. "I'm not that rich." He walked further inside to where the conductor stood to collect train tickets. Franko held out his ticket.

"We will depart in ten minutes," the conductor informed. Franko nodded and headed inside the train, sitting down next to the window in an empty compartment. A few minutes later, he was heading towards Ether, the City of Gold. As the train started, he took out a sandwich from his bag and started eating it, thinking about Liam's foolishness. Finishing his sandwich, he felt a warmth burning in his coat pocket. *The pocket watch.* He grabbed the bronze watch, lighting red and warm to the touch, and opened it to reveal a small paper coming out of the red portal with a *triquela* sign on the edge of its burnt edges. *A message from Adrik.* He took the paper that flew out in front of him and closed the pocket watch. *I will never get over this great invention.* Franko thought as he grabbed the paper and started reading it.

I am heading to Lunar Castle. The plan is in motion. Don't fail in Ether. And no detours either.

"Of course, boss." Franko shook his head, shaking the paper three times, making it disappear in the air.

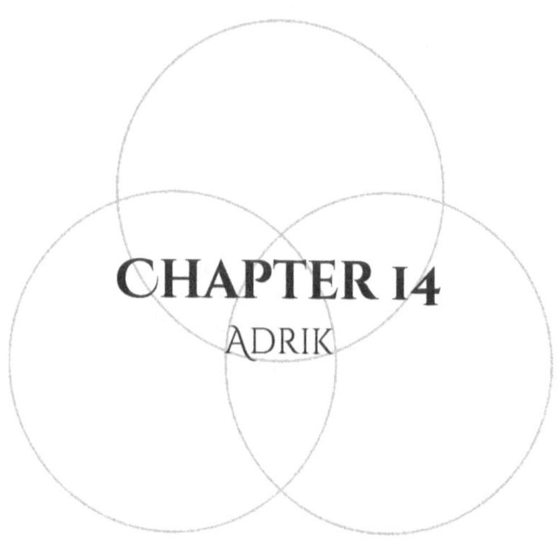

CHAPTER 14
ADRIK

NEWS OF TERRANCE'S DEATH had reached the entire castle right at sunrise. Adrik entered the noisy grand meeting room. Axel had knocked on his suite door in the morning, following orders from Kaan.

"Suicide?" Isaiah was speaking, tilting his head. "You think he wanted to die falling off a balcony..."

Kaan nodded. "Yes, I believe so. Guards are searching the castle for any suspicious activity." Axel walked up the dais and stood in front of the table, crossing Kaan. Adrik noticed he was always there, besides Kaan, in every important matter. They all stood up, thinking. It wasn't until Kaan looked at him that Adrik made a slight nod.

"I have to leave for Lunar Castle today. The plan must keep going," Kaan said, turning to look at a frowning Isaiah. "Isaiah..."

Isaiah looked up. "I am listening."

"You must stay here. Send a messenger to both Castles and inform the Courts about the tragic incident. I won't have time to inform them all."

Isaiah made a nod, walking down the dais and heading out of the room. Adrik could tell Isaiah did not believe Terrance's cause of death. Kaan waited until Isaiah had left the room to speak.

"There is an assassin in the castle," Kaan said, looking at both Adrik and Axel. Only for a millisecond, Adrik thought he had been caught. He didn't feel an inch of regret. Kaan continued looking at Adrik with a frown on his face.

"He didn't take his own life?" Adrik asked.

"No," Axel responded, his voice quiet. "He was poisoned."

"With what?"

"*Volka*," Kaan said.

"What is *volka*?"

"A type of new drug."

Adrik shook his head slightly, making sure not to ask any more questions that would raise suspicion. He already knew what Kaan wanted from him. "You want me to find out who did it."

Kaan nodded. "Yes, but no rush. We are leaving for Lunar Castle. When we come back, we can't have a traitor alive."

"Certainly." Adrik nodded.

"The carriage has been ready, Sir," Axel informed Kaan, walking down the dais. Adrik turned around to leave as well.

"Wait," Kaan stopped before Adrik could leave. "You must know that I don't trust no one. However, I have chosen you both for an important matter. Don't make me regret my choices."

Both Axel and Adrik made a slight nod. As far as Adrik knew, he was the only one who didn't mean it.

CHAPTER 15
FRANKO

THE FIRST THING THAT Franko did after getting off at Ether Station was the first thing Adrik told him not to do. He couldn't help it. The City of Gold was far better than he had seen during his last visit two years ago. A bit more modern and populated by more modest people. Sadly, there wasn't any modern machinery yet: cars, airplanes, computers, or anything similar that Franko had read about in some books. He dreamed of one day getting out of Kosmos. Yet that day could not come until he had gained enough money and finished his work with Adrik. *Soon*. He thought. One day, he would get out and do everything he ever wanted. One day, he would be at peace.

He walked out of the station, looking at the people who wore modern, shiny clothing. Some Arkadians wore cheap modern clo-thing, but nothing compared to the clean clothes that Etherians had. Others still wore dresses or professional suits like the old standard days. Franko saw himself as he was. With long dark coats, trousers, and messy brown hair. It was the comfort that made him who he was. He passed money exchange stores. Businesses that change Kosmos *Kosniz* to currency from other countries. Not a lot of people stood in line at the closest store, and Franko decided to head there after his first mission. It was rare for Adrik to send him out for currency tasks. That was usually Orson's, and Franko didn't mind the switch in responsibility. With the tech store and running other main assignments for Adrik, money was not too safe in his hands. At least not yet. Franko turned away from the exchange store and kept walking, trying to remember whether specific structures had been there before. Most of his memories of Ether had been hazed over the last two years.

"Excuse me, Miss, may I know where the Ether Council is located?" he asked a lady in a yellow dress selling bread on the sidewalk.

"It is downtown, in the city center," she responded.

"In the city center of Ezim, correct?"

"Yes. Ezim. There's a tall golden building. It is certainly not difficult to see."

"Right. Tesekkurler ederim," Franko thanked. "I'll buy a loaf of bread."

"Great!" The lady smiled, getting a bag with a loaf of bread from the food stand next to her. "Here you go. Five *Kosniz*, por favor."

Franko paid the lady and walked forward, eating bread as he did. It was then, when the clouds had moved away from the Sun and he moved further down the street, that he saw it far away. The golden tower. It was the greatest new building he had seen in Kosmos so far, and he wondered whether it was actually made of gold. He was going to figure it out soon.

Just like Azra, the city center of Ezim filled up with people. A park and a water fountain stood in front of the golden tower. Everything was full of color, as if the Sun had chosen to only shine in one city of Kosmos instead of the other. Franko felt he had traveled from death land to the land of the living. Kids played around the fountain while their mothers screamed at them to calm down. People stood in their stands selling souvenirs, bracelets, gifts, international food, etc. He glanced at a light-brown coat, thinking it would match his skin tone if he bought it. *Where have I been this entire time?* He shook his head slightly, not believing his eyes. *If a city like Ether could turn into this,* he thought. *Then I truly wonder what the outside world looks like.*

"Pass?" one of the guards said as Franko approached the entrance of the golden tower. He shook his head in confusion.

"Oh my? I need a pass..." he said. "I was not aware. Where can I get a pass?"

"Only the Ether Council can give you one," the guard informed, his eyes looking up and down at Franko.

"Well then, don't I need to enter to get a pass?"

"No. Over there." He nodded towards a blue stand a few feet away. "You will have to fill up a form and wait for approval in three days."

"Three days?"

The guard assented.

"Mister..." Franko looked at the guard's badge. "Mister Lee...

I have an important matter with Ether Council. Is there any—"

"No." The guard shook his head. "Over there and that's that."

Franko nodded, turning around. "Three days..." he whispered, walking away to the street next by the tower. "Well then... I tried the nice option. Now comes option number two: taking a page out of Mister Montova's handbook."

He walked around the golden building, posing like Adrik while he analyzed everything surrounding it. But no matter how hard he tried to remember each small, tiny detail, he couldn't, it made his head hurt. Franko liked the unexpected. *Spontaneity* was his middle name. He didn't like plans that stressed him most of the time. Sure, he could handle them, but for him, nothing was better than surprises and fast thinking. Somehow, he was going to get into the building. Each door was individually guarded, unlike the entrance, where three guards stood. He could climb, but yet again it wasn't his best suit either.

"It has to be done," Franko talked to himself, walking around the stands and thinking of a plan that equaled getting into the building without hurting bystanders.

"Hello, kids." He smiled at two small boys walking around the fountain, selling *sulya* cakes. "Don't you think the guards would like *sulya* cakes?"

"They don't want anyone near them..." one of the small boys said.

"Well, I did hear one of them say it was their favorite dessert. Maybe if you offer them some later when the sun comes down and they are less uptight, they might even take a *dozen*."

The two boys looked at each other. "Maybe," the other boy

said. "Thank you, Mister." They walked away, watching the guards and arguing about who to ask first. All Franko had to do was wait and hope that the *sulya* cakes didn't let him down.

CHAPTER 16
ADRIK

ADRIK'S BLACK CARRIAGE arrived at the same time as Kaan's. In the blazing Sun, the metallic brightness of Kaan's four-wheeled vehicle drew attention. By the sudden silence of the road, he must have followed a different route. No surprise, Axel had traveled with Kaan. Adrik suggested he should travel alone, to which Kaan accepted with a frown. He didn't trust the businessman yet. Not until his job was complete. Probably not even then, because considering Kaan's quiet and ordered life, it appeared he trusted absolutely no one, except his thoughts.

That is the only thing that Adrik could see he had in common with Kaan. The acceptance of isolation for self-trust. Adrik understood it, and because of it, he knew Kaan had dark secrets. *Volka* was one of them. But years of living brought years of changes, and Adrik wasn't sure whether he believed Terrance about Kaan's involvement in the village fire. He needed proof, the absolute truth.

Once outside the carriage, Axel walked up to the coachman guard. "Go to the back entrance," Axel demanded. The guard nodded and left with a few other Lunar guards staring at the carriage. Lunar Castle was exactly its name. Midnight. Dark. Like Arkadia. With dark blue, black, and silver designed rugs on every floor and walls that seemed to hold the night hostage. Opposite to Solar Castle or Adrik thought based on the paintings at Stellar. Yet everything was light enough in the afternoon, making the walls lighter to a gloomy chestnut color.

"Axel," Kaan started, walking closer to the first set of stairs. "Show Mister Montova his suite. I have matters to attend to." Axel nodded. Adrik did as well, looking at Kaan as he walked down the main hall and turned left.

"I'll give you a tour in an hour, if you like," Axel said. "It will be easier if you know every inch of the castle." Adrik agreed with a mental picture of the castle's blueprint in his head. They walked up the stairs to the fourth floor.

The suite was almost similar to the one in Stellar Castle. Only this time, Adrik resided on the east side of the castle, with a view of the horse stables. He paced back and forth. *Thinking*. Without being at Stellar, there was nothing more he could figure out about his potential enemy. As far as the Lunar Castle plans showed, there was no archive room anywhere in the castle. No records of anything regarding Illuminators and their alliance with supernaturals. Nothing that could help him know who his real enemy was. He waited for Franko's response about Ether Council. But being Franko, he suspected he was waiting for nightfall to make his big smoky entrance. Adrik knew he had no choice but to follow whatever Kaan's assignments were. Still, he couldn't just sit around waiting like a puppet. Adrik's plans were numbered and just like numbers, they were endless.

Lunar Castle was emptier than Stellar, making it seem haunted. Even with some Illuminators residing just above the fourth floor, it made no difference. The witches' alliance with them only held each other with a thin thread. It was only a matter of time before witches would make their extravagant showcase to the new generation. Workers walked around the castle quickly, going back to their invisible rooms. Adrik walked down to the first floor, looking around for any sign of a Lunar Court member. He remembered James, the Stellar Court purple-coated man with glasses from the grand meeting room. He asked for more information than the ladies. On the first floor, Adrik walked down the main hall, following the movement that came from the hall Kaan had entered. When he passed by, at the end of it stood a silver door with a Moon design, closed shut. He could hear talking coming from it, but nothing was clear to understand. The handle of the silver door shook slightly. Adrik quickly walked further down the main hall, turned the corner, and waited. One minute later, the creaking of a door opening and footsteps filled the solemn air. Adrik peeked from the edge. Exactly six people in their colored coats walked out of the hall, whispering to each other. They walked down the main hall, dragging their feet on the carpet. Two of them turned sideways to talk to each other. *Lunar Court.* Adrik recognized the three Stellar Court members: Davina in green, Ingi in orange, and James. Their eyes appeared glazed under the light. *They are drugged.* Lunar Court walked upstairs, their confused but awakened faces matching Ether Council members' expression. Whatever Kaan was planning, Adrik thought, was for something far mysterious than he imagined. Curiosity rose through Adrik's mind like wildfire. There was nothing he didn't plan, not even when it came to multitasking. His mental planner filled up many tasks automatically, each of them marked off successfully by the end of the day.

Adrik stood up straight, his back to the wall, ready to turn the corner and walk into the silver room hall.

"Adrik." Adrik turned to see Axel behind, walking towards him. Axel wrinkled his brows at him, looking at the main hall. "Kaan, huh?" he said, looking at Adrik with curious eyes.

"What about him?" Adrik asked.

Axel half-smiled. "You know... it took me a very long time to get where I am."

Adrik stared at him, his jaw tightening. He had expected it. The quietness of Axel was not only a mysterious trait. "Why is that of any importance?"

"Just informing..." Axel crossed his arms.

Adrik stood up straighter, making sure to look into Axel's squinting eyes. "For your information, I have no intention of taking your spot. And if I were, trust me, I would have done that already." Adrik expected the question to come from Axel's mouth. "What exactly are you doing here then? If it's not to take my place?"

"Money," Adrik replied. "I have a family to manage for."

Axel nodded. Without another glance at him, Adrik walked out into the main hall. He was seventy-five percent, Axel believed him. After all, he wasn't exactly lying. Axel was like everybody else in Arkadia. All talk but no action, and no proper attention needed to them. Yet, seeing Axel standing there with questions flowing in his mind, the businessman understood he needed to be cautious.

CHAPTER 17
FRANKO

S ULYA—an extreme, addictive wine beverage made with chocolate and sweet fruits. *Sulya* cake—a cake drowned in an extreme, addictive alcoholic drink made with chocolate and sweet fruits. To Franko's surprise, the night had fallen rather quickly. He wondered if the tipsy guards felt the same. Some people had their theories about the origin of *sulya*. Nobody had known who had made the addictive drink, only that one day, boxes filled with it had appeared outside restaurants and shops. The appearance of these boxes happened every other month. Though no one had found out the creator, he or she had sent envelopes expecting a share for *sulya* exchanges. With that, the creation of *sulya* cakes came along. Some said that the *sulya* was made of a magical liquid, others that it is a deadly drug, or that it comes right out of Kosmos soil. Either way, there were no actual answers, and years back, Kosmos courts had banned the selling or consumption of *sulya* in the cities. In the years to pass, they stopped implementing the law. Only some bars and shops sold them secretly, like the two boys who had just sold more than two dozen delicious-looking cakes to the guards at the golden tower.

Franko wondered what the entrance guards saw; they giggled and walked in a loppy manner as people organized their stands to go home. Slowly, Ezim had become emptier that afternoon, and only the laughs or music from parties were heard farther away. A few people walked around, going on date nights, talking with no care for the world around them. *I'm starting to feel lonely.* Franko walked around the nearby streets, waiting for midnight. He turned around, going back towards the golden tower. He passed an alley he had walked by earlier, but this time, shuffling came out of it, *a small growl, and... the sound of a candy wrapper?* Franko stepped forward to see closer into the alley. A golden puppy came running towards him, licking his shoes playfully.

"Aww... look at this little cuteness..." he said, bending down to pet the puppy. But as he did, the dog walked away from him, curling up by the wall, scared. He quietly played with a red candy wrapper. Franko walked up to him, bending down again.

"Hello, there... are you hungry?" he asked, taking out a piece of a sandwich from his bag. "Here, you definitely need it more than me." The puppy bit the sandwich, eating it slowly while looking back and forth at Franko. Having a pet, a confidant, was something that Franko dreamed of as a kid. *I'm not a kid anymore.* He stood up and walked away from the alley. Seconds later, he stood by the golden tower, feeling something touching his shoe. The puppy had followed him all the way.

"I don't want you to feel bad, but don't you have an owner to go to?" Franko looked at him dearly. The puppy whined. "No? Ok, then you can follow, but you'll have to listen to me."

The guards stood up, their backs against the walls and eyes nearly shut. One of the back entrances was unguarded. He walked up towards the door and tried to open it. *Closed.* The guard next to it slept with his back against the wall, drunk, his badge visible. Franko took a look around first, slowly grabbed the badge with the keys, and headed inside the tower, glancing back again once. "Stay here," he whispered to the puppy, who just sat by the door watching Franko disappear.

The inside of the tower was larger than how it looked from the outside. Instead of it all being gold, like Franko imagined, everything was a mix of black, white, and silver halls. More light bulbs than candle lights. Franko stared around in shock at the furnishings and decor materials, he had only seen modern machinery in all the picture books he read and his imagination. Now he could see a glimpse of the modern world. The tower was empty with suited men going up and down the middle stairs while others entered the electric elevator. Franko waited until someone else entered the lift. *Wow, an elevator.* Franko couldn't believe he had just entered an actual elevator. Thanks to Adrik and the tech store, Franko had used some of his money to order technology and modern books. He had become friends with a book owner, who sent him book crates through a delivery service. From Ether to Arkadia, boxes of books arrived at Metal Tech once a month for Franko. It helped him a lot. Adrik had suggested it was a good idea, knowing he had to send Franko to Ether someday for an actual mission.

The man next to Franko wore a business-like suit. He looked ahead, holding a black briefcase, then pressed the *27th* button, the last floor of the golden floor.

"Excuse me," Franko started. "Do you happen to know where I can find Ether Council? I was sent for an errand, but I don't know much about the building."

"I'm heading there for a quick meeting, you can follow for sure," the black-haired man said. "The building has a lot of floors, so it's easy to get lost." His voice was calm and genuine. Franko wondered what business he had with the Ether Council.

"That would be great," Franko responded with a smile. On the twenty-seventh floor, they got off. Similar to the lower floors, the halls and reception remained somber. The man headed to the reception with Franko following behind him, looking around at the white maze-like hallways.

"Hello, Sir. Mister Steve Sinclair?" the receptionist greeted.

"Yes, it is me."

Franko waited behind the man, watching the hallways and the men standing at the corner of the small lobby. They stood next to a steel ladder, holding wires and other tech, which he recognized could be used for the installation of cameras. Franko raised his brows. *No windows in the tower or telephones, but yes to camera devices?* He looked above in every direction, hoping they hadn't placed cameras elsewhere yet.

"You have the last meeting with the Ether Council, correct? Please sign here." The receptionist pointed at the paper and looked back at her computer once Steve Sinclair signed. Franko had never seen an actual computer up close, despite knowing a handful of tricks on using one. "Here is your key to the last floor." *Last floor? Isn't this the last floor?*

Sinclair nodded and looked back at Franko. "I have a meeting to attend..."

"Thank you, I've got it from here," Franko said, watching Sinclair heading to a black door elevator at the other end of the main hall with a key card in his hand.

"How can I help you, Sir?" the receptionist asked.

"Hello," Franko started. "I am a new employee. Here to organize the archives."

The receptionist frowned. "I didn't know they were looking for new employees. May I see your employee badge for the thirtieth floor?" Franko felt the guard's badge in his pocket. It wouldn't be of help with the word *Guard* in capital letters.

"I lost it."

"As a new employee, you should have read in the handbook that you are not allowed on floors twenty-eight through thirty-three without a special badge."

"I'm easy to forget... it is rather a large handbook."

"In this case." The receptionist nodded. "I suggest going to the second floor and requesting a new badge, since you are new, they might give it to you right away with proper identification."

"Ok, great." Franko nodded. "Do you happen to have a restroom here?"

"Yes, on that hall to the left."

"Thank you," Franko smiled, heading to the hall the receptionist pointed at and going inside the restroom. He walked in circles thinking for a few seconds, admiring the designs and structure of the restroom, then looked at himself in the mirror.

"I knew I looked great with this red coat," Franko said, fixing his black shirt underneath. He felt a sudden warmth hitting the side of his stomach. *The pocket watch.* A message from Adrik. He opened the red blinking watch, and a note flew out into the air. Franko grabbed it quickly. *Tell me you have any information.* Franko sighed, watching the note disappear in the air after shaking it three times. *Now,* a blank piece of paper appeared in front of him as magic, the words in his mind writing themselves down. *Not yet, boss.* Franko thought. *But almost. I'm inside Ether's golden tower.* He pressed the crown of the opened watch six times until the inside turned into a red portal, then threw the paper in. He waited for the portal to vanish and looked at the actual time. Realizing the lateness, he walked out of the restroom, looking for the stairs that would lead him up to the thirtieth floor.

"There have to be some stairs," he whispered, passing empty halls and closing empty office rooms. Usually, there were stairwells next to the elevator, but there were no doors close by. He walked to the corner of the end of the last hall as soon as he saw the small *Stairs* sign written backwards. He understood why that would be confusing. But even if people had noticed the intentional mistake, the door to the stairs was locked. He still needed the keys, and he had no choice but to steal them.

"Excuse me, Miss?" Franko said, heading to the receptionist from the same hall where she had last seen him going.

"Yes."

"Um." Franko half-smiled, his hands feeling cold as ice. "There seems to be something wrong with the restroom, I believe there's a leak." The lady frowned, and Franko continued. "It is flooded."

"What? That's strange." The receptionist quickly got up to check inside the restroom with Franko following behind. "You were inside for a very long time... when did this start?"

Franko shook his head as if he hadn't spent the entire time flushing a bunch of paper into the toilet. "Ooh, about five minutes ago, I was trying to figure out what was wrong, but..."

The receptionist shook her head. "I understand. I'll have to go down and get maintenance immediately before the whole floor floods." She walked towards the elevator.

"Of course." Franko watched around for the camera installers, but they were gone. Wires hung from a hole in the corner of the roof, he guessed they had given up on the technology.

"Do you mind staying and checking..." The lady asked, going inside the elevator just ahead.

"Not at all." Franko smiled, waiting for the doors to close.

Once she disappeared, he grabbed the keys labeled *Stairs*. It wasn't long before the silence greeted his ears. Going up the lift would have been nerve-racking and noisy. Now, he entered the thirtieth floor. *Archives*. A sign read on the wall between the elevator and the stairs. On the entire floor were only two black halls that led to other rooms. Franko walked to the first door on the left, and he couldn't believe his eyes. The whole room was filled with monitors, glass boards, and keyboards that changed color. He looked up at every ceiling corner for surveillance cameras. There were none. He could tell how *secure* the tower was. *Or maybe they don't want to go overboard with modernity just yet.* Franko thought, hearing the pocket watch tick with every second that passed.

With a sigh, he closed the door and headed for the other one. A room filled with actual paper files inside. He felt a little relieved that he was looking at the past and not the future. Still, a single computer stood in the corner, and file cabinets were all around the room. *To look for archives, search for keywords.* The message on the monitor read. The only thing that Franko knew was that Adrik was looking for an event that had happened about ten years ago, including a fire and witches. But no matter how long he looked into each drawer manually, there was nothing related to a fire ten years ago. Only an abundance of business papers and trades with other countries filled each file. Franko had no choice but to check into the other room.

Even though he was glad he had read many technological books, enough for him to learn how to use an unlocked computer. Reading about it and learning how to do a task were entirely different things. He did the same he had done, putting keywords on the first computer he saw. Nothing. No fire from ten years ago. No information about Stellar Court and its members. No drama with witches or the Supernatural War. He scrolled and scrolled quickly, but nothing. And then he stopped, catching a glimpse of something he had heard of before. A name that, even if he hadn't heard of it before, would catch his attention anyway. An agreement had been made between Ether Council and the HSS ten years ago during the Supernatural War. *The HSS?* The acronym sounded familiar to Franko; he had heard of it before. *What did it stand for?* He tried to remember, yet it wasn't necessary, when underneath a signature was written. The cursive handwriting was difficult to read and understand, but in bold print letters, it read: *Atticus Mon-cler. Current director of the Hunter Secret Society.*

PART SEVEN

EIDETIC HOLDER

CHAPTER 18
ADRIK

THE HUNTER SECRET SOCIETY was the only place that Adrik hadn't tracked down. It was a secret, a place out of reach and out of Kosmos. He hadn't put enough time into it yet, seeing as everything he thought he needed was in Kosmos. The outside world had become a strange place to him. Part of him missed it because he sometimes imagined Italy. The beautiful villa that his family had. The warmth of his mom and the safety of his dad. The salty air of the ocean and the sweetness of the greenery. He remembered all the solo trips he would take; he remembered it all. But as he passed the silver door the day after Franko told him what he found, he knew one thing. Someone, whether it was Kaan or anyone from the Courts, was hiding something about the village fire. And they had done well at hiding it.

After years of sending Orson to figure out the Archive room at Stellar Court every year, which Adrik had checked multiple times during his visit, there was no actual clue of anything he needed to find. Most of it must have been discarded after the Supernatural War. Evidence could've been destroyed, but not the truth. *Someone* had to know something, and he wasn't leaving until he figured it out.

Kaan waited for Adrik inside the silver door room. He sat down at the edge of the wooden table. The room was no larger than a living room. A study room, to be precise, with books surrounding three of the walls and silver chandeliers hanging from the ceiling. Kaan was looking down at the drawings and handwritten work on the table. Then, he looked up when he heard Adrik enter, fixing the sheets into a pile.

"Adrik," he started. "Please, sit."

Adrik glanced at the pile, standing at the foot of the table across from Kaan. "I am fine standing."

Kaan half-smiled. "Ok, then," he said. "I saw you were getting down to business already, spying on the Illuminators."

Adrik nodded. "That was the deal." He had spent all morning walking around the lonely Lunar Castle looking for signs. Anything suspicious, he had to know. He saw Illuminators just outside practicing their powers: the Earthkalais controlling Earth's elements, the Joviankalais experimenting with the science, and the Celestialkalais exercising the mind. From his window, he saw Kaan going to the stables with guards earlier. Throughout the entire day, he had seen workers, Axel, and about two businessmen roaming around the castle, and nothing more.

"Have you learned everything you need to know about them? About their powers?"

"As far as I know. Yes."

Kaan nodded, looking back at the papers on the table.

Adrik frowned. Kaan was looking for something. He was searching. "Is there anything in particular that I should be looking for?"

"Yes, there is." Kaan looked up and hesitated for a second. "Therefore, anything out of order or suspicious about any Illuminator at all has to be reported to me. Any other questions?"

"No." Adrik was about to turn around then decided otherwise. "What do you know about the Hunter Secret Society?"

The question awakened Kaan. He stood up straighter and furrowed his brows. "Why are you asking?"

"I've heard about it once at Ether. I was on a secret task for one of the council members, he wanted to know what his son was up to."

"Let me guess, Mister Brenner was it, the worried father. He had guards for his son every hour of every day."

"Yes," Adrik said. It was long ago when Craven had sent a spy to Ether. Adrik was there, in Craven's office, standing on his left side as he heard the deal made between the council member and him. Mister Brenner trembled slightly, walking through the people in Craven's bar with the loss of *Kosniz* in his mind, at least Adrik knew so. He had offered to do the job, but Craven had other plans for him and never ended up going to Ether.

"Do you have anything to do with the HSS, then?" Kaan asked.

"No. Curiosity, that's all."

"The HSS exists, Mister Montova. Somewhere in Paris, France and it is completely alive, since the Supernatural War, might I add."

"They worked with witches against vampires, didn't they?"

"In some cases, they did." Kaan shook his head. "But I've never met them. After all, I'm not that old."

"Of course not." Adrik watched Kaan's movements, yet he looked peaceful as a leaf. "By the looks of it." He turned around the moment Axel entered the silver room.

"Sir—" he started to speak, until he saw Adrik in front of him. Adrik retreated with a nod and left the room, with Axel closing the door behind him.

Adrik could have stayed and listened closely behind the door. But he walked away, knowing that whatever he needed to know, he would find some other way. He didn't believe in the universe showing him signs or helping him. He only trusted himself... and maybe Franko, if he could just get more information. The last time Franko had sent a message was an hour ago. He was able to get out of the golden tower and find a place to stay before going back to Arkadia in a few days. In the meantime, information about the HSS was all Adrik needed. First, he had to find a way to get close to Kaan, discover his secret, and who he really was while also pretending to get his job done. With Axel in between, there was no way that he could get that close. There had to be a way to get it all done before he left Kosmos.

Once he was back in his suite, he sent Franko a list of things he needed to get from Ether. *Be quick. Time is ticking.* He wrote. *Of course, chief. As always.* Franko responded a few minutes later. Adrik hated pacing in the room. He wasn't used to it. To some extent, he missed Arkadia and the freedom of it. Being stuck in a room without knowing how exactly to move forward felt suffocating, like he was back in that small closet hiding with his sister. Like, at some point, the whole castle could collapse into flames. He finally stood on the balcony watching the light from the lighthouse go around in circles, illuminating most of the grounds. The air felt fresh and peaceful, it smelled like home. Not Arkadia. *Italy*. That was home. And Arkadia had just been a small stop, a planning area, to head back. He had left all of his heart in Italy and in his perished family.

Adrik was still awake when Axel knocked on his door past midnight. "Kaan requires you," Axel said. Now, they walked down to the first floor, turning around the hall, and going into the silver door room. Like earlier, Kaan sat in the same place on the table with papers all over and a map. Two young men in orange clothing stood next to him. Across Kaan, on the other side of the table, stood two guards with someone standing in front of them. Adrik couldn't see who was in between until he passed by them and stood closer to the table, a few feet away from Kaan and the guards. It was a girl who stood in the middle with caramel brown hair. Her green-gray eyes passed over Adrik quickly, glancing at his silver rings, then looked away as Axel and Kaan spoke.

"Shall I send word to Stellar Court about this incident, Sir?" Axel said, standing close to Kaan.

"No, it is not necessary. Not a word to anyone," Kaan said,

then looked at Adrik, who only stared back. "Adrik, escort Miss De Rose to one of the main suites... on the fourth floor." Adrik nodded, looking back and forth at Kaan and the curious girl, wondering what had happened.

"Why am I being held hostage?!" Miss De Rose said, frustrated. The guards shuffled behind her, probably wondering whether to hold her, but they didn't fully move.

"Take it as a small vacation, Miss De Rose." Kaan smirked. "Anyone in your place would have been extremely excited." Adrik watched him. Kaan was enjoying it. Maybe the girl had something to do with his plans. *But what?*

"My friends will be looking for me," the girl responded. She looked frustrated and angry, somewhat desperate but composed in place.

"They will understand." Were Kaan's last words to her. Kaan nodded to Adrik to take her away.

The girl winced as Adrik grabbed hold of her arm. They went up to the first floor. Noticing his grip, Adrik slightly released her arm. He may have been uncaring, but he knew how to respect and treat innocent people right. He didn't have anything towards the girl, but he was pretending to do as Kaan said. The girl gazed around, watching Adrik without even trying to hide it.

"Don't try to escape. You'll waste your time... and mine," he said once they stopped in front of a suite on the fourth floor. He released her, nodding for her to go inside at once. Adrik recognized the anger in her green-gray eyes before he closed and locked the door behind him. Kaan had made her a hostage. She was important to him.

Without wasting any more time, Adrik walked down to the first floor and into the silver room where Kaan and Axel were talking.

"Everything is in order," Adrik said, closing the door behind him.

"I will need you to keep an eye on her. You will be her guard. Check on what she does or if she plans anything. You will be held responsible for what happens to her," Kaan ordered. "You may leave." Adrik headed out of the room, and this time he waited to hear what Kaan and Axel had to say. Their voices sounded like a whisper behind the door.

"Now," Kaan started. "How did you know she was an Illuminator, Axel?"

"With the book, the *Illuminated*, it had disappeared from us..."

"What do you mean disappeared? We have had that book for years, transporting it to new Illuminators."

"Yes, Sir," Axel paused. "We were keeping track of it. Taking it to the Illuminators we saw on the map made by the Arch, as you ordered, but when we had gone to find it from the last Illuminator, it was gone. I found it at a library with a tracking spell, which happened to take hours. That's when I saw her; she had seen the title, and that's when I knew who she was. I allowed her to take it."

There was a long pause before Kaan continued. "The book must have magic of its own."

"But Sir, how is that possible? We've had that book for years. Nothing like this had happened."

"Not until now... that could only mean one thing," Kaan paused. "Clara De Rose is a powerful Illuminator like nothing else. It might be she who can give me infinite power."

"She *is* a Celestialkalai Eidetic," Axel commented. "What do we do now?"

"We train her, Axel. Make her trust us. And then I will take what should be mine," Kaan said, his voice sounding firm. "In the meantime," he continued. "It is time to distribute the *volka*. Make sure everyone at Kosmos, especially the Illuminators, receives it. Except for the few people residing in this castle and Adrik, we need right-minded people here for now." Footsteps approaching the hall made Adrik shuffle; he composed himself and walked away, passing one of the young men in orange who had been inside the study room with Kaan earlier. He didn't pay much attention to him, and neither did he. *Clara De Rose*. Who was she? How did Kaan want to gain power from her? For what?

Throughout Adrik's prominent gangster life, he had heard a lot of truths from members and those whom he had spied on. Two lightbloods created Illuminators. The rarer that lightbloods were, the more rare did Illuminators became. As far as everyone knew, Illuminators were the only supernatural beings to be scarce and exceptional. Yet within the Illuminator order of Celestialkalais, there was one species that even people thought didn't exist, the Eidetic Holders. Celestialkalais with memory and forgetfulness powers, connected to the dwarf planet Pluto. Legends throughout the years had rumored of the chosen ones, a curse, spirits, religion, etc. Some thought that an Eidetic Holder might be an angel, a saint, or a demon itself. But there was no proof, and as years passed, the rumors did too. No one with that power had existed for decades.

Not until now. So, what did Kaan, a Stellar Court member, a lifetime witch, want to do with the girl? What did *volka* have anything to do with it?

With Clara around, Adrik's work had doubled. He hadn't been able to sleep and stood up early in the morning, ready to follow Kaan's orders. He headed to Clara's suite.

"I will be back in five minutes. Kaan requires your presence," he said, then waited outside until she was ready. They walked down to the first floor, where Kaan waited inside the dining room. "Enter," Kaan started. "Please sit." Clara slowly walked inside as if Kaan were a monster that could kill her right there and then. Adrik wouldn't have been surprised. She sat at the foot of the table facing Kaan, who wore more modern clothing: black pants, a dark blue-black sweater, and a black-cord necklace with a white crystal. The first time Adrik saw Clara, he knew she had come from the outside world based on her choice of clothing. Kaan had either grown up in the modern world or was only trying to make her feel comfortable.

They talked for a few minutes. And even though Kaan nodded at Adrik to stay some feet away from the conversation, he could hear them clearly, watching them through the archways of the dining room.

"My apologies for my unmannerly behavior last night. Country policy changes have been taking up most of my time. I'm Kaan, a member of Solar and Stellar Court. Nice to meet you, Clara

De Rose. Everyone else is at Stellar Castle, therefore it's just us this morning," Kaan informed her, as if it wasn't already obvious. "Suit yourself." Kaan nodded towards the set of food plates around the table. Clara stared at him quietly. "Or not."

"Why am I here?" Clara asked, now her face with a slight curiosity.

"You willingly entered the castle."

"Why am I held *hostage*?"

Kaan smirked, taking a bite from his fork. "People would die just to enter the castle, and you want to leave so soon?" Adrik never watched gang fights for entertainment. But he stood there, watching the dining room like a drama and action combat.

Kaan shook his head and cleared his throat. "I never said you were a hostage, Miss De Rose. You are a guest."

"The lock on my door says otherwise."

Clara stared at him, waiting for an answer. She was easy to read sometimes.

Kaan shifted in his chair, his back becoming straighter. "We haven't seen an Illuminator with memory powers for years."

"How do you know that?"

"Witches have records for every supernatural species," Kaan smirked. "For safety..."

"Or for power." Clara watched him carefully. "It isn't a secret that witches have been trying to ally with Illuminators."

"That is indeed true. Witches have been trying to *maintain* peace with other species for years, and allying with Illuminators will be the best for everyone. Don't you think so?"

"I'm supposed to believe *you* want the best for your long-last-ing vampire enemies?" Clara asked, shaking her head.

"I'm not the enemy here, Miss De Rose." Kaan smiled.

"You are not the ally either."

"But we could be."

"I don't think so."

"Very well then, I don't think you have much of a choice." Kaan stood up at once. Taking it as a sign, Adrik stood by the dining room doorway right away when a guard appeared next to him at the same time. Adrik moved inches away from him before their shoulders touched.

"Excuse me, Sir," the guard said, looking at Kaan. "We have found the um..." He looked at Clara but proceeded. "The person you sent us to..."

"Finally," Kaan responded with a smile. The guard started to leave as Kaan left the dining room for the main hall. Clara did the same, exiting from the other doorway where Adrik had just stood for a few seconds.

"Tell Axel to meet us in the library and to bring the house-keeper as well," Kaan said to Adrik, glancing at Clara. She stood silently watching Kaan walk out of the castle from the main entrance.

"Come with me," Adrik said, walking to the stairwell. He looked back at Clara, who was following Kaan's steps. "What are you doing?"

She ignored him.

"You can't go outside," he warned, walking towards her before she took another step.

"Don't worry," she half-smiled. "I'm not planning to run away... yet." Adrik frowned, but Clara continued talking. "You are more than a bodyguard, right? Based on your choice of clothing and not-so-respectful manners to *Sir* Kaan, it appears you were hired for something else. Aren't you *a bit* curious as to what Kaan is up to?"

He had never met anyone so annoying but quick-witted at the same time. Franko was close, but the young girl somehow had enough courage to talk to the one person Arkadians feared. Despite that, she didn't know that yet.

"No," Adrik lied. "And I can't let you figure it out either."

"So, you like being treated like a puppet then? Are you that loyal to him? Is money that important to you?"

"The only person I am loyal to is myself. And it's none of your concern." He grabbed Clara's arm, and she began to step back.

"I'll go. On my own," she said, walking forward and rolling her eyes at him. It was at that moment that Adrik swore that this would be the first and last time he ever did a job as a bodyguard.

PART EIGHT

REALITY OR FAKE

CHAPTER 19
NEIR

"WHY ARE WE GOING THIS WAY?" Erin asked, walking quickly behind Neir.

"Erin, don't ask questions. I'm in charge, *remember*," Neir responded. She had looked around more than three times already. Her apartment was on the same street as the bakery, just around the corner.

"Your apartment is just—" Erin started, confused as to why Neir had gone the other way, passed three streets, and turned, making a whole circle to get home.

"*Shut up*," Neir whispered at once. She turned around, looking at Erin. *Out of all days.* She wished that Erin could have gone with his mom instead. Briz had an afternoon shift at a bar. She worked two jobs, including at the bakery. Yet usually, she would get a random shift on the weekends, and Neir was left to care for Erin when the thirteen-year-old didn't want to stay home.

"What?" Erin whispered, looking at Neir's alert, bright eyes.

"Someone has been following us."

"Since when?"

"Since we got out."

"And how do you—"

Neir looked at the still-open restaurant cafe just a few feet away. "I will need you to go inside and wait for me to come back."

"What are you going to do, Ms. Bakery Girl? Fight the person who is following us?" Erin crossed his arms.

"Something worse…" She pushed Erin towards the restaurant.

"What do you mean, *something worse?*"

"Hurry up," Neir said, waiting for Erin to get inside. When he did, she started walking again, and a release of worry fell off her shoulders. It was still daylight, sundown to be exact. Why was a light vampire following her? Lighters never really followed hunters; it was mostly nighters. And if they did attack, it would have been at night, when no eyes saw past the dark. Yet there she was, turning down an empty alley again. She could finally feel its presence just behind her. The only times she had a hard time telling between vampires and hunters was when they were all close by at the same time. She could've been better at distinguishing if she hadn't fully left hunting years ago. Being back felt like *deja vu*.

"You chose the wrong person…" Neir said, turning to face a very glaring vampire.

"I think I have the right one," he hissed, eyeing Neir without blinking. He was lighter. Neir could tell in the way his eyes lit up from the normal brown to bright yellow as he started against her.

Something clicked, a memory from a few days ago. A night

vampire had been killed by her. Probably thinking Neir was human, he had proceeded to attack her with two of his other friends in the middle of the night. One of the friends had been a lighter vampire with yellow in his eyes rather than red. Before Neir could continue her hunting, Briz's call had brought her back to the bakery. She had never seen the lighter or his friend since.

"Came back for revenge?"

"That's not even close, hunter."

"You may be a lighter, but I'm still stronger..." Neir didn't move, she stood her ground. She knew she was strong. A new lighter usually practiced going out into the Sun again or learning the powers gained from the Illuminator they've murdered. A phase of rebirth all over again. She wondered what the case was for this one, but the vampire didn't speak or reveal any signs of power. He was thinking, waiting to make the right decision. Then he moved fast as lightning, hitting Neir in her face first. But she was faster and punched him straight in the stomach right after. Her soft, light skin was still healing from the last vampire fight. Now, the cut on the forehead and lip was bleeding again. She kicked the vampire twice, preventing him from standing up. She moved on top of him, grabbing a bloodstained stake from the inside of her coat pocket and dragging it through the vampire's heart. He shook at first, his face turning pale and blue as the stake hit his heart. In seconds, he was dead. Neir stood up, leaving the stake in his heart. With the stake intact, the body would evaporate by itself, disappearing into the air after a few hours. When the stake was taken away, it decomposed as normal. She moved the body towards a dumpster, making sure it was fully hidden behind the trash bags. After

Carden's visit, she couldn't have more witnesses see the dead vampires before they dissolved. Losing the Illuminator and light-blood-stained stakes wasn't even a problem, she had much more at home to use. She started moving the body next to the wall, then stopped when she sensed someone around. A hunter.

"Bravo!" Carden appeared from the street next by. "What a great show, sister. I almost got fooled and actually thought he was dead. Oh wait. He is." He smirked. "Say hello to the cameras for me." He pointed up to the gray building next to him. Neir stood her ground, her green eyes following the top of the building. A man stood by the edge with a camera in his hand. He wasn't a hunter or a vampire, but a human whom she couldn't sense. Carden was using evidence against her.

"I see I don't need to explain myself," Carden started. "So, I'll say this briefly."

"What? Are you going to send me to the HSS prison now?" Neir said.

"No, I had a *better* idea." He took out a piece of paper from his coat pocket and threw it to Neir. She caught it swiftly. The paper was a contract signed by him, the director, and a few HSS council members. "You have three weeks to leave Paris and never come back. As long as you don't step in the city or country, you are safe... take it as compassion for being my sister."

"I'm not leaving Paris."

"Yes, you are," Carden said. "Or I'll make sure to ruin your life."

"I am not leaving," Neir responded, looking at the piece of paper and tearing it apart into tiny pieces.

"I have more copies at the headquarters." Carden smiled, turning around to leave. "You have *three* weeks." He nodded at the man on the building; he disappeared right after. Carden left around the corner without turning back. Neir knew he was scared. He didn't want her to be a prisoner at HSS because he was afraid she would get the upper hand. But now, he wanted her away from the only place she felt at peace. The only people she felt close to.

"I think I underestimated you when you said 'something worse'," Erin appeared behind a nearby passageway by the exit of a shop. "I mean, I read comic books... but this. This is *cool*."

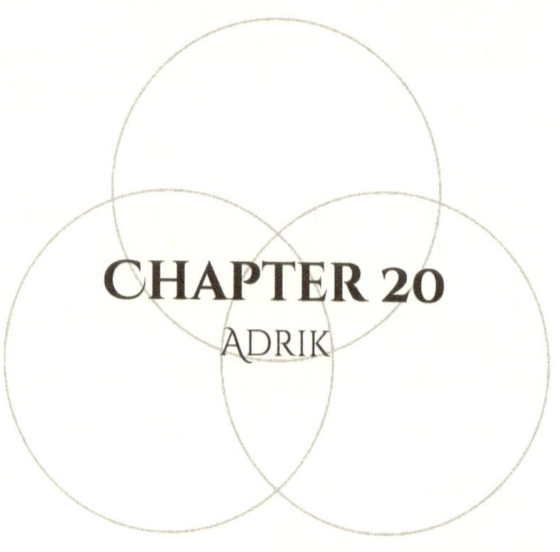

CHAPTER 20
ADRIK

ADRIK FELT THAT TIME was moving faster than normal. He spent the entire day guarding Clara after her meeting with Kaan. They had gone to the small library on the third floor. Kaan wanted to see her powers. And he had... but ended up getting taunted instead. His power over her was slipping.

"Why don't you like chocolate?" Clara asked Kaan. Something in Kaan's eyes lit up. He knew what memory of his she was talking about. "You should try it, but I doubt that it can take your sour mood away." Clara sat up, staring at a bothered Kaan. Adrik stood firmly, looking at everyone's reactions. Lia, whom he'd seen days before with a disapproving look after he'd quickly sent the worker away, was wide-eyed at the scene. Axel stared at Clara intensely and at Kaan without care. Adrik was surprised at Clara's bravery and appearance of not being afraid. Kaan admitted he believed she was lying. He believed she had more power to show.

But she stayed quiet.

"Escort her back to her room," Kaan said to Adrik. He moved further inside and stood by the door as Clara got up from her chair. He could feel her eyes watching him as he walked in front of her, hearing her footsteps behind him.

"Why *do* you work here?" she asked.

Adrik didn't respond after a few seconds. "I assure you that is not to make friends." He disliked being reminded of his past, even though it never really left him. Especially, when he was now standing on a thin rope. The mission wasn't like stealing or opening locks. It required patience, and Adrik had done enough patience for the last ten years. He went back to his suite after leaving the girl. Franko had sent a message. He was still looking for the items Adrik had indicated. By tonight or tomorrow, Franko will be gone back to Arkadia. And Adrik had to leave soon after.

He remembered what Terrance had said about Kaan and Isaiah not being in the Court ten years ago. After watching them, he wasn't sure. The only way to fully find out was to contact the HSS. Kaan was no fool. He planned to control the people of Kosmos, something that had to do with Clara's power. Adrik had gotten close enough to know his thinking. But he had to know for sure. He needed proof of what had happened. Terrance was gone. Kaan, Isaiah, and Solar Court members remained. But only one had given the order.

It was late at night, and a few minutes passed after Adrik had gone out to check Clara's suite. Everything was quiet as usual. Adrik had gone out to the stables, walking around the castle grounds and looking at the hotel room lights where the Illuminators stayed. He had seen them earlier, during training sessions. If it weren't for their colored uniform, anyone could have guessed that they were an army of soldiers ready for a physical battle. The *volka* had done its job just like Kaan expected. The Illuminators made the guards look like puppies. They stood yawning and talking in whispers as Adrik headed inside the castle from the restricted west garden entrance. He headed back to the fourth floor and stopped as soon as he heard Kaan and Axel's voices above. Their steps didn't sound far. Adrik followed them. Kaan and Axel entered the small library. They spoke quietly, but with the complete silence of the entire castle, Adrik was able to hear them clearly; he stood behind one of the hidden library entrances inside the third-floor hall.

"The *volka* was distributed, Sir," Axel said. "By now, more than three-quarters of the whole country is under your control until upcoming orders."

"What did you find out about Miss De Rose?" Kaan asked.

"She lives a normal human life. Has two light-blood parents, a sister named Aurora, a few friends... the rest you know," Axel paused. "That's all, Sir."

There was silence for a second. Adrik paced quietly around the library. "Figure out more. Do it soon."

"Yes, Sir."

"If Clara has memory powers, then there has to be someone who has the opposite ones. Her balance. Find that person and bring them to me," Kaan demanded. "We will need both to move forward with the plan."

"Yes, Sir."

"Also, start with the *other* plan. Everything has to be ready for when we have both holders of the Eidetic powers."

Axel repeated. "Yes, Sir. I will start as soon as possible."

Adrik wondered how much money Axel would have now after repeating the words over and over. He would have been rich. He would have been what other people believe in. *Luck.*

Kaan started pacing again, his footsteps magnifying with every step. It wasn't only Kaan who walked around; someone else was close by. Adrik stood up straight, listening to voices in the next hall.

"What are you doing?" Adrik asked, seeing Clara and the housekeeper, Lia, going upstairs. Clara held cleaning supplies while Lia held a food tray.

The housekeeper spoke first. "I accidentally dropped Miss De Rose's food—"

"I was helping her," Clara interrupted. "Am I going to be scowled at for being nice?" She showed no uneasiness.

"Come on. Let's go," Adrik said to Clara, then turned to look at Lia. "You can go later to clean."

"Food fell, Adrik... to the floor," Clara grimaced. "It's not *my* room, but it shouldn't stay unclean for so long."

"She will go later," he repeated, turning to Lia. "You will certainly need more than a bucket with a few supplies."

"Yes, I'm aware. I was going to return after... for more," Lia muttered, nodding her head. They switched the cleaning supplies and tray. Adrik walked ahead of Clara, her hands holding the meal tray as she glanced down to the third floor, back at Lia. They smiled slightly at each other, giving Adrik a sense of an alliance between them. *Good. Try to run, Clara.*

Once Adrik locked Clara's door, he walked back to the third floor. He was late. Kaan and Axel were already heading out from another exit. Adrik waited until they descended the stairs to head back to his suite. Clara must have heard the same thing he did. He wouldn't be surprised if she tried to leave. If it wasn't for the pretense of doing Kaan's job, Adrik would have left already. He needed a way to leave, to get out of Lunar Castle or Kosmos. Every second he spent in the castle felt like a waste of time. Time that he needed to use on his actual mission instead of bodyguarding. But he was already on Kaan's radar. Now, it was time to get out.

CHAPTER 21

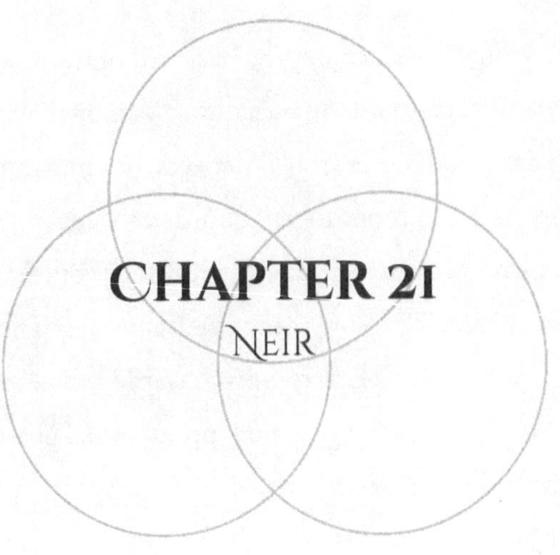

NEIR

ALL THE LIGHTS WERE OFF when Neir entered her apartment. Even during the day, it was rarely bright, and she always had one lamp illuminating the living room at night when she got back from work. She headed towards it, seeing through the dark, and turned on the lamp. Erin turned to lock the door, squinting his eyes and flopping onto the couch. Neir closed the barely open white curtains over the balcony doors, not before looking out and checking that everything was normal. Paris streets were usually filled, where Neir's apartment was situated, but today it was rather lonely with only a few cars passing by. She had intentionally chosen that apartment; the more people who walked by, the less vampires would appear in plain sight. And in case they did appear, she would make sure to vanish them.

"What did you see?" Neir asked, standing in front of Erin, who just sat looking for the remote control. "How did you get into the alleyways?"

"Everything. I walked out the back exit of the restaurant," he responded. "What are you? Supernatural? Vampire? Vampire hunter? Oh, a werewolf?" Neir rolled her eyes, heading to the kitchen just across the living room to get a bottle of water. "This is not a game. You won't tell anyone, Erin. Not Briz or your friends..."

"I get it, Neir. Who am I going to tell anyways? They probably won't believe me and take me to a psych ward or something..." Erin half-smiled. "Besides, what you did is pretty cool, I guess, as long as you kill the bad guys."

Neir held out the water bottle for Erin. He grabbed it, still searching for the TV remote around the couch. "A vampire *hunter*. And the remote control is there." She pointed to the drawer in the gray table beside the sofa. Erin was shocked in place, not reaching for the remote control to watch his favorite comic show.

"Really? A vampire hunter? *That* was a vampire in the alley? The one you staked?"

"Yes."

"Then who was the man with glasses? The one who gave you a sheet of paper?"

Neir sat down on the couch next to Erin. Her head started to hurt, but she didn't know why. Maybe she hadn't eaten enough, maybe she was tired, or maybe just completely angry. "That was my younger brother," she responded.

Erin sat straighter. "Your brother?"

"You ask too many questions, Erin." Neir stood up, going back to the kitchen to grab a glass of water. "I'm taking a shower. Stay put... and don't touch any of my stuff." She headed to her room past the kitchen, watching the TV turn on and looking back at Erin before entering her forest green room. She sensed that Erin had more questions to ask, but she disliked his curiosity and headed away before he could continue ranting.

CHAPTER 22
ADRIK

SLEEPLESS NIGHTS WERE taking a toll on Adrik. He wondered how long it would take for him to finally lose more of his mind. He moved out of the castle's kitchen and wished he had slept better the days before. The two cups of coffee had eventually woken him up. He walked out of the silent castle and towards the stables. He tossed and turned earlier, trying to go to sleep, when he heard a voice calling him. At first, he thought he was dreaming, then he guessed he was hallucinating from sleep deprivation, but now he followed the voice to the stables. He was fully awake now and completely sure he wasn't imagining things. Inside the stable was dark; only the moonlight and the lighthouse lit the inside. He walked further, hearing the muffled voice say his name, until the breathing of the horses and crickets chirping filled around him.

Whether the voice was a woman's or a man's, he couldn't tell. He listened closely, finally realizing it sounded like a girl's voice. It spoke low and eerie, almost like a whisper or a thought. Adrik stood in between, inspecting each stable. All of them were closed except one. Yet a horse just stood there waiting patiently. When Adrik stepped closer to it, he heard the voice again, now out in the open. If there was anything that Adrik disliked was the mystery of magic. He disliked how it made him vulnerable, but he was curious about it all. The voice *had* to be magic, a trick, or a game. He didn't believe in saints, spirits, angels, or ghosts. It was magic. It *had* too.

"It's magic, *alright*," he whispered to himself. He grabbed the horse in front of him, got on, and headed straight to the forest, following the suspicious voice.

Everything got darker the further he rode. Light rain flew with the breeze, and the hooting of owls increased as Adrik rode deep into the humid forest. He slowed the horse to a stop, waiting for a few seconds to hear the voice again. When minutes passed without a similar human sound, he decided to turn and go back to the castle. The horse walked in a slow space next to Adrik. He walked around, examining the space around him, but the voice was gone. Everything seemed to be back to a normal night. It wasn't until Adrik heard shuffling again that he stopped in his tracks. *Leaves rustling, but the wind was calm. A breathing sound that wasn't the horse's or his.* Adrik tied the horse leash to a nearby tree and followed the sounds at once, stepping quietly on the grass. A dark silhouette stood just a few feet away from him. He didn't recognize her until she turned. *Clara.*

Without missing a second, he grabbed hold of her hands, not letting her use her powers on him.

"I don't want to hurt you," she said, trying to pull away.

"That implies I'm capable of being hurt," Adrik responded.

"You should rethink that." She hit Adrik in the leg, making him stumble, and he did the same trick to her with his other leg, making her fall to the ground.

"To your *functional* power, it was demanded that I take you back to Lunar Castle unharmed." Adrik held out his hand to help her up and noticed her looking briefly at his silver rings before taking it.

"You don't seem like the type to hurt me, even if you had the chance to do so," she said, standing up. She underestimated him, but to some extent, she was right. He understood why she wanted to run away. As far as he knew, she was part of Kaan's insane plan. If she left, he would be done as a bodyguard and free from Kaan. He would play the part and had to let her win.

Her eyes showed she hadn't finished fighting yet. She tried punching him but missed. He tried to grab her wrist again and failed on purpose. What he hadn't expected happened too fast. Adrik felt something missing in his hand, the second Clara created a purple-blue protection wall and walked away from him.

"You should be afraid you won't get far," he said, looking her straight in the eyes. She showed the silver ring in her hand. One of Adrik's silver rings. The one with vines designed around it. The one that belonged to his sister.

"This is important to you, isn't it?" She inspected the ring. He guessed what she was trying to do. A bargain.

"I'll hunt you down until you wish you had gone to Kaan instead if you don't give me the ring back." He meant the words coming from his mouth.

"I'm sorry," Clara continued. "But you can either find the ring before it gets lost in the mud or let me go." There it was. The threat had worked. Because the second Clara threw the ring out into the air, Adrik was ready to look for it, and she managed to run away.

PART NINE

OUTSIDE WORLD

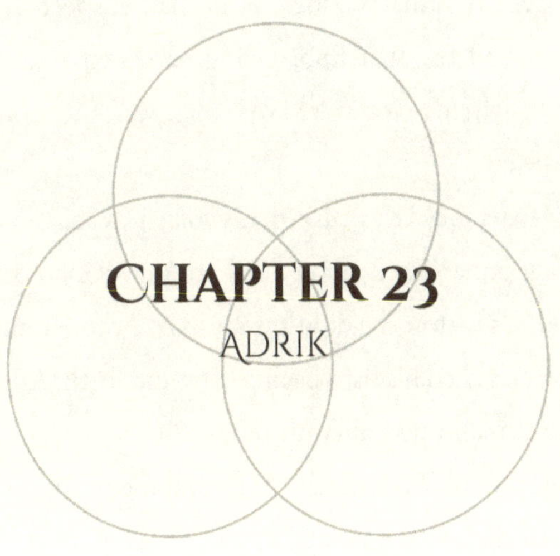

CHAPTER 23
ADRIK

IT WAS A WIN-WIN SITUATION. Adrik flashed the pocket watch to the ground and bent down, getting the silver ring that stood next to a white flower. Another invention from Franko that he had silently thanked. *Just don't ask me how I did it.* Franko had said, when he showed him the tricks of the pocket watch: tell time, a compass also used as the locator, message portal, and colored lights. One would have to keep the pocket watch closed, press it three times on the side, and a bright light would ignite from the inside. Besides the normal usage, the compass on the left worked as a locator if the owner intended to be found. *Better yet.* Franko continued. *It's not even that heavy.* Adrik had to admit he was even surprised and slightly curious. But he never asked how and trusted that Franko was a good metal tech inventor.

Adrik placed the ring back in his right hand, on the ring finger where it had been. He traced back his steps towards his horse and headed back to Lunar Castle. As he had suspected, Kaan was walking around the first floor giving orders to Axel and all the guards. The witch's eyes waited for an answer, the moment Adrik came into view.

"*Where* is she?" Kaan asked, his voice was cold and tense.

"She is gone. Took a horse and ran into Ring Forest," Adrik responded. "It is clear she didn't want to be a captive anymore."

Kaan clenched his fists, pacing back and forth. Adrik watched him. He was planning something else.

"I did my task," Adrik said. "The deal was to spy on the Illuminators, including Clara. Being her guard was more than what was bargained for."

"You let her go," Kaan shot back. "I overestimated you." Adrik held back a smirk.

"She *is* an Illuminator," he explained. The excuse of her having greater power would help him.

Kaan half-grinned. "No need to explain, Mister Montova. I *clearly* know what she is. That is why I want her." He turned to face Adrik. "But you are correct. We made a deal." He picked up a briefcase that had magically appeared beside him and handed it to Adrik. "But the job is not done. This is half of what was promised."

Adrik took the case slowly, looking at Kaan and making sure that there wasn't an inch of trickery. "What is the other part of the job? I suggest choosing your words wisely." Adrik gripped the case at the side of his black business coat, testing the heaviness of it.

"You will continue to spy on her. I need any important information," Kaan started pacing again. "You will be my second pair of eyes. Deal?"

Adrik nodded, stagnant in place. "Yes."

"She will get out of Kosmos. Once we receive the notice, you will follow accordingly."

"It's a deal."

Kaan half-smiled as Adrik turned to leave. "See you soon, Adrik Montova."

It wasn't long until Adrik had turned the corner and passed Axel on his way to see Kaan. He frowned at the sight of him, but Adrik ignored him and walked towards the castle's exit. Like he had expected, everything had gone exactly like he thought, and now he didn't have time to waste.

CHAPTER 24
FRANKO

T HE BOY IN THE BLUE SCARF had eyed Franko the second he had passed by. He was distracted, looking at the bookshelves and whispering *Explosives* when he noticed the golden-haired boy ruffling his hair.

"Don't eat anything? Am I supposed to starve?" Franko spoke to himself as he walked through the bookshelves. He contemplated Adrik's food poisoning warning from earlier. With only three of his homemade sandwiches left, he wasn't entirely sure how his stomach would take the starvation. "Here it is," Franko whispered as he entered the alley *Chemistry Books*. He searched for anything that would help him with knowledge. "How to make better bombs? How to make... anything that can be made? How to..." He felt a warmth coming from his chest and realized a second later. His pocket watch glowed red. The watch cooled at his touch, he opened it, and a paper flew in the air, floating for a few seconds until

Franko held it. *Be in Arkadia by tomorrow. Don't forget anything and... stop detouring.*

"How did he know?" Franko said to himself, looking around while shaking the piece of paper in the air. He almost jumped when he saw the golden-haired boy standing in the corner, furrowing his brow, watching the piece of paper disappear in the air. Franko watched back and forth at the disappearing ashes and the boy's expression.

"Magic," Franko said before the boy quickly disappeared without ever being seen again.

Franko continued looking for more books he could find before he headed to Arkadia in the next hours.

CHAPTER 25
ADRIK

THE CLOUDS HAD HIDDEN THE Sun once again in the City of Silver. As if the city itself knew of Adrik's arrival and the loop had started all over again. The stares, the talking, and Adrik's annoyance. The lights in Metal Tech were already on. He could hear Franko's voice clearly once he entered.

"He *hired* you? For what purpose?" Franko questioned the man in front of him.

"I already explained..." the small man squeaked, his back slowly losing composure as he turned around at the sound of the door.

Franko looked at Adrik at once. "You *hired* someone else."

"For a job," Adrik replied.

"What job?"

"One that you can't do."

"I can do *any* job."

"Are you a witch?"

Franko hesitated. "No."

"Exactly." Adrik looked at the man and handed him a bag filled with *Kosniz*. "You'll get the rest after this is all over." The man made a slight nod and took the bag, his hand slightly shaking. "Did you get everything?" he asked Franko.

"Everything is here." Franko pointed at the corner of the room. Bags, suitcases, and boxes stood next to the man. Adrik didn't ask how Franko managed to get everything to the tech store.

"Here," the man said, giving Adrik what seemed to be a small piece of paper. "It is reusable. Write a note and I'll get the message. The paper will disappear and appear as desired."

Franko frowned. "Magical witch paper? Why would you need..."

"We are not taking anything. Which means we need someone to take care of all of it here and be able to transfer it once we are out of Kosmos," Adrik explained, then turned to the man. "There's an empty room upstairs." He nodded upwards. "If anything goes wrong, I will hold you responsible, Duran." The man nodded rapidly and disappeared at once to the second floor. Adrik headed to the bar, where his sword stood neatly inside an untouchable glass case. He opened it without trouble and held the sword, looking at the *triquela* sign carved at the grip. For a second, he remembered what his father had told him. *A knife is for a man, someone like me. A sword is for a warrior. If you ever manage to own one, make sure you use it right.* The sword felt like a feather in his hand. A mere prop for power. *But* his father continued. *There is no warrior without a good mind.*

Everything was packed and fixed for the outside world. Most

importantly, the sword inside a case filled with maps. All Duran needed to do was portal it once they settled in a place.

"It's time to leave," Adrik said to Franko, walking out of Metal Tech. A thought in his head. Was he a warrior, a hero, a villain, anywhere in between? He didn't know. All he needed was revenge, and as long as he accomplished it, nothing mattered more. "It will take us a few hours to make it to Bore Port, but we will make it in time."

"Or..." Franko smiled, closing the door behind him. "We will make it there earlier."

From around the corner, a horse appeared, behind it a carriage. "Meet Midnight."

"Impressive, but not surprising."

"I forgot you aren't that fond of animals... what a shame," Franko said, opening the carriage door and proceeding to get in, not before looking back at his dear tech store. He glanced at the man on the coach box. "To the North Entry, Hugo." The coachman nodded, avoiding Adrik's eye contact as the duo entered the carriage.

CHAPTER 26
FRANKO

F RANKO WASN'T ENTIRELY SURE whether he was awake, asleep, or both. Not long ago, he had started to daydream about a mansion and an animal farm made with tiny sandwiches. At the same time, he could feel the rocky road making the carriage move harshly every five minutes. Adrik sat awake, drifting in and out, closing his eyes every ten minutes. He wondered what else he was planning. Whatever Adrik was thinking confused him every second. All he knew was that they needed to find the Hunter Secret Society. Even after going through the plan, the details were up to the person in front of him. His mind had already begun to shut down again when he saw Adrik compose himself. It felt like only a few minutes had passed by when the carriage stopped.

"We are here," Adrik said, his stern voice shaking Franko awake. Lights greeted them outside the carriage. They were in front of the North Entry station. Boreas Port, to be exact, was known for the management of trade coming from Europe. The international trade cities of Arkadia and Ether used Bore Port for most of their business issues.

"Hugo, take care of Midnight. Something happens to him… I'll consider killing you," Franko said, giving Hugo, the homeless man he saw at Ark Station, some *Kosni* bills. He saw him again after returning from Ether and decided he could be helpful, if Franko didn't say for whom he was going to work. Even so, Hugo nodded and headed off, back to the dim roads of the Ring Forest.

"Consider?" Adrik slightly frowned at Franko, who just half-smiled and shrugged.

The clock had barely hit twelve when they entered the station. Workers got out of the train carts in a hurry to the edge of the ocean for their daily assignments. It was easy to recognize the Illuminators, of course, they either wore green, orange, or purple uniforms while the light bloods and humans wore brown or black clothing. A trio of men stood outside smoking cigarettes and taking a break from their finished shift. Adrik nodded at Franko and disappeared into a hall that continued outside the station building. Franko let out a sigh and looked ahead. *How do I get myself into these situations?*

"What the hell are *you* looking at?" one of the men said, his dark eyes barely capable of staying open.

"Leave him," the man beside him said, barely paying attention to Franko. He looked around, probably not wanting to cause attention. Franko looked away uncaringly, walked by them, and hit the tempered man with his shoulder.

"Sorry… not sorry," Franko said without looking at them.

"What the hell is wrong with you, man?" the angered man said, ready for a fight. His friends started to appear alert. Franko ignored them, walking fast towards the exit ahead of him until he was out of the station. The men didn't take another second and followed him into the Ring Forest, whispering words under their breath.

"Where did he go?" one of them said when they couldn't see Franko anymore.

The other started, "I have no—" but didn't finish his sentence, when he was hit from behind.

"Men and their temper," Adrik said. "Completely predictable." Franko nodded in agreement, following Adrik's action and punching one of the men until both were unconscious on the ground.

With a little more crouching, Adrik and Franko passed up actual seafarers. They walked up to the ship gangway, a brown uniform jacket over their dark clothes. They approached the old guard, holding their fake identification in their hands. *What are we going to do? We look nothing alike?* Franko had told Adrik earlier. He complained. *Say we lost weight. Changed physical identity with magic if that's possible.* Adrik replied. He kept his composure, giving Franko a hint that he had a plan. That's until Adrik started coughing, the exact time that people behind them had started to fill the gangway. As far as Franko knew, Adrik never got sick. He could have easily dealt with a knife to the gut or a bullet wound. But *sick*? It was almost impossible. Yet there he was, starting to cough more harshly as he stood upon the guard. Adrik shook with worry and panted.

"Excuse me, Sir, are you alright?" the guard said.

"I think I'm fine," Adrik tried to say, handing the identification. The old guard had a slight concern upon his face, watching Adrik cough again and again.

"I need a restroom," Adrik panted, handing his black coat to Franko. He shook, his face pale. The guard turned to call security from inside the ship. As they tried to take Adrik inside, he let his identification fall to the ground, washed off by the current of the sea.

"May I?" Franko added hastily, showing the guard the identification and making sure the photo was half-covered. "He is a friend." The guard nodded in a hurry to attend to the people in line before sailing. Franko followed inside behind the security guard and waited outside the restroom. Adrik got out a few minutes later.

"Can I have a glass of water?" Adrik spoke to the security officer, who gave a single nod and disappeared down the hall.

"You're actually sick?" Franko frowned. "What did you eat?"

"Horrible sandwiches while I waited at the Ring Forest. Would have been surprised if I didn't get food poisoning."

Franko crossed his arms, thinking he had cleaned out all the trash from Metal Tech earlier. "I'll give you a nine-half out of ten."

"What about that half?" Adrik walked out of the hall and onto the main deck.

"For not telling me about the plan."

"Your reaction wouldn't have been as realistic."

Frank nodded slightly and frowned. "How useful..."

Adrik ignored him, continuing to walk outside towards the main deck. About fifty total cargo containers stood on each corner of the ship, with a few wooden boxes around. Walking in silent footsteps and holding their heads low, no one wondered about the two troublemakers. After a few seconds of walking around the grounds of the ship, Franko knew Adrik had memorized each twist and turn. The clock on the red wall showed five minutes for sailing to begin. Franko made small conversations with the other workers, getting information about their daily jobs in case there were any sudden stops. He watched Adrik wander around the ship for about more than five times.

"Avoid drawing attention." Adrik had told him minutes earlier, but Franko nodded and disappeared moments later after Adrik started to pace around.

"Hello there," Franko waved at three of the workers eating lunch from plastic containers. They all had introduced each other and talked about the difficulty of labor with low wages. From afar, Franko saw Adrik glare as he explained that his tedious 'job' had left him completely exhausted. Then Franko nodded as Adrik showed him his pocket watch under his shirt. He had lost track of time.

"In a few seconds now," Adrik said after there was a small shift on the ground. The ship had started to sail slowly and then faster with each millisecond that passed. Once at a certain length, the red and purple magical walls appeared. Everyone in the country knew about Kosmos' magical barriers. The red one, as Franko had read, was a portal made by witches. As long as you passed the portal with a clear mindset, it was achievable to teleport to a desired destination. The purple barrier, however, was the Celestialkalais' protection wall that kept beings out of Kosmos. In other words, everyone could get out of the mystical country if they were able to reach the barriers themselves. Some experienced witches—like Duran, Franko realized—could automatically teleport from inside Kosmos. With their help, Illuminators were welcomed to do so as well. After all, thanks to them, Kosmos was well protected against 'evil'. It was rumored that Stellar Court tracked all the portals manifesting in the country for that exact reason.

Franko felt goosebumps on his arms underneath his dark coat as they passed the purple protection wall. A stronger force was felt, even Adrik seemed to shift, when they passed the red portal. A tinge of magic hit each of their cells, and just like the unimaginable. Their bodies were no longer seeing the view of Kosmos' shore.

PART TEN

BLUE, WHITE, RED, AND TWINKLING LIGHTS

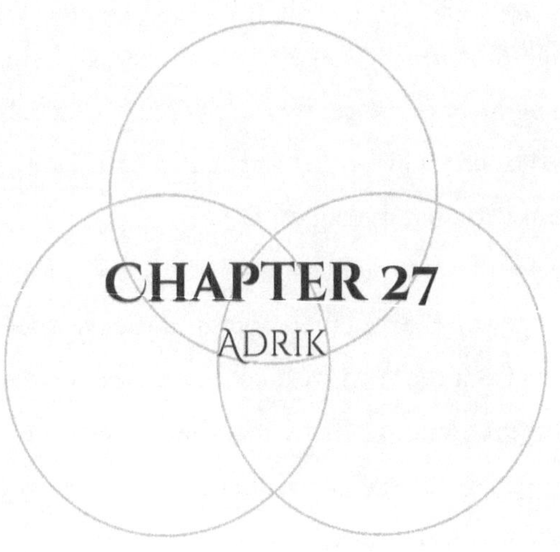

CHAPTER 27
ADRIK

A WHOLE NEW WORLD. One Adrik could no longer control. But control was no longer Adrik's issue. He needed a way to find the city's secrets, starting with the HSS. He had been thinking and found a million drawbacks. *Theft?* Different security systems. *Murder?* Different country laws. *Espionage?* Too many watchdogs. *Allies?* Who would ally with strangers dressed in black? They showed no threat to Adrik. All these drawbacks had a simple solution: watch, learn, and scheme.

"The map says this way," Franko said, pointing at the map in his hand. Before the ship had touched France's shore, Adrik had heard a few workers talk about Le Havre, one of the ports closest to Paris, France. After carrying a few heavy boxes at the port center, changing back to their original clothes, and Franko managing to steal a map from a small stand with the help of a distraction, they headed straight to the train station. Adrik had stood by a building, watching Franko contemplate how to steal from the old man. With not enough time, Adrik walked towards the stand, the man's full attention on his appearance. He didn't even need to talk to the old man, who glanced at his pocket watch, and started with a past story about items with sentimental value.

The weather was neither sunny nor gloomy, Adrik preferred it to stay that way. He read the map, turning it over to make sure he was reading from the 'You are here' angle. Odd weather, different names, culture, language, and inconsistent clothing. It was all expected, manageable as long as they looked like they could fit it. He faintly thanked himself for knowing the unexpected and preparing for the sudden burst of changes in Kosmos. At least he had learned... in a very crucial way. Franko couldn't help but look around as they walked to the nearest train station. He nodded with wide eyes at each modern-looking item inside the shops and smiled at each person who walked by.

"Stop looking overjoyed." Adrik looked at Franko, walking closer to the shade of the building next to them. "You are attracting unwanted attention."

"This is paradise," Franko replied. "Don't pretend you aren't slightly shocked."

"I'm not. I can't afford to be blindsided," Adrik said, looking around at modern machinery, electronics, jewelry, and clothing. "Do you have the Euros?"

"The what?" It took Franko a second to realize. "Yes. *European currency*." He opened the inner flaps of his coat, getting a pack of Euro bills out of his coat pocket, and made sure all his tech was neatly placed inside the silk lining.

The train station wasn't far from the Port of Le Havre, they only had a few minutes to get there and buy some tickets. A few people stared at Adrik and Franko, looking them up and down. Adrik continued walking until they had finally reached the booking counter.

"Two tickets to Paris. The earliest you have," Adrik started.

The woman dressed in a white long-sleeved shirt and red vest smiled. *Laura.* Her name tag read.

Laura made a nod. "Are you guys part of a play?" She stared at both troublemakers, frowning.

"No, but we are in a rush." Adrik crossed his arms upon seeing Franko's slight smile.

"Ok," Laura said, her French accent distinguishable. "Two tickets to Paris. The train leaves in an hour." She handed Adrik the tickets to which he took quickly as he nodded. From the corner of his eye, he saw Franko still grinning at her.

"Thank you, *Laura*," Franko said. "My costume is amazing, right?"

"You look nice..."

"Of course I do! But do you know any good fashion stores nearby? There is a certain item I'm looking for."

"Yes, just outside..."

Adrik headed to the exit of the station at once. There was only an hour for him to use. He waited five seconds until Franko finally stood next to him. "Fashion store? Blending in. Now we are thinking somehow the same."

"Blending in?" Franko frowned. "That's not... I need a change of clothes. I can't wear this for twenty-four hours *or* wait twenty-four hours to get my clothes teleported here."

Adrik rolled his eyes. "If you don't shut up, I'll kill you in less than twenty-four seconds."

Franko shook his head. "You would not."

"I've done worse with less time."

They took a turn down the next street, not far from the station. As it turns out, Laura was right. "I'm definitely not wearing that," Franko said, staring at the window of a Le Havre gift shop. A mannequin with a blue shirt and khaki pants mocked them.

Adrik turned at once, heading back into the train station. "When you find something useful. I'll be surprised." Franko ignored him and continued walking down the path of gift shops. Adrik had already checked Le Harve's map earlier. It was no use. There was no sign of modern stores, only the oldest streets of France. He read it over again as he waited in the train station, when someone stood in front of him.

"Hello," the little girl said, showing him a red lollipop. "Open. Please." She said, a lopsided smile on her face.

"Lily!" a woman screamed from afar in an English accent. "What did I say?! Don't speak to..." Adrik looked up at the woman, whose face turned slightly pale.

"Excuse me... sir." She grabbed the little girl and walked away quickly, disappearing around the corner of an exit. The little girl waved goodbye, her light brown hair flowing in the air. *Light-brown*. That was his little sister's hair color. The last thing he saw before he was taken away from her. The last thing he saw through the fire and smoke in his home. In annoyance, he pushed the thought away, deciding to stand up from his seat and analyze what modern structure France offered. White windows on the rooftop illuminated each inch of the station. A mix of brown and beige wallpapers surrounded all the walls. And even though a huge brown clock stood on the main wall with the 'Trains au depart' sign, Adrik couldn't help but check his pocket watch.

Kosmos, standing on the North Atlantic Ocean, close to Africa, Portugal, and Spain, was about one hour behind France's time. But the watch had fixed itself on the current time automatically. There were only twenty minutes left when passengers were called for the departure to Paris. Adrik headed inside the train, wondering when Franko could ever be on time. He sat down by the window, watching how the gray seats became filled with people. It was all similar to Kosmos. There was no way he could stop comparing the old and the modern. Born in America and residing in Italy for seven years, Adrik was no stranger to the modern era either. He had not stepped an inch into Ether, and he hadn't needed to. Arkadia managed most of the illegal trades that the City of Aurum hadn't figured out. Secrets, lies, and misleading alliances. From dangerous gangs to invisible modern supply stores, including Franko's tech store. He had learned, watched, and read enough to understand what the electronic screens in the back of every seat were. A food advertisement had just shown up, a man promoting his bakery and comparing his products to others. Adrik glared at the sight of the cakes, cookies, and many other sweets that showed up on the screen.

"*Seat 135.*" He heard Franko say as he sat on the seat horizontally across from him. "This gives me *deja vu.*" He held a sandwich in his hand.

"You're late," Adrik said.

"I was hungry... but this sandviç isn't as good as the ones I make. The lady at the stand was looking at me..." Franko showed the sandwich and took a bite. "Here." He extended his arm, showing Adrik another sandwich. Adrik stared at it for a few seconds. "It's not poisoned, you know."

"I would kill you before you try to end me," Adrik responded, taking the sandwich.

Franko shook his head. "I already know that, boss." It wasn't that Adrik didn't trust him; to some extent, he did. Who he didn't trust was everybody else. Even the most normal-looking people were out for vengeance. And analyzing Franko, he didn't exactly seem the type to kill someone... not out of vengeance at least. Not when Adrik had already done background research on him.

From the Paris train station to its abundant streets, it was a nonstop of *Wows* and *When did they create that?* from Franko. Adrik was slowly losing his calmness when Franko started to ask another question.

"Are those the new cellphones everyone keeps carrying and holding to their ear?" he asked, staring at everyone who held a phone.

"Yes." When the invention of modern phones arose, Adrik's parents were skeptical about buying one. Living in a small town in Italy and not having many family members, they never exactly found purpose in owning any communication device. Yet Adrik was always curious, and he had learned as much as he could. He had almost forgotten those devices existed and was surprised at the amount of change the world had taken outside Kosmos.

"Where can we get one?" Franko asked, excitement in his voice.

"We don't need one. Devices like those make it easier to track us down."

"Track us down?"

"Everything modern is controlled. We already live without it, therefore, it is not needed."

Franko tilted his head at first, almost in disagreement, but then nodded in understanding. They walked down the crowded streets of Paris. Each store was filled with people who looked like soldiers ready to fight inside the stores that had a 'Sales' sign. Adrik knew that entering each store looking like a murderer from a play would bring unnecessary attention.

Franko shook his head at the store they walked by. Now, a mannequin with a plain white T-shirt and black pants stood on display. "As I said before... I am *not* wearing that. That is an embarrassment to my very soul."

"Are you sure," Adrik responded. It was less of a question and more of a statement. Beyond him, a fancy suit store, something Arkadia definitely couldn't afford. Without question, Franko stepped in, Adrik following behind him. Fresh air and quietness greeted him like stepping into a cooler from a chaotic, humid bar. He could get used to fresh air all the time, but the humid, windy air of the City of Argenti lay in the back of his mind. Nothing compared. No matter how modernly different the new city was. The inside of the store reminded Adrik of Lunar Castle or a replica of it. The brown walls, dark chandeliers hanging in every room, and windows that looked out onto the streets of Paris. An abundance of displays with suits hung in all the corners of each room. It made Adrik feel at ease. On different walls hung different sets of colored suits: black, blue, and gray. In a matter of seconds, Franko had disappeared on the opposite side of the store, where all the colorful suits were stored.

"Can I help you, sir?" a man standing like a statue in a black suit asked.

"Yes," Adrik spoke clearly. "I would like to see your simple coats and suits, preferably black, vintage, and tailored suits."

The man looked Adrik up and down. "This way." And lead him through the wave of darkness.

It wasn't even five minutes in when the man had displayed about ten vintage suits to Adrik. Each had its own style of different designs, buttons, sleeves, etc.

"All of them," he said, after inspecting each suit for the third time. The man left with a silver rack towards the register as Adrik headed to the last room, passing the colorful suit room.

"There's no doubt. You are allergic to color," Franko said, standing by the archway and looking at the table with...*no surprise*... red and blue ties. Like the other rooms, even the ties were structurally organized by color and design. After rolling his eyes, Adrik walked to the dark-colored ties. He could feel the presence of the store clerk behind him right away.

"Five gray and five black. Different designs, if possible," he stated.

"Right away, sir." The man nodded, getting neat ties in a hurried manner. Adrik headed to the register. Franko followed behind him with about five ties of different dark-shade colors: red, orange, blue, purple, and silver.

"Is that all, sir?" the cashier at the register asked Adrik.

Adrik slightly smirked. "For today."

CHAPTER 28
FRANKO

THE EIFFEL TOWER didn't match the beautiful view of the golden tower of Ether. *Or is it the other way around?* Franko couldn't decide. If a few months ago someone had told him he would be in Paris carrying ten bags of luxury with Adrik doing the same, he would not believe it. *Adrik is carrying ten bags of suits. No, I am carrying ten bags of suits!*

Downtown Paris felt completely unbelievable. Every ten minutes, he would ask Adrik to pinch him to make sure he was not dreaming. After Adrik's continuous response of "I'll punch you instead." Franko was sure he was not.

People stared at them as they passed the Eiffel Tower, east of the city, in search of a hotel. Finally, Adrik had stopped in front of what Franko believed to be the most luxurious hotel in all of Paris. To Franko, even though he had never seen Stellar Castle, he was sure it could not top off a hotel like that.

"Are we—" he started, amazed.

"Wouldn't want to burst your silly dreams, but no," Adrik said. "We can't attract attention."

Franko shook his head, letting out a sigh. "Then where are we staying?"

"Just a few streets ahead." Adrik continued walking ahead, where more buildings stood. Franko slowly walked behind him, taking every inch of splendor in sight. Women in pearls and men in great suits walked in and out of the amazing hotel. He wondered when he would be at that stage of life. Standing in front of the small but livable white building, he was not exactly close. The black doors to the ground floor opened to a courtyard in the middle. Nature and four picnic tables surrounded most of the outside. They entered the reception area just to the left side of the building. Decorations of red and brown filled the entire area. No one seemed to be around just yet. Not even in the small dining room to the right.

"Bonjour, comment puis-je vous aider?" The old man smiled behind the walnut desk, leaving Franko confused. He stood up, holding a book that seemed to belong to the hollow part of the bookshelf behind him. Franko was about to respond in simple English when Adrik said, "Bonjour, I am looking for two decent rooms on the highest floor, s'il vous plaît."

"Aah, English." The man nodded, his accent noticeable. "French, not bad." Adrik nodded once, placing his bags on the floor. "Two *decent* rooms, high floor. These are charges." He gave Adrik a piece of cardboard with prices written. Adrik merely looked at them. Franko looked at his surroundings. He noticed the white ceiling with flower-like designs, to the coat holder, only two feet away from him, filled with umbrellas.

"Pay the deposit now or end of the day," the man continued. "Full charge before leaving."

Adrik nodded, giving the man the Euros for the deposit. "Keep the change."

The man handed him two brown keys and smiled. "Bon Repos."

"Merci," Adrik said, grabbing the keys once and heading towards the stairs to the left of the area.

Franko shook his head out of slight shock. "You know French?"

"Enough to hold a conversation and understand some words."

Franko felt, *no*, he knew that there was nothing Adrik didn't know. Well, except what he was currently trying to figure out. Besides that, every time he felt hesitation going through his own mind, there was none from Adrik. No mess or fault that made Adrik fall. He somehow always expected everything. Always had a scheme.

Walking through the hallways of the hotel was like being inside a wooden cabin. There was just too much brown and too many old antiques. He waited for the time he would see something newer and better. Adrik didn't flinch. There was no shock or surprise at anything. On the highest floor, Adrik walked to his room, ready to open the door. Franko walked to the next door, the room next to Adrik's. Once entering, there was no surprise. Blue and yellow greeted him. The room was a decent size with a restroom to the right. *At least it is cleaner than anything I've seen in Arkadia and slightly better than Metal Tech.* He thought. He placed his business bag on the table, along with the things that made him feel heavy in his coat: bombs, smoke grenades, metal gadgets, knives, etc. Besides the wooden wardrobe, something quickly caught his eye. He had seen them at the train station and around shops but didn't want to ask.

"An *actual* television," he said out loud. He had only seen one or two in his entire life. The modern world was filled with them. Looking around the television, he started pressing buttons to find a way to turn it on. Then he saw the remote control with the same name as the TV and started pressing those buttons instead until the television turned on. He barely remembered anything past being five years old, but he recalled how he wished his actual parents could get him one. His well-off adoptive family had a TV in their living room, but Franko stayed in his room. Toys untouched, lights turned off, and hearing the voices of his old and new family making decisions for him. For two minutes, Franko spent changing the channels, watching small parts of news, stories, and drama.

"This is one of the most brutal wars in the country..." the news reporter said, proceeding to show videos and pictures of a country currently at war. Franko shook his head in disappointment, turning off the TV at once and inspecting more of the room. He headed towards the brown door to the left, thinking that it was some type of closet. Another room similar to his was just on the other side. Adrik's room. It was somewhat bigger and spacious. Adrik stood on one of the two balconies from his room. He turned around, hearing the door close behind Franko.

"Did you know this door connects our rooms?" Franko smiled. "That is great."

"I'm locking it."

Franko sighed, looking around and heading to the other balcony. From where they stood, the Eiffel Tower was visible. The beautiful lights had been turned on as the sunset had started to set and dusk fell over the city. Watching and hearing all the people was unbelievable. An actual dream. Cars and trucks of different colors passed through the street. Some automobiles looked the same, and others had different sizes. He couldn't believe he had missed so much. Born in a village in Turkey, he had missed it all. His biological family had been poor, as far as he could remember. His parents couldn't give him enough to survive. He remembered seeing them one last time. He was eight when he met his adopted family, who had tried to raise him. Two months after his eleventh birthday, he was in Kosmos with an unknown light-blood Uncle, who was closer to death than living, and a bag of money from his adoptive parents. Franko had forgotten most of his childhood memories. Not that they weren't that bad. In fact, everyone was decently nice to him. But because most of the time, he felt like a burden to anyone who cared for him. His adoptive parents had come to pick up Uncle for his biological parents' funeral and take them back to Turkey for a while. They've died from a disease. His Uncle left the world with a similar fate a month later. Thirteen-year-old Franko never went back, leaving a note for his adoptive family in his Uncle's tiny house and disappearing into the chaos of Arkadia. And now, somehow, he stood on a balcony overlooking Paris, knowing independence had been for the best.

"The plan is in motion. Get ready. We will be hunting in an hour," Adrik said, bringing Franko back from his mind. He watched as Duran's magical paper disappeared and appeared again in a second, till a sudden red portal materialized behind them.

DEAD CIRCLE

CHAPTER 29
NEIR

T HE DOORBELL CHIME RANG through the silence of Lumière du Jour. Briz walked into the bakery, frowning.

"What are you doing here? I thought we were close," she said, hands waving in the air. Neir sat behind the rustic counter, tapping her pen on the notebook in front of her. She knew Briz would have come inside at some point. It was the only way to her other job.

"We are," Neir responded. "I'm trying to get ideas on more pastries."

Briz looked down at the empty, dotted with ink, notebook. "Looks like that is going well for you." She walked to the counter, set her things on it, and sat on the stool next to Neir. "Are you okay?"

Neir closed the notebook. "Don't you have a night shift?"

"They called me to go in an hour." Briz sighed. "Don't change the subject. Come on, tell me what's wrong."

"Nothing's wrong. You know I don't get sad. I'm stressed."

"I didn't say you look sad. You look like you are about to kill someone."

Neir half-smiled. "That's a pro."

Briz got up all of a sudden. "Come on. You need a drink, and I know where I saved a bottle." She left for the kitchen, coming back a few seconds later with a wine bottle and two glass cups.

"I never saw *that* bottle." Neir tilted her head. She knew Briz would stress a lot with work and Erin. *Alcohol keeps me awake. It's the only solution.* She had said a few months ago. *It's not the only solution. Coffee?* Neir had passed her a cup of black coffee instead, throwing out the wine in the kitchen sink. "Not to be annoying, but I thought you said you were going to stop drinking."

"That is my New Year's resolution." Briz poured wine into both glasses. Neir raised her eyebrows. "Oh, come on. I haven't drunk in a while." She slightly shook the bottle. "See! The bottle is almost full, and it has been here for a month. This is just for emergencies."

Neir took a sip of her drink, watching Briz chugging hers in a second. Even though she was four years older than Neir, she looked the same as when they met two years ago.

It was around midnight when Briz had sat alone, drinking coffee and cheesecake at the bakery. Now and then, Neir watched as she added alcohol to the cup from a hip flask. Briz hadn't moved an inch unless she came to the counter and asked for more coffee.

"I didn't count, but an excess of coffee *with* alcohol is bad for your health," Neir said, cleaning up the messy counter before closing the bakery.

"Well, thank you for your concern, but I am paying, aren't I?"

"Yes," Neir responded. "But I don't have time to head to the hospital in the middle of the night, and you probably have family worried about you."

Briz laughed. "I do have a kid to maintain... and not a single job. I think you understand why I'm drinking."

"Do you need a job?" Neir asked. "I'm looking for employees."

"Would you hire a drunk woman like me?"

"As long as you are hardworking." Neir proposed. "I won't judge, but I don't want death in my hands either."

Briz took a last sip of her coffee-alcohol, standing up, ready to leave. "At what time should I be here tomorrow?"

"Eight in the morning."

"See you then." Briz smiled, getting up from her chair and walking as if she were sober.

"Do you need company?" Neir asked. Briz shook her head. "See you tomorrow." She had come the next day, sober and with a wide smile.

Now she sat next to Neir, staring at the bottle with a frown. She had hung out with her a few times outside the bakery. Going to brunch or to the park for exercise. Briz was her only friend. Well, one of her friends, if she counted Erin.

"It's Erin, isn't it?" Neir took another sip of her drink, glancing at the entrance door for a second. Briz shook her head slightly.

"I feel like I have failed him somehow. Like he would be better without me."

"Failed him?" Neir said. "I say you are the best mom I have

ever met."

"You are only saying that to make me feel better," Briz raised an eyebrow. "He is homeschooled and lonely every day. He has friends he meets at a bookstore or gaming stores. Hell, he plays poker at the bar with other men."

Neir smiled, remembering Erin's comic book addiction and his reaction to Neir's secret. "Erin is a very bright, mature kid, and that's because of you," she said. "Besides, if he ever gets bored, you know he always appears wherever I am. So, you have nothing to worry about."

For the first time that day, Briz smiled. "I thought you didn't care about Erin."

"Oh, I don't," Neir replied. "I wouldn't want his death in my hands either."

"Sure, right." Briz laughed, standing up from her chair, grabbing her bag, and heading toward the door. Neir did the same, getting the bakery keys from the counter and turning off all the lights. The night had gotten colder, making her slightly shaken.

"See you later, boss," Briz said, glancing at Neir, locking the door. "You got mail, by the way."

"See you later. Be safe." Neir watched as Briz walked away from her, hearing the sounds of her shoes fade. There was a carton box next to the entrance door. A small sticky note with *De Van* written on it. She picked it up, looking around before heading to her apartment.

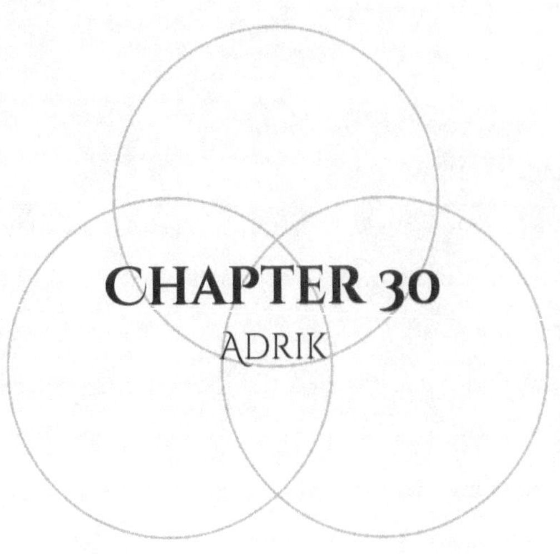

CHAPTER 30
ADRIK

VAMPIRES LIVED DISCREETLY around France. *How ironic.* Adrik thought. Seeing as the headquarters of the Hunter Secret Society was exactly there. It didn't add up. Even by Kaan's flat tone of voice, he avoided talking about it. He must have known more about the Society. Both had the same common enemy after all.

Franko walked next to Adrik, fixing his dark blue coat. With holidays coming up, an abundance of people walked the main streets of Paris.

"The Eiffel Tower is that way," a girl said happily to her friends. Wearing a black coat with silver designs and wool fabric gave Adrik an advantage. No one stared at him like a threat. No one cared about him except for his choice of clothing style. No one got in his way. And the duo would have drawn less attention if only Franko could ignore the city itself.

"Now," Franko nodded at the group of girls. "*They* set their priorities straight."

"We can't set any *priorities* if we aren't drowned in gold," Adrik responded sourly.

Franko made a single nod, following Adrik's steps and turning the corner of the street. "Tesserkurler, chief. For the hourly reminder."

Duran had overestimated the looks of the museum, but he was correct in some aspects. It was a considerable place for monsters to hide. A few feet away was the entrance to the grand museum and hotel. The large black gate was opened, and people came in and out of the huge courtyard. It was the largest building Adrik had seen in Paris, but not larger than any castle in Kosmos. Inside, the atrium was almost packed. Some people, dressed in their lavish coats, stood out as they walked around, while others entered the museum through any available entrance on the three sides of the building. The white building itself looked like a castle with a dome in the main entrance, where most people seemed to enter first.

"This place doesn't match Stellar Castle. Does it?" Franko asked, wide-eyed. Adrik shook his head, looking around and inspecting every person he could. At the entrance, they met with a large open hallway. Paintings and statues stood on the white walls, feet apart from each other. A ballroom with black and white tiles on the left and more white halls on the right. More people walked ahead toward the 'Tomb of Napoleon' under the golden dome. He had read about it in the guidebook and articles displayed at the entrances, enough to make a distracting conversation if someone asked questions. Two groups of ten people walked ahead of the duo with a guide.

"Ici dans les tribunes du milieu..." The French guide on the left started. *Here in the middle stands...* 'Napoleon's Tomb'. The other guide from the group translated into English. Everyone in both groups nodded, and no one raised their hands. Adrik and Franko walked past the mass, entering another white hallway to the right. Paintings hung on the wall. Adrik felt the stares of the black-suited guys standing at every corner of the museum. No, he didn't feel it. He knew they were watching them, over the crowd of people that moved down the hall and into the maze of color. Even in a suit, it was almost impossible for him to fit in. He just had that curious attraction. Other men in normal suites walked with either a wo-man, a champagne glass, or uninterested, sleepy eyes. A waiter walked by Adrik.

"Would you like a glass, sir?" he asked. Adrik grabbed a glass, unbalancing the tray. Franko quickly grabbed the remaining glasses before they collided with each other and fell to the floor. The crowd started to get ahead with people walking by the duo. Franko walked in sync, bumping into another man laughing about a joke Adrik had no humor for.

"What the hell, man?" The blonde man immediately turned around, his gold jewelry flashing in the light.

Franko chuckled, shaking the two glasses in his hand and pouring some of the contents on the man's suit. "Sorry, mate..."

"You have no idea how much this costs, jerk." The man took a step back, grabbing his handkerchief and wiping the dirty suit.

"Obviously, you don't." He eyed Franko judgingly, and even Adrik couldn't help but glare at him.

"Let's go. There are certainly a lot of ignorant people here..." Adrik said, standing next to Franko.

"No." Franko threw the three glasses he held to the floor. "I won't leave without a nice apology." People backed off from the chaos, creating a circle around them.

"An apology?" The man laughed. "As if that's going to happen." He proceeded to turn away from the duo, but not before Franko grabbed his arm abruptly and punched him in the face. Adrik held the temptation of doing so too, knowing to stay put instead. The guards had taken rather a long time intervening. Now, they walked into the circle, grabbing Franko first.

"You are going to..." the man started, held back by another guard.

"Stop," the guard holding the flush-faced man said. "Or I would ask you to leave now."

"Let's go," the guard holding Franko said, glancing at Adrik as well. They were pulled out of the circle with two guards behind them.

"Idiots!" the man screamed as an unsteady Franko walked around the corner, behind him, Adrik followed. The guards led them up to the third floor, down a hallway, and into an office. Franko flopped into a red chair by the large brown desk.

"You have ten minutes to freshen up," one of the guards said. "Another strike won't end well."

Adrik inclined as the guards turned to leave. They glanced back for a few seconds, closing the door. Franko stood up at once, walking back and forth in a straight line. And again, Franko was right. There was nothing money couldn't do in this world.

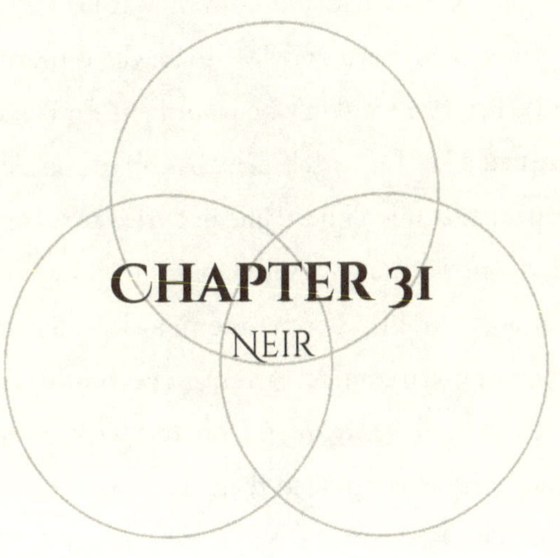

CHAPTER 31
NEIR

AN EMPTY BOX. *What the hell?* Neir stood in the middle of the secret room, surrounded by shelves of self-defense items, handmade wooden stakes, and jars of anti-vampire garlic liquid, better known as *allium* mixture. The brown carton box sat on the wooden table in the middle, wide open and empty, with a folded note inside. A dragon drawing in the middle of the paper. Neir opened it at once. *This is where your heart will be buried, Hunter. Once we burn your corpse, just like you did to everyone else.*

"Vampires." The last standing members of the Paris clan were coming to get her. The last time she checked, she had killed fifteen of them. The first nine were when she was a valued agent of the HSS, and six had been recent. And that was only counting the Paris clan. She didn't know if there had been new members. A vampire clan tended to add more once there were only ten members left, including the leader. Her brother had given her time to get out of

Paris. She only had a week, and nothing was packed. Something told her she should leave and live somewhere peaceful. But it wouldn't be her. She wouldn't be who she is. In France, she had already created a life for herself. The bakery. Business with other food companies. It was all hers. She had tried to leave her hunter days behind, but watching vampires in plain sight was no help.

She headed out of the secret room, locking the door behind her. The white unread contract agreement her brother had sent that morning to the bakery *again* sat on the kitchen island. They haunted her, so she had stashed them away just as she was doing now. In the drawers, they went. Never to be seen again. She decided to start making scrambled eggs for dinner when her cell phone rang. *Briz.*

"Hey, Briz—" Neir hadn't even finished her sentence.

"Neir! They got my mom! *They* have her!" Erin exclaimed.

"Erin, *slow down*. Where are you?" Two knocks were heard at the door. "At the door."

Erin stood there, his face red, sweaty, and out of breath. Rage. "No one followed." He entered as Neir looked around the empty hall quickly and closed the door.

"What happened?"

"The vampires have her. I saw it all." He held Briz's black purse in one hand and her phone in the other. "I was going to the bar to play cards. When I saw red-eyed men take her down the alley. They were too fast, and I was too late."

Neir could lie and say she couldn't believe it. But she did. She knew the risks of being a hunter. Worst if she killed them.

"You need to stay here," she said at once, grabbing Erin's arm and taking him towards the couch. He stood still, unmoving. "What? *No.* I'm going with you. I'll be the one to kill them."

"No, it's more dangerous if you go. I don't need distractions."

"I'm going, Neir," he demanded. "You are acting like I'm a little kid. Like I haven't held a gun at a person before. Like I'm weak." Erin was no kid. Neir knew it so well. Even before all the stories Briz had told her about Erin's fights, speeches, and deals. Erin was mature. A fearless, brave young adult.

"You can't go," Neir repeated. Erin shook his head. "Listen, Erin. You need to stay safe. Understood? For once, follow the rule and do what I say."

Erin gave a single nod. "What are you going to do? Torture them first? That would be great." Neir walked to the kitchen counter, getting a key from a drawer, then the key necklace in her pocket, and the last key inside the air vent beside the secret room.

"What I do best," she replied, opening back up the secret room. "Kill them... and then burn their leader alive." She unlocked the padlocks first and entered the four-digit number on the digital lock. *1216.* "I have about six more to go anyway."

CHAPTER 32
FRANKO

FRANKO COULD HAVE BEEN an actor if he wanted to. At least that's what he thought. Yet he stood at the corner of the golden-decorated hallway, checking for possible guards and people heading towards the museum's third-floor private stairwell. A huge 'No visitors allowed' French notice hung on the door. He nodded at Adrik, signaling him to walk across. Adrik proceeded with caution, nodding back at Franko to follow him. He closed the door behind him quietly. Their footsteps echoed around the entire white walls. With a very slight help from Duran's memory, Adrik managed to figure out new secrets and passageways.

During their walk to the museum, Adrik explained the plans he had in mind. *We'll go inside and find an entrance to the floor. If everything goes accordingly, good. If not, wait for further instructions.* He'd explain. Adrik had inspected around for a few minutes before entering, following the guides to each corner of the museum. Taking into account the statue guards, he whispered to Franko about a change of plans, following the guide through the Paintings hallway. Franko had faked a smile at the waiter while Adrik pretended to take a sip of the red wine, only letting the contents in the glass touch his lips until the guard in the corner finally looked away. He then passed his glass to Franko for him to throw away. The front crowd had started listening to the guide explaining the history of the paintings. Franko stayed behind the crowd, stood beside a plant that sat next to a bench, and threw the glass contents away from all three glasses he held. Easy enough since Adrik had already bribed the guards at the entrance to let them stay even if his 'alcoholic friend' went temporarily rogue. Their luxurious clothes and offerings helped after all.

Now Adrik continued upstairs, looking up and down the stairwell every flight of stairs. They ascended to the fifth floor. A floor that was hidden away from the public. As the grand golden public staircase in the middle of the museum building only led up to the fourth floor. Adrik nodded at Franko, proceeding to open the normal-looking double doors.

They were greeted by gold hallways similar to the ones from the museum down below. The only difference was the number of rooms on each side of the hall. Music and voices came from each room. The more they headed down to the end of the hall, the louder the noise increased, and the more halls appeared. Gold wallpaper colors quickly transformed into red. A great disguise for lost humans who'd accidentally entered the floor. Finally out in the open, a large room with chandeliers stood in the middle of the red floor. Some people stood around as music played, and others headed to the reception on the left or disappeared into the hall maze. *A hotel party?* Franko asked himself, wondering how no one below could hear the vast noise.

"Excuse-moi, madame," Adrik started as a waiter walked by with a tray of red wine glasses.

"Qui," the waitress responded, looking back and forth between Adrik and Franko. "Can I help you?"

"Do you know where the main office is?" Adrik asked. The lady shook her head. "Your *boss*. He is expecting us."

"Right," the waitress looked around. "Through that hallway, in the end, behind the red double doors." Without thinking twice, Franko grabbed a glass of wine, watching other people holding one for themselves as well.

Adrik nodded. "Merci." They watched the waitress head to the table she was being called from a few feet away. She set the tray down on the small table and touched her wrist, the scars under her sleeve easily noticeable.

"That is not wine," Adrik warned. And headed straight, passing the groups of people talking in small whispers. Franko gulped, feeling his stomach turn. He followed Adrik, quickly leaving the glass at an empty table, and tried not to breathe as he passed another table filled with a bunch of cups. Adrik didn't even squint.

The double doors stood out in bright red at the end of the hall, which was strangely more silent than the other ones. Once at the doors, Adrik knocked twice. Franko glanced behind him, making sure no one was around. He became completely aware that down the hall, hundreds of bloodsucking nighters stood partying. He had heard stories about them before. Or likely had seen them up close.

He wasn't sure… maybe he had. They looked exactly like humans. Looked like them. Moved like them. Some had strange, old accents he hadn't heard of before. Most spoke English while others spoke French. As far as Franko knew, vampires couldn't smell a human's blood. Not unless it was out in the open, had an emotional connection to them, or had been around a specific human being. Hundred-year-old vampires could probably tell right away. Even if vampires were starving to death, they would only crave it but not smell it inside someone's skin. Franko hoped that one bit was true as the red double doors opened. A man stood in a white coat in the middle of the dull room, watching a set of papers on a brown desk. Adrik held a straight face with both of his hands to the side. He could've passed up as a vampire, especially how emotionless he was.

"You can leave," the white-suited man said, shaking his hand towards a young man across the desk, rushing him away. "And who are you?" He looked up, fixing his golden-blond hair.

"Adrik Montova," said Adrik, his hands behind his back.

"You've got the look of a businessman—but not one I've heard of," the man remarked, tilting his head and studying Adrik carefully.

"I assure you that is unlikely in this country."

"Mmh…" The man nodded, glancing at Franko. "If it is unlikely, that means you are new here. What is the reason for your presence, Mr. Montova?"

"I don't have time for small talk. I'm here for business." Adrik stayed unmoving.

"Funny enough, neither do I." The man shook his head.

"I'm looking for your most famous vampire hunters."

"What is a person like you hunting the hunters for?"

"There is information I need to obtain. For a good price, of course."

A knock was heard at the door. The young man who had been there earlier appeared through the small crack. "Sir, I've got news…"

The man nodded in annoyance. "What is it?"

"The package was received. The side target was taken…"

"And the main one?"

"Has fallen into the rabbit hole."

The man smiled, teeth white as paper. "Mission accomplished. Tell everyone to be ready in fifteen minutes." The young man nodded, heading out.

"Seems you are in luck, Mr. Montova. Name your price."

Adrik nodded to Franko. "My partner is a chemical and technical expert."

"Specialty in bombs," added Franko. "And anything metal. Not to brag."

Adrik continued. "We sell in packages. These items are rare. Easier to reach your target effortlessly."

"A business deal and fewer deaths… well, for my clan. Interesting." The vampire nodded, considering. "I'm Nikolas Mondragon. A display it is, Mr. Montova." He held out his hand.

Adrik only nodded, ignoring it. "Good, I'll be here tomorrow after sundown. Just outside the gate."

"I will be there."

"Very well," Adrik turned around. Franko followed, not before seeing Nikolas wink at him a second before.

PART TWELVE

BUSINESSMAN

CHAPTER 33
ADRIK

SOME MAY AGREE THAT money can't buy happiness. Adrik thought differently. It made the road to vengeance easy, if only one knew how to use it wisely. And that right there was close enough to satisfaction.

Franko shook his head, walking beside him. "What happened to the plan? I don't even have that much tech anymore to sell it?"

"That was the plan," Adrik responded. "You don't need to."

"And the deal?"

"There was no deal."

"No deal?" Franko furrowed his brows. "Wait. You... never shook his hand. Did you?" He shook his head. "How did you know he would be convinced?"

"I didn't." Adrik fixed the pocket watch on his coat. "I'm a businessman. Look like one and others will know of it too."

"Boss, you are unbelievable... in a good way, of course."

"There was no need for a deal. We have all the information we need."

"The target. Do you think they meant a hunter?"

"I know they meant a hunter. They wouldn't need much searching if they were looking for a human." Adrik looked around, making sure no one followed them as they walked to the next street towards the hotel.

"Everything is set, chief. All you have to say are the magic words."

Adrik felt the mischief go through his mind. "It's time."

Franko smiled, starting to walk to the other side of the road while Adrik looked around one more time before heading inside the hotel. He checked the pocket inside his coat, making sure that the roof keys were still inside.

"Bonjour," the old man, whose name was Henri, said with a sour smile on his face. Adrik only stared, heading straight for the stairs until ending up at the roof door he had found the previous day. After midnight, the hotel was much emptier. Just as Henri headed to the dining room to take a break last night, Adrik was already behind the counter. It seemed that everyone still used the same old trick of hiding valuables underneath wooden floors. The hollow hole held a regular metal safe filled with organized documents and keys, each folder with named and labeled keys. Finally, he had come to the conclusion that Henri was somewhat deprived of sound.

From the rooftop, the foggy nights of Arkadia had turned to lightened gatherings in Paris. The infinite chaos was the only thing both cities had in common. Mondragon and his clan had chosen a wise area to hunt their prey. The leather case stood behind a stack of blue chairs next to the rooftop access door, just as Adrik had hidden it the day before. He grabbed it, placing it on the table a few feet away. He laid the written maps out. The ones he had analyzed for days until they lay in his mind like the palm of his hand. Red dots took over most of the zone: human deaths caused by vampires in the past three years. Not counting the forgotten ones. According to Duran, these were the estimates of deaths that the witch historian had discovered through years of rumors and news. Adrik had spent time in Arkadia looking for the best allies. People who came and went from the City of Argenti, even if the numbers were less than twenty a year. He watched, heard, and shook many hands. That's how he found Duran.

Paris could be modern, more vigilant, but no different. One last time, he made sure everything was set. That the dark alleys knew who their new master was. Adrik looked up, inspecting the area he was within. The building under his feet sat in the middle of all the deaths and the chaos. He checked his watch; by now, the vampires must have expanded along the streets. Adrik put everything back in his place, so that no sign of living was shown on the rooftop. He wouldn't be there for long either way. Down below, he saw Franko standing at the corner of the right street, east of where the hotel stood. Adrik closed up his pocket watch and pressed on it three times, letting white light shine that only Franko could see from where he stood. Franko activated his watch as well, making Adrik's light shine a warm yellow color. A signal of beginning and action.

Adrik watched Franko moving east from the rooftop, looking

at the other side of the street, across from where the museum stood. He nodded, signaling Adrik that the Clan had started moving. Adrik moved further to the other corner of the roof, his eyes squinting at the sight of a group of people heading in different directions in sets of two. They seemed to be heading east, as Adrik predicted, towards his way. He walked back to the other corner, nodding at Franko to start crossing the street. The garden down south was still open. Adrik expected Franko could act well enough like a normal tourist if he ended up passing the two vampires. He would enter the garden and hide for a while after they passed. That way, Franko would stay behind them, and Adrik would be ahead of them.

At last, he would see the vampires walking on the street below, finally passing the hotel. As he suspected, they were moving west from where he stood and east of Paris. Adrik waited until they headed closer to the intersection of the closest street, then he started walking to the edge. And ran. He jumped above each roof in front of him, passing the walls of each building. His mind was ten steps ahead. *Over the metal box. Duck under the hanging clothes. Ignore the muddy water.* Adrik felt the adrenaline coursing through his feet. For a second, he had thought he was still in Arkadia. The perks of Paris were its streets. The way the buildings were close enough for him to jump with no problems. Once in the last building, he walked back, getting ready to jump to the building across the street below. Cold air met his face as he jumped, making a front flip, and landing on his feet. Only hitting his back in the slightest and continuing to run. He moved more towards the edge, watching the vampires every five seconds. When they started to look up, he hid out of their sight. They pursued the same direction for ten minutes straight, blending into the people and shadows. Between dark alleys, they walked. Until they stopped to a halt, waited for others, and entered a five-floor parking building. Adrik jumped buildings once again until he was above the parking garage. He looked down. Franko entered through another entrance on the other side.

A slight silence greeted Adrik, he walked down the staircase closest to him. He'd seen four vampires standing on one corner of the building, while the other six entered the building. Only the sound of the wind hit the open, exposed walls. Down below felt more clustered, and footsteps started to echo. The closer Adrik got to the third floor, the louder the echoes increased. He stopped on the third floor, seeing silhouettes on the other staircase across the building.

More footsteps were heard from the stairs under him. They were surrounding the building from every possible corner. Adrik would have no choice but to hide inside the electric room a few feet away. Yet there was no way he could hide inside and listen clearly. He slowly headed downstairs, the vampires coming into sight. Adrik hid behind the nearest wall. A set of footsteps approached the stairs below. He looked over the edge. Two vampires. Before he could jump over the stairwells, a low hissing sound exploded. Franko appeared, running up.

"*Allium* bombs. They actually work." He grinned widely. "Brutal but effective."

"Try again," Adrik said, quickly passing Franko and taking one of the small gas bombs in his hand. Behind, one of the two vampires stood up, his weak movement ready to hit Franko. Adrik punched him in the face, pushing him down the stairs and throwing the gas bomb towards him. Some older and more powerful vampires were able to counteract the effects of the *allium* mixture. New ones became easily weak and useless for a fight.

"We were lucky." Franko stood up. Adrik passed him, going back up to the third floor.

"Luck doesn't exist. Only precision."

"Hiding already? Come out and face me, Mondragon. Or are you going to send your stupid amateur vampires to fight me instead?" A fierce voice shouted. *A girl's voice.* The young lady stood in the middle. Her blonde hair moved in the wind. He couldn't see her face until she turned at the sound of the elevator moving up. It was full of anger. *They are surrounding her.* Adrik thought, looking at the girl's eyes. *What did a girl like her have to do with vampires?* She looked around with concentrated eyes, almost calculating. Analyzing. She was no ordinary person.

The elevator opened, doors creaked in the tense silence.

"Where is she?" the girl asked the moment Nicholas Mondragon appeared out of the elevator.

Nicholas smiled widely, clicking with his mouth. "*Neir De Van.* No need to rush."

The young lady, *Neir De Van*, crossed her arms. "Is it because you don't want to die so soon? I understand." She faked a smile. "I'll give you five seconds to say your last words before you do."

"You won't kill me, hunter. Not until you have what you want."

"Then stop playing games, vampire. *Where* is Briz?" She took a step closer. Two vampires at the other stairwell moved behind her quickly, their rigid stance showing they must be stronger and older than the reborns.

"You are surrounded."

"I'm aware. You kept your Clan vampires below. Four to be exact. These are the amateurs and two old ones. I can take them in less than a minute." The four vampires behind her hissed in annoyance, standing in two groups.

Nicholas smirked. "Don't doubt it. Considering you already killed half of my Clan."

"Then why now?" Neir asked. "Why have you decided to take your revenge now?"

"Now, I am not alone. I have allies from other areas. With one call, they'll be here in less than *thirty* seconds."

"That's against the laws of the Society..."

"I know you are not part of the Society anymore, little hunter."

"That would be cowardice on your side."

"It would be bravery, Ms. De Van," Nicholas said, taking a step closer to her. "I don't intend to kill you. You will die. *Yes*. But you'll certainly be *alive*." Neir stumbled backwards at the words. Her eyes filled with rage.

"Hold her," Mondragon spoke to the vampires. They held her left arm first. She didn't move or fight. The vampires were too distracted to notice her right hand moving something out of her pocket. "How many bombs do you have left?" Adrik asked Franko.

"One."

"Throw it. Head down the stairs and wait." Whatever the hunter had planned, she needed a distraction. At once, fire erupted from the middle of the floor. Following Franko's *allium* bomb, more smoke appeared from the ceiling. Adrik headed to the middle, hearing the grunting and fighting noises. If he could see through the dark, he saw through the smoke. He saw Neir fight the two amateur vampires almost with ease, killing them by dragging a stake through their hearts. Mondragon was nowhere to be seen. Four more vampires appeared around them. Two, he recognized, were the ones Franko tried to fight on the staircase earlier. The other two, as Neir had said, were part of the Clan. They ran straight for Neir. Adrik headed just behind her. Neir turned for a second at the sudden sight of Adrik.

"Who are you?" She frowned, getting ready to fight the Clan vampires in front of her.

"A businessman," Adrik responded, heading straight for the other two in front of him. The *allium* air around them made them weak, but they were still certainly strong. All he needed to do was distract them until the hunter got rid of the others. Through the smoke, he fought them. Their red eyes appeared everywhere like a flash. For a minute, it was all well. Until the smoke assimilated itself into the deepest parts of Adrik's lungs and the memories went straight into his mind.

Smoke and fire ignited his surroundings. Screams of the people he loved infiltrated his ears. For a second, he saw her sister being taken away. Away from him and life itself.

Then he was back on the gray floor of the parking lot building. Now the vampires he was fighting seconds earlier were against Neir. She fought them easily. One by one until she staked the last one. Adrik tried to stand up. Neir suddenly appeared by his side.

"I don't need allies." She grabbed Adrik's arm, helping him stand, which he frowned at and pulled away as quickly. "This is my fight to take. And I am capable of handling it myself." With that, she walked away into the midst of the smoke, jumping out of the parking lot building and disappearing into the wind.

PART THIRTEEN

EVERYTHING BLACK

CHAPTER 34
FRANKO

THE TECHNICAL INTELLIGENCE of Franko's mind was at stake. After all the fighting, thinking, and receiving a note from Adrik to follow the potential hunter, who held the next answers they needed, he was *hungry*.

His watch had glowed red earlier while he walked to the corner of the street. To avoid the vampires below the building, he walked out the same way he had entered, following Adrik's orders to stay close. Franko hid in the doorway of a closed structure as the piece of paper flew in front of him from the pocket watch. *Follow the hunter. West side of the building. Blonde hair. Everything black.*

Franko looked up, watching the people around him. *Blonde hair and everything black.* He was already at the corner of the street, in view of the west side of the parking lot building. The men in black that stood a few minutes earlier were gone. If Adrik had asked him to follow the hunter, then he suspected that she parkoured out of the building, had gotten out of the exits down below, or both. Just as he was about to cross the street where the garden was located, he saw her. Blonde-golden hair shone under the street lights. She was a few buildings away. *Or both.* Franko had been sure to watch all the parking lot buildings. Besides the alley he had gotten out of, there couldn't be a way the hunter had gotten out unless she had parkoured down to the street.

With a bit of squinting, Franko was able to see her dark colored clothing and the way she looked around before getting into a taxi. He signaled for a taxi, standing by the sidewalk, just as a yellow car came into view and turned the corner from the preceding street. The car made a stop. It took a second for Franko to open the door, remembering everything that he had watched around the *outside* world. Like opening the door, smiling at the driver, and responding when he said "L'emplacement?" To which he guessed meant *location* in his English.

"Taxi," Frank said, pointing to the taxi the hunter had gotten into.

"No French?" the man questioned Franko, driving ahead.

"Qui," Franko responded, remembering the words Adrik had said when he meant *Yes.*

The man smiled and nodded. "Aah." And that is when the hunger started. Not only because he was physically hungry but because he was getting anxious watching the taxi driver slowly lose track of the hunter. *How do you say hurry up in French? Better yet, how to say stop driving like an old man in French?* Taxis and more cars followed in front of them. In his eyes, Franko saw the hunter's taxi take a turn to the right. But he didn't think the driver had seen, taking a turn to the left on the upcoming street instead. Far away from his assignment.

"Taxi. Taxi." Franko pointed behind him.

"Taxi." The man pointed at one of the two yellow cars ahead. Franko panicked, slight frustration rising in his head. He pressed the button in the door with an unlock padlock drawing and headed out of the taxi without turning back.

"Hé! Mon argent! Euros!" He heard the man scream.

He turned as he walked, watching all the taxi windows down.

"You're not a very good driver anyway!" And ran fast to the end of the street, turning the corner, and hiding in another door-way.

Boss. His mind wrote on the vintage piece of paper. *I hope you have a backup plan because... I lost her. Tell me you have another plan.*

CHAPTER 35
ADRIK

ADRIK ALWAYS HAD A PLAN. *Plans* as a matter of fact. His plans had *plans*. He hadn't waited a second following the hunter. After getting out of the parking lot, she walked to the next street and got into a taxi. He suspected Franko wouldn't have much of his 'luck' following someone in a new and strange city under pressured traffic. However, Adrik adapted fast to new environments. After growing up in Arkadia and living dangerously, it was in his nature to do so.

With the city traffic increasing every minute, it was easier to follow the hunter's taxi up north to the Seine River. When the taxi continued to a bridge, he had no choice but to get into a taxi himself.

"Suivez ce taxi," he told the driver, the moment he entered.

The driver nodded, glancing at Adrik now and then, until Adrik turned to him without breaking eye contact.

"Y a-t-il un problème?"

The man broke eye contact soon enough. "Non Monsieur."

I have a plan. He responded to Franko. The vintage piece of paper wrote in itself Adrik's thoughts. *The locator is activated.* The paper flew inside the watch and into the small portal, closing itself, then blinked a warm green around the edges. With Adrik's intent, the locator activated itself, letting Franko know where Adrik was or where he headed with the help of the compass. The taxi continued north, up until the hunter's taxi stopped in a less chaotic street in the 9th arrondissement of Paris.

"Gardez la monnaie," Adrik said before getting out of the taxi, handing him a hundred Euro bill. Then Adrik headed out, proceeding to climb the nearest and isolated building until he was on the rooftop. He followed the hunter's footsteps in the cool breeze. She turned into a dark alley, taking out two keys, and entered one of the back entrances of a shop. Adrik climbed down a building and walked toward the shop the hunter had entered. *Lumière du Jour.* The sign above read. The first time Adrik remembered he entered a bakery was to demand a loan payment on Craven's behalf. The second time was to help the bakery owner pay his dues in exchange for information. The third time was just the same. Another day, another agreement.

The bakery was the only shop open on the entire street. The hunter was not only his climbing, parkour *amateur* component, but was a baker, nonetheless. An entrepreneur. A smart one at that, because she knew he was following her. Or else she wouldn't have gone past the counter, turned some of the lights on, and unlocked the shop in the middle of the night. Adrik waited for two minutes, watching her pace behind the counter.

He entered the shop casually, like he had been there before. From the windows, he had inspected the inside a few seconds earlier. The bell hanging from the door rang. *Brown clean surfaces. Colorful red and green holiday decorations.* He sat down at one of the tables, the one closest out of sight from the window view. The brown curtain, which he suspected was the doorway to the kitchen, opened.

"I thought I was clear." The hunter stood behind the counter, black bow in hand, arrow pointing straight at Adrik. "I *don't* need any allies."

"Never said I was." Adrik looked at her, without moving an inch of his fixed stance. "I am here to make a deal. If you want your loved one back, I would suggest putting the bow down."

The hunter stood her ground. "What's in it for you?"

"The HSS." Adrik started. "I need to get inside, find information. And you are the one who can get me there." Upon hearing the HSS, the hunter finally backed down, putting the bow and arrow on the counter.

"Continue." She sat down in front of Adrik. "What is the deal?" Her curly hair shone bright gold, and her voice was between rough and smooth. He didn't like sugar or sweetness, but if it tasted the way her voice sounded, he wouldn't think twice.

"You will gain assistance in getting your loved one back," Adrik said. "I heard you aren't part of the Society itself anymore. There must be a cause for that, and the effect that you might want to get back at them."

"Their current leader, Alaric De Van, has exiled me from the

HSS. And *Craven* De Van, from the city itself. I need to stop him and everyone with him. I need to show the truth of who my brother truly is."

"Your brother," Adrik said, more of a statement than a question.

"I'm Neir De Van. His *sister*," Neir revealed.

"In that case. We both know you can't take him alone. Not with the Society and vampires against you."

"What's in it for you then?" Neir asked again.

"Get me inside the HSS. Getting into the archives is all I need."

"Can I trust you?"

"No," Adrik shot.

"I wasn't going to."

"You shouldn't."

She stood up straighter, looking straight into Adrik's eyes. "Can I trust you to finish the deal?"

Adrik slightly tilted his head. "Creating and finishing deals is my purpose. You can fully trust in that." Neir smirked and nodded once as if thinking.

Adrik got up from his seat, watching out at the darkness outside the window, and took out a piece of paper from his pocket. "Meet me at this place tomorrow. Make sure no one follows you."

She stood up, putting her hand in front of him. "It's a deal then."

"It's a deal," Adrik repeated, shaking Neir De Van's hand with ease.

CHAPTER 36
NEIR

T HE BAKERY LOOKED DARKER and lonelier, knowing that Briz was not around. Neir closed the entrance door and got out the back door the moment the supposed businessman, whom she realized she didn't know his name of, got out of the front entrance. She'd been alert since the parking lot building. A taxi had been following for minutes and seeing the reflection of the man's silhouette at shops blew his cover. He didn't mind her knowing he was following her. He made a deal; one she couldn't refuse.

She had small hope that she could go home to Erin and tell him good news. Yet all she had was anger and desperation to hunt down all the vampires in the city and show them no mercy. The second she tried to unlock her apartment door, it flew open. Erin looked at Neir, then around her, and into the hall.

"Where is she?" he asked. "Where's my mom?" Neir didn't respond, moving inside the apartment and locking the door.

"I couldn't find her," she said, placing her bow and arrow on the kitchen counter.

"What do you mean?"

"The vampires have her. I know she is alive, but I don't know what they want in exchange," Neir explained.

"They want to kill you," Erin murmured. "Don't they? *You* for her."

"They were trying to hold me hostage. That's all I know. All the information I could get."

Erin walked towards Neir, eyes dark and cold that no young teenager should ever hold. "Neither you nor my mom is going to die, Neir. I'll make sure of that."

Neir shook her head. "No. You won't do anything. With you in between, it will make everything worse. I need you to leave."

"No," Erin shot. "I won't leave."

"I need you to go to the police department."

"No."

"File a report for Briz and explain to them your family situation. They will take you somewhere safe," Neir continued. But Erin kept shaking his head in denial. "In the meanwhile, I won't have to worry about you, and I'll find her."

"I said *No*," Erin now shouted. "So they can arrest me for all the illegal stuff I've done. You know, some people have filed complaints against a thirteen-year-old. They'll recognize me right away. Put me in jail forever."

"You've never been caught, Erin." Knowing the department, she guessed that no one had taken any robbery or disrespectful complaints truly seriously. "You are leaving."

"No."

"I need you to leave."

"Why? I can help you! You know I can!"

"No, *you* can't," Neir struck. "You are just a kid. I don't want you here. I never wanted you here. *Leave.*" She knew the only words that could cause Erin heartbreak. *Leave.* The feeling of complete loneliness turned true without anyone to be around him. And even though she shared his hurt and had known it for years now due to her own family. She couldn't feel pain. She *wouldn't* let it control her emotions or decisions. Of course, being around them, she had learned to care. It was because she did... that on the upcoming decisions, she couldn't care at all. Erin had to leave. So, he did. Neir had to move on to new tactics and finally get enough mental strength to do what she *knew* had to be done. So, she did too.

PART FOURTEEN

PARTNERS IN RETRIBUTION

CHAPTER 37
FRANKO

THE SOFT DRIZZLE couldn't make Franko's day any less unpleasant. He loved rainy, cold days as much as he loved Sun rays and sandwiches. They reminded him of the days in Arkadia, where even though the Sun shone every now and then, the smell of humidity and soil filled the air. The only problem with gloomy days was that they usually made him sleepy; he desperately needed a distraction.

Last night, he had stood outside Lumière du Jour, hiding in the shadows of the street across and looking at his watch. From the window, he saw her. The person he guessed was the hunter, talking to Adrik. She stood her ground at first, then slowly backed down, putting what seemed to be a bow down. He paced around the lonely street. Waiting until Adrik had finally gotten out of the bakery and crossed the street towards Franko.

"I knew you had a plan," Franko began.

Adrik walked next to him. "We made a deal."

Franko smirked. "Of course, you did. I saw you shake hands."

He didn't ask further questions as they headed back to the hotel. Adrik held his devious face, meaning his mind didn't want to be interrupted.

Early in the morning, Franko headed down the stairs of the hotel, yawning for the fifth time since he woke up about an hour ago. The clock in his room read that it was about to be noon when he had finished getting ready. He knocked at the shared door his room had to Adrik's. No one opened, and no sound came from the other side.

Probably on the rooftop. Franko thought as he headed out of his room and downstairs. The drizzle stopped once he stood by the hotel entrance.

"Bonjour," Henri, sitting in the reception area, greeted. He sat by the brown front desk, reading a book from the bookshelves behind him.

"Bonjour," Franko said back. *Bonjour. Hello or Good morning. Got it.* Franko took a blue umbrella from the little bucket at the entrance. It made his green coat stand out. The sky still looked dark, so he guessed it might rain more later. From what he recalled, that was what the news on the television had said earlier. Something about seventy percent precipitation in the area.

He headed out of the courtyard, planning to eat lunch on one of the white tables later. Just as he turned the corner, he regretted walking in new boots. Cars passing by made the water run down the street, splashing onto the sidewalk.

"Modern cars. Lucky, it's a great invention," Franko shook his head, glancing down at his shoes. He started to walk to the right, closer to the building walls, not noticing the blond young woman walking in front of him. He took a step to the left to avoid hitting her but stumbled back into the street where a car passed. The girl grabbed his arm quickly, pulling him back to balance before the car could hit him. Franko moved forward, too.

"By the universe—" He sighed. "I almost had a heart attack, and *how* did you do that?"

"Fast thinking," the blonde girl replied. It wasn't until he looked at her clearly that he realized he'd seen her before. Franko furrowed his brows, noticing the tiny scratch wounds on her face. "Wait a minute. You're the *hunter*."

The hunter tilted her head, eyes suddenly fixed on Franko's. "What are you talking about?"

"You made a deal last night—" Franko stopped, "—well, with my colleague. A *friend*, you could say. Sounds better that way." He looked at the roof of the hotel. "And you are early. That's good."

"I didn't think your *friend* had friends," the hunter insinuated.

"Ooh, he doesn't. Trust me." Franko agreed, turning back toward the hotel.

"I don't trust anyone."

"You sound like him." Franko shrugged.

"Trust is a dangerous value. *Trust* me."

Franko smiled, shaking his head. They walked inside the hotel, entering the reception. The old man greeted them again, furrowing his eyes at the hunter. The duo headed up the reddish, carpeted stairs.

"Franko Sezin, by the way," Franko said over the shuffling of their boots hitting the carpet.

"Neir De Van," Neir said. "Nice choice of coat. Is there any way I can get one? You know, to stand out more?"

"Yes," Franko said, the side of his lips turning up. "There is this one store..."

Neir grinned, glancing at Franko's coat and then at him.

Franko tilted his head. "That was a joke. Of course, you wouldn't want to stand out, *hunter*."

They were finally on the last set of stairs. "Told you. You shouldn't trust me."

"Oh, *you* are cruel," uttered Franko, following Neir to the rooftop door. A slight humid wind flowed through the air, moving Franko's colored coat and Neir's blonde hair. Adrik stood next to a table, analyzing the maps of Paris he'd received from Duran, about every hour. He didn't look up when they walked out until the duo finally stood a few feet away from the table.

"Took you long enough," he said, finally looking up from the table.

Neir stood next to him, looking at the map as well. "France is a large country. It might take a while to learn everything."

"That would only apply if I were learning it," Adrik clarified, moving the map of France to the side, revealing an entire world-wide map with red, yellow, and blue dots on different places.

"Are we hunting the entire world now, boss?" Franko asked, looking at the map.

"Not yet."

"What do the dots mean?" asked Neir.

"That's not important right now," Adrik responded, going back to the Paris map and moving it on top of all the other maps. "Our mission is here." Franko moved forward, watching the lines and shapes of the map. A star where they stood and a triangle in red to what he guessed was the vampire area. Another star by Lumière de Jour.

"First, I need to know what you know." He looked at Neir. "We have to move forward."

"First, I need to know your name," Neir replied.

"Adrik Montova."

"Ok. Good to know."

Franko stared back and forth, both looked at each other expressionless, wondering who would break first. "So... boss, back to earth." He pointed at the map. "What are we going to do?"

"Every second you take telling the truth is a second our enemies move forward. You can fail alone or get revenge right-fully," Adrik said to Neir.

Neir cleared her throat and started. "The vampires you saw yesterday took one of my... colleagues from the bakery. My brother, Carden, vice-director of the HSS, exiled me from not only the Society but the country, too. He made my family and the entire Society against me. Made them believe I was a threat and he a hero. Word spread among the Clan that I was out; it was only a matter of time for them to get revenge for all the lives I took among them. Not that they were alive anyway."

"What makes you believe the HSS isn't allied with the Clan?"

"No. It's not possible. The director or council won't destroy their sole purpose."

"Most cases suggest that the enemy of your enemy is *your* enemy," Adrik stared at the map. "And to know where your colleague is and what everyone else is planning, we will have to enter their lairs."

"Into the Museum *and* the HSS." Neir nodded, looking at the map. "When do we start?" she asked, eyes fixed on Adrik.

He looked up at her, their faces filled with revenge. "Tomorrow morning."

CHAPTER 38
ADRIK

"WE HAVE NO TIME TO WASTE," Adrik addressed, his eyes watching Neir. Her dark green eyes showed more emotion than anything else. She nodded.

"What is the first step, chief?" asked Franko, looking at the map intently.

"Getting our weapons ready." Adrik glimpsed at Neir. "Chemicals, arrows, climbing walls. What else can you do?"

"Wields knives. I'm a hunter. I can do everything that is needed to hunt."

Adrik nodded. "Franko, do you have all the elements and chemicals to make nine bombs?"

"I might need some powders."

"I may have some of the chemicals you need," Neir informed. "*Allium* and other useful mixtures."

"Our first location is the museum," said Adrik. "Stay out of sight. Everyone should believe you are alone, Neir. Nicholas Mondragon knows about us."

"What? How?" Her eyes furrowed.

"We went to the museum to look for someone like you. That's all you need to know." Adrik proceeded to roll all the maps, saving them back into the brown case. "Do anything you need to do today. Bring everything you can before sunset. We will start on the plan here."

"Right away, boss," Franko said, turning around to leave.

"And Franko," Adrik started. "Do mind being late. So, don't be."

"Adrik," Franko paused. "If I'm ever late, it will be at my funeral." He turned, leaving the rooftop. Neir followed after him.

"Neir," Adrik blurted. "Lay low." Neir nodded and turned around without any words to say. Her eyes were still and almost unreadable. Yet Adrik had seen eyes with a flicker of light just like hers, trying to hold on to some sort of hope as they looked into the mirror. The flicker of light that faded away from his eyes a long time ago. He took the large case and hid it back into the corner, underneath all the newspapers by the chairs. Anyone who even tried to dig into the papers would find nothing but a pile of emptiness underneath.

Desolate hallways saluted Adrik in the hotel, just as the reception and the dining room. Only the faint classical music of the people in the kitchen by the dining room sounded, with only two guests coming into the reception and two others checking out in the span of thirty minutes. In silence, Adrik drank black coffee and avocado toast. He enjoyed it. Perhaps more the silence than the breakfast itself. For about an hour, he sat alone, thinking and planning. Drawing out the maps in his head. Remembering twists and turns.

Then, knocking on the door was heard and the old man at the desk at the reception shifted awake.

"Excuse-moi. J'ai un colis pour Monsieur Baudelaire," the young man in blue standing in the doorway said. Adrik got up and walked toward him. "Monsieur Baudelaire?" The man asked, hands shaking from the cold. Adrik nodded. "Qui."

"Signez ici, s'il vous plaît." The man passed Adrik a clipboard for him to sign, which he did in strange cursive, the word *Baudelaire*, then he passed Adrik a cardboard package.

"Merci," the man thanked, leaving Adrik's sight and disappearing into the street. Adrik headed upstairs, package in hand, to leave it in his room and come back downstairs. Just as he descended the first-floor stairwell, a fire alarm sounded from the ground floor.

"Feu." Someone screamed.

"*Fire*." Someone else screamed in English. Adrik wasn't sure if it had been a hallucination of his mind, imitating voices within the fire alarm, or real. It wasn't until he got downstairs that he saw the commotion in the kitchen. Light smoke was coming out of the kitchen doorway, and a young man in an apron carrying a fire extinguisher was quickly putting out the fire from the stove. Some people from the ground floor had come out of their rooms to see what was going on.

"You foolish boy. They shouldn't have hired you in the first place," the lady who had been next to the young man said, her native French accent distinguishable.

"Désolé. I'm sorry, everyone. False alarm," the young man said. The lady had started translating the apology to French for those who didn't understand, but Adrik was long gone up the stairs again and through the creaky roof door. He dug through the pile of newspapers, grabbed the large case, and opened it. Then, he moved aside the neatly folded maps out of the way, placing it over the newspapers, leaving the case empty. He moved his fingers over the inside edges of the case until he found the loose cardboard that was covered with the same colored fabric as the entire briefcase.

The cardboard loosened from one side, then the other, revealing a hollowed gap. Not long ago, he had told himself that his enemy would die with his hands. That his sword was a mere prop. Now he had more people to take care of. Enemies of his ally and wicked creatures were in his way. And the one who would die in his hands was not yet to be found. Till then, in the daylight, the silver sword sparkled. The sword, he kept like a trophy and had been used on various occasions. The only sword that answered to *his* name, the sound of his voice, his blood, and followed the movement of his hands under the black gloves. His mind knew the moment he touched the grip. Anything, especially the way to vengeance, could always be done a little bit earlier.

CHAPTER 39
NEIR

THE LAST TIME NEIR had worked as a team was with her brother. She was Carden's *partner in crime*, as he used to say, just as he was hers. And the last time they had worked together, she had been stabbed in the back by his own teammate. Ironic, since he was the one sticking closer to her. She had always been a solo hunter since she was a child. She liked it better that way and had adapted to it. But Carden was always a follower. Her *follower*. Her *partner in crime*, in most cases.

More drizzle hit the white tables in the hotel's courtyard. She was glad to have worn her waterproof hiking boots. For a hunter, she tended to check the weather, making sure that even in the pouring rain or hottest of days, she could still climb buildings and parkour through the city. Or make more efficient routes for her mission. Many members of the HSS had experimented on the best footwear to use for climbing. From research to projects, there was never truly a formula for the best parkour shoes. Neir had chosen a specific footwear brand that made her feel comfortable. Yet only balance and the climbing of the hunter itself resulted in a less dangerous journey. That's unless, of course, she found herself with the undead.

"Neir," a voice spoke from behind her. She turned around, watching Franko approach her. "Would you know any place that sells delightful breakfast sandwiches?"

Neir tilted her head. "Is that where you were heading to in a hurry this morning?"

"Yes?" Franko responded, furrowing his brows. He walked toward her, grabbing the same blue umbrella he had earlier from the bucket at the entrance doorway.

"There's a place just a few streets from here," Neir said. "I can send you the location. What is your phone number?" She took her black phone out and waited for Franko's response.

"I don't have one," Franko said, nodding at the phone.

Neir frowned, walking into the courtyard. "Other than the fact that they can track you, find you easily, it is distracting... why?"

"Exactly all those reasons," Franko said, following and walking out of the courtyard as well. "You can come with me, you know?" Neir doubted making any type of relationship with her new ally. It was early, and she still hadn't eaten anything. She could easily go down the street and buy anything to eat as long as it gave her energy.

But Franko continued. "We are going to be partners..."

"Don't say in crime."

He smiled. "Colleagues, then?" Neir crossed her arms, thinking.

"Ok, let's go," she said. "But we don't have time to waste."

"I heard that, too. Many more times than I'll admit."

"Ooh," Neir started. "Don't crash into a car. I'll probably not save you this time."

Franko beamed, fixing his dark green coat as he headed onto the street. "The first time was clear. Death is definitely not my thing."

Neir expected and had hoped for silence as they walked. But every now and then, Franko would greet strangers or comment on something new.

"Like your purse." He smiled at one of the ladies walking by.

She half-smiled. "Merci."

Neir shook her head. "You don't have to compliment *everybody*."

"That's what you do, if you want compliments back or meet new people." He greeted another guy passing by. "Hey man, I like your boots, and your coat is nice."

"Tellement bizarre," the young man murmured.

"*Such a weirdo*," Neir translated. "I don't think that's a compliment. Not everyone wants to make friends, Franko."

"Like you?" Franko asked. "I am very noticeable and observant myself, Neir."

"We are just colleagues. You do understand that?"

"I understood *bizarre, merci,* and many other words."

Neir crossed her arms and turned to Franko, deciding to ask the question she meant to ask minutes ago. From the place she'd only heard magical stories about. "You are from Kosmos, right?"

"Is it that *noticeable*?"

"You said so yourself," Neir responded, taking her phone out of her pocket. "You don't have one of these. The way you dress is decent, but not modern enough. You stare at people, at things like you haven't seen them before. Should I continue?"

Franko laughed, putting his arms on his hips. "No, thank you."

"You're welcome," she said, slightly nodding at the shop in front of them. "This is it."

Neir walked inside first with Franko following behind. The bell on the white door rang as soon as she opened it. She felt *deja vu* as she looked around the shop. Still vaguely the same, there were hardly any changes in decorations and prices of refreshments and meals. She remembered coming here a few months ago to get inspiration for her bakery and recipe ideas. It felt like it was yesterday, shunned by the HSS and trying to live a normal life out of her environment. But watching the impostors in the shadows of the sunlight and the monsters under the moonlight, Neir could not hold back. She had to balance her old life with the new one, even if the old one didn't want her back.

"Have you decided what you want?" Neir asked, standing next to Franko with her arms crossed. It wasn't until she realized that she had her arms crossed that she nudged Franko back to earth and uncrossed her arms.

Franko tilted his head. "Is the whole menu an option?"

"No."

"How about a hundred of those ham and egg crispy sand-wiches?"

Neir looked at him, squinting with annoyance. "Just choose."

"Alright then," Franko said. "Three of those sandwiches and an orange juice." They were up next in line. Most people ordered to go and left, so there were only four tables filled out of ten. Once Neir ordered in French and got their bag of food, she and Franko sat at one of the corner tables. She ate her omelet and hazelnut iced coffee in silence, watching the people out the window living their human lives.

"This is one of the best sandwiches I've ever tried," Franko said, eating his last sandwich out of three. "I should've ordered more..." He continued, but Neir was too distracted watching people coming into the shop and ordering. A woman and her child started to sit on one of the tables on the other side of the shop. The woman set the bag with her order on the table, which Neir guessed was meant to go, but maybe she had decided to eat there instead since they sat down with ease. They seemed happy as they started to eat their food from the Styrofoam containers, especially the kid, who smiled at her mom. She smiled back. Yet her eyes seemed distant. Then her phone rang, a piano music tone filled the space within the talking and whispers of people. She answered her phone at once and nodded. Whatever news she had heard, they were either important or bad. She closed both to-go trays. "Laissez-nous partir. Maman doit travailler." *Let us go. Mom has to work.* Neir could hear her say. The kid shook his head, his face filling up with tears as her mom grabbed his hand and led him out of the shop. Down the street they went. The little boy cried for company, and his mother was worried about work.

"Adrik said tomorrow morning," she spoke out loud.

"Is that a question or are you stating?" Franko ate his last bite.

"Both."

Franko nodded. "Then yes. Tomorrow morning."

They still had hours till morning. Too much time to use and waste. "Why not start now?"

PART FIFTEEN

PLAN VERSUS ACTION

CHAPTER 40
FRANKO

*D*URING MIDDAY IS WHEN THE *Sun shines the brightest*. Franko remembered Adrik telling him the second day they had been in Paris. Even within the scattered, gloomy clouds, rays of sunlight hit the city. The best of both types of weather. It surprised him that he hadn't even yawned yet, but he knew exactly why. He was wide awake, with Neir walking straight by his side. She hadn't spoken since getting out of the shop. "We are going to the museum now. We can get the floor plan ourselves."

"Of course, we can," Franko responded. "But are you sure?"

"Yes."

Now, they turned the corner of the street and walked towards the museum. Neir hadn't spoken since then.

"I'll help you with anything, but are you positive?" Franko asked, after minutes of appreciating the sights alone.

"My answer hasn't changed since minutes ago," Neir said, fixing her curly hair underneath her black jacket.

"Ok." Franko slightly nodded. "I have armor inside this coat. Two bombs: one *allium* gas and one grenade. A small gun with about three bullets and a knife."

"Can you shoot or throw?"

"Well enough." Franko shrugged. "My expertise is creating, fixing, and destroying materials."

"Fair enough," Neir said, turning the corner toward the court-yard of the museum as she got Euros out to pay for the entrance at the black gate. "Let's hope acting is one of your specialties, too."

"About that..." Franko began. "They might not let me inside for that exact reason." In short sentences, he explained to Neir what had happened in the museum last time he had entered.

"I'll think of something," Neir said, once Franko finished. "You look the part already. Follow my lead." They were now in line, waiting to go into the building. With the black glasses on all the guards, Franko couldn't distinguish them. He hoped in his luck that they didn't recognize him either. He fixed his hair to look less messy than it was.

"How do I look?" he asked Neir.

"Decent."

"Dear, I certainly look more than decent."

"Sure, honey," Neir agreed wryly, as soon as they approached the manager, alongside a guard, at the entrance.

"Bonjour," the manager greeted. "Tour guide or guide-book?" She held out two guidebooks towards them.

"Bonjour. A guidebook will be fine," Neir smiled. The first smile Franko had seen since he met her. They entered without any glances from the guard.

"So, you *are* capable of smiling?" Franko smiled at her.

She smiled back. "Shut up, Fran."

"*Fran?*" Franko tilted his head. "I like it."

"Just an act, *Franko.*"

"So, what is the plan?"

"There's no plan," Neir admitted, opening the guidebook. "You'll be a distraction, and I'll head into the office, which is on this floor, based on this *inauthentic* map."

"Neir, the entire museum is filled with guards. They respond to any bloody commotion. I say by experience." Franko hadn't noticed it before, not until Adrik mentioned it last time. But most of the guards wore glasses and stood completely frozen. Adrik had theorized that some of them must've been vampires, and if not, they were humans, most likely aware of the deadly creatures. He wondered if the hunter beside him could tell. "I have a question."

Neir turned to him. "What is it?"

"Are the guards vampires?" Franko whispered, following her slow pace.

Neir glanced around the halls, at the guards, and the artifacts. "Only a few. I've counted about five now, others are human workers. Some might know the truth, I can't be sure." Franko nodded, wishing he could tell who was what.

"We'll get into the office first. Then deal with everything else." Neir continued beside him, reading or pretending to read the guidebook. Then, she looked up after a few seconds. Looking back and forth. A tour guide and his group stood at the center of the room. Neir and Franko passed them, entering the Statues area. The large room was emptier than the Gallery Hall. A few people stood around looking at the sculptures and down the next room of armor statues. A young man stood in the middle of the isolated room, inspecting an armor statue while looking at a guidebook.

"Wait a second... is that—" Franko started, making Neir look up from her book again. "Adrik?"

They approached the man wearing fitted and silk clothing. Franko couldn't believe it.

"What are you doing here?" Adrik glared, closing the book. He wore a fine black suit, his hair neatly in place, a new shiny silver watch on his wrist, and of course, the gloves still on his hands with the three silver rings.

"Who are you?" Franko asked, still in shock. "And what have you done with Adrik Montova?"

"What are you two doing here?" Adrik repeated.

"Doing something," Neir responded, her arms crossed. "I'm not going to stand around and waste time."

"We had a plan," Adrik reminded.

"Yeah, *Adrik*. That you didn't mind sharing with the rest of the group."

"She is right," added Franko.

"You let your emotions control your actions," Adrik continued, looking at Neir.

"Aren't you?" she responded. "What was your solo plan? Try to get into the office in the hopes that no one will stop you?"

"There is no hope, Neir," Adrik said, his voice cold. "I would have gone into the office. Kill anyone who needed to be killed. I have nothing to lose. Only revenge. And I have come to collect the debts my enemies owe me. Whether I'm alone *or* not." He stared at Neir, not looking away from her. She looked back at him, eyes flaring like forest fires, and Franko felt like it was time to intervene.

"Look," Franko interrupted, trying to get their attention. "We won't solve anything if you guys start fighting like a married couple. Neir, we both know Adrik had a plan. Let us hear him out first, then we can act on it." It took them a second to react to Franko's proposal.

"Fine," Neir said, looking away. "What was the original plan before you decided to go on a killing rage?"

"Yes, boss. What is the plan?"

"Nothing we haven't done before," Adrik answered them, turning to Franko. "This time, you'll just have to draw blood."

Neir held the small ticket in her hand. She was just as good a thief as she was a hunter. Yet Franko felt it was definitely her nice hair and posture that made her trustworthy. He even considered dying his hair blonde, but that would be a waste of such nice original hair.

"How did you do that?" he asked her when she came back from bumping into one of the ladies who had barely left her coat in the coat room by the entrance.

"I just asked her about makeup," Neir said. "I find a lot of people have millions of makeup collections. She showed me the lipstick in her bag, and I offered to hold her ticket. I may have only needed the number, but she forgot about it." They headed to the coat room.

"What is your number?" the assistant standing inside the room asked.

"*1216*," Neir responded. The assistant nodded, heading to the back of the clothing racks and coming seconds later with a black hooded coat. He handed it to Neir.

"Thank you." She faked a smile, looking back at Franko. "You'll think she will notice her coat?"

"With everything that's about to happen?" Franko said. "I don't think so."

"Very likely." She walked to the hallway, where the restrooms stood, fixing in place two knives, one stake, and three darts inside her jacket.

Franko stood in front of her, making sure no one saw.

"Is that all you have?" Franko asked.

"I have one more stake inside my boot and two more *allium* darts." Franko opened the left side of his coat, showing two bombs, a gun, and a metal knife.

"I'm ready."

"So am I." Neir put on the coat over her black jacket, making sure to unzip it so it would look decent enough.

"In that case..." Franko put his arm out to lead Neir back into the gallery. "*Action*." They went to the hallway of the museum, now with a new and improved mind.

"Would you like some wine?" Neir asked as they passed the waiter with glasses of water and wine.

"Sure. Why not?" Franko responded, starting to get a glass of wine from the tray Neir did the same. Franko drank it all at once without taking a breath.

"Fran, slow down. You know the wine doesn't do you any good," Neir warned.

"Don't worry. It will be fine."

"What are you doing?" Neir asked. Franko walked away, his head started to feel loopy. "Where are you going?"

"Getting another one!" he exclaimed, loud enough for everyone in the hall to hear. "Waiter! Where is that guy?" One of the waiters appeared around the corner. "Give me another." The waiter nodded as Franko grabbed another wine glass. "Now this is actually wine..." He smiled, but he was yanked from the arm by Neir.

"Can you stop?" she shot.

"Let go of me." Franko took a step back, slightly hitting the plant pot behind him and spilling wine on the floor. "Ooh, hey, I *remember* you." He talked to the plant, touching one of the leaves.

"Fran, stop it. Come on. Let's go," Neir suggested, but Franko shook his head, walking away and bumping into the crowd ahead.

"This feels familiar," he murmured, feeling Neir pulling his arm.

"Hey, you!" Someone from the crowd screamed. A guy from the tour group said, moving out of the crowd. "Drunkards like you shouldn't be allowed inside. You almost bumped into all of us, who actually want to learn here." He spoke in another English accent that Franko had heard of before. *From Britain*. Franko thought, remembering how some people from Arkadia talked in a similar accent.

"Excuse me? *That* is offensive to everyone drinking wine right now? You are holding a glass yourself," Franko gleamed. "How ironic."

Neir nudged him. "Fran, let's go. We don't want to cause any trouble." Franko shook his head and started to step back. The guy seemed to have a very short temper and headed straight for Franko, punching him right on the face. People started backing away. Franko grunted, walking toward the guy and punching him back on the shoulder. He could feel the adrenaline and pain rushing in all at once. Still, he couldn't stop. The guy punched him in the stomach just as Franko tried to pull him to the ground, the guards started to move into the crowded circle. But the guy punched him hard on the face again, and so did Franko. He felt fluid on his forehead and rushing out of his nose. Then, he looked up. The guy in front of him had a cut on his forehead and blood on his lips. Blood was drawn. And most of the guards had started walking away. Only one stood close by, hand signaling the other ones to move back or upstairs. Neir nodded at Franko. He moved back, and the guy suddenly backed down, disappearing into the people who were now moving into the other side of the museum or decided to head out. More guards moved away from the hallway, leading the people out of the bloody hall.

"Wait a minute." The guard coughed. "I remember you. You like causing trouble, don't you?" Franko didn't speak, only half-smiled. The guard closest to them started coughing continuously until another guard grabbed him from the arm and pushed him away, only turning around and saying, "You. Get. Out."

"Get out," another guard started as he passed by. "You are now banned from the Museum."

Neir shook her head. "Excusez-moi? He didn't start the fight.

He was only defending himself."

"Rules are rules, Miss. S'il te plaît, sors. He has to get out of the Museum. With all due respect, *you* can head to the other halls as this one will get sanitized." The guard stood there, waiting for both of them to move out of the hall. Neir nodded at Franko. They walked out until they were back at the entrance.

"Keep watch outside. I'll head inside from the other entrance," Neir said, looking at Franko. "And you should probably clean that up."

Franko touched his forehead. "Is it that bad?"

Neir nodded. "Could be worse."

"That makes me feel better," Franko said, walking to the restroom and glancing at Neir heading out the main entrance of the museum.

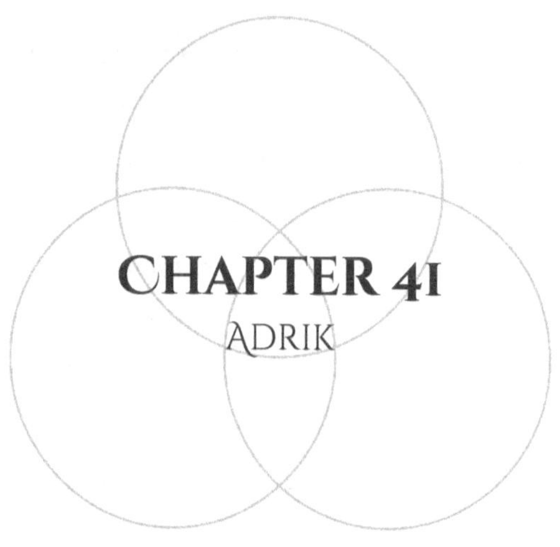

CHAPTER 41
ADRIK

LIKE PLANNED, the guards had left as soon as the commotion in the Gallery Hall was heard. Even the guard standing by the office had stepped out of his post to figure out what was going on. Standing in the corner of the Statues area, close to the armor statues, was easy enough. No one would have taken much consideration of their peripheral view as they walked through the main corridor. Two guards and a few people who had heard the fighting had walked quickly towards the Gallery Hall. Adrik headed to the left, away from the commotion and into the Office Area. The corner of the Museum had three break rooms, with the main office being on the corner. One of the entrances was right across, but the entire area was empty. Adrik headed to the counter, where a lady in a black uniform suit sat, the phone to her ear.

"Oui. Je leur dirai d'aller là-bas," she said through the phone. *Yes. I'll tell them to head right there.* Due to the chaos, Adrik guessed they would need the janitors to head to the Gallery Hall. It would be some time before they found them. He'd been explicit in telling them to cut out the recording cameras and hide for ten minutes if they wanted to get well compensated.

"Excuse-moi," Adrik started, proposing a donation. "Je voudrais faire un don très généreux."

"Désolé monsieur. Veuillez patienter quelques minutes, s'il vous plaît? Je reviens tout de suite." She smiled, getting out her chair.

"Bien sûr," Adrik responded. Of course, it would be his pleasure to *wait*. Quiet and composed. He almost smirked as the lady disappeared around the hall, keys dangling in her hands. He waited ten seconds, then headed straight for the locked white door. Behind its glass window, he could see the hall with rooms on each side. He took out a bobby pin from his pocket instead of the lock-picking gadget that Franko had given him. *Fifteen in One. Special Edition.* Franko had said. It had helped Adrik in some cases. Yet he stuck with the bobby pens, sharp-thin knives, cards, removing the hinges, or anything he could use for lock picking. He shuffled around the pin inside the lock and listened closely until the click of the lock turning sounded and the door became loose. Adrik opened it, heading inside the hall and closing the door behind him. He looked at his watch. *Nine minutes.* He walked fast, glancing at each room and sign. *Office. Break Room. Lunch Room. Library. Storage and Records.* At the end of the hall, the Records room stood. Pin in hand, he checked the knob. *Locked.* Then proceeded to work on his hobby. Inside, the entire room smelled of papers and files. Organized papers. Desks stood on the edges of the room with stacks of carton boxes, while in the middle, large wooden cabinets filled the space. Adrik looked around the room, seconds ticking in his mind until he could find the large drawer labeled *Plans* in French.

Four minutes. He had four minutes left after he locked all the doors and stood by the counter again. Neir was already there, holding a black coat over the counter.

"Did anyone see you?" Adrik asked, getting out safety pins from his pocket and opening the folded map he held gently. Neir shook her head, watching Adrik place the map over the inside of the coat. He passed safety pins to Neir. They pinned the edges of the thin map to the coat, then Neir put it on.

"Noticeable?" she asked.

"No," Adrik responded.

Guards stood in each entrance while guests asked them what was going on. Adrik walked behind Neir, hearing the complaints and questions. They passed through the small crowd. The people who had been inside earlier were being led out to the courtyard. It wasn't until they moved out of the crowd and walked toward Franko by the gate that Adrik looked around them. Smoke was coming out of some of the archway entrances of the Museum. People started to move back as the fire alarm began to sound.

"Let's go," Adrik said. He looked back one more time. *Chaos.* Everyone was too distracted to see them leave.

PART SIXTEEN

SOMETHING ABOUT RAIN

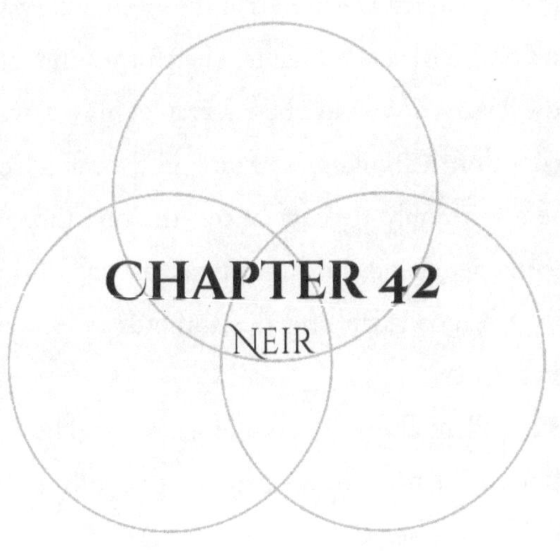

CHAPTER 42
NEIR

THE BUSINESSMAN'S PLAN was smart, Neir admitted. Hiring the janitors to control the cameras and using smoke grenades, including the man who punched Franko, wasn't entirely necessary. Hers would have worked just fine either way. She would've easily distracted the front desk and stolen the map herself. Sometimes not overthinking about something helped. She let the adrenaline control her. That's all she needed to move forward.

Afternoon had set in as the taxi turned the corner two streets away from the bakery. At the passenger's seat, Neir glanced at Adrik, he watched around the busy streets of Paris. Then looked at her twice through the entire ride. Not even Franko spoke, but she could hear his sighs as she saw him watch out the window from the corner of her eye. They got out of the taxi after Neir paid the driver, and she moved onto the street toward her apartment.

"This way," she spoke quietly, taking a turn into an alley by the corner of the street. She liked that the green building seemed to change to a dark coal color at night. They turned the corner.

"Now, I see why you live here." Franko mused, watching the entrance door of the building standing in the middle of the dark alley. There were only two entrances, the one they were going through and one behind the dumpster at the end of the alleyway. As far as Neir's knowledge, only the landlords and she knew about the secret entrance.

The confidentiality of the building itself had been one of the most important elements in the beginning months of living independently in a city she didn't want to leave. Only now was she hiding in the darkness of the HSS but in plain sight of the vampires she wanted to hunt. The entrance's double dark fiberglass doors, the limited number of apartments and tenants, and the quietest place in Paris, the building settled in, made it extremely easy for Neir to choose her new home. After working, sleeping in the seats of the rented bakery shop, and walking around for two weeks, she had found it.

She'd wondered whether Adrik was impressed with her choice of living, yet she couldn't tell his thoughts as they walked up the stairs to the fourth floor and the last room at the corner of the building. Watching his analyzing expressions and Franko's *Wow* stances every minute was almost laughable.

"Here we are," she said, opening her door and letting them inside. Neir tried not to smile.

"Nice place, Neir," Franko said, his hands on his waist.

"It's decent enough," she responded.

"That's a shadow of the truth," added Adrik.

"You can sit down," Neir suggested to the duo, walking to the kitchen. She grabbed bottles of cold water, a mirror compact from the kitchen drawer, and an ice bag from the fridge. Then, headed to the living room where Franko sat on one of the black sofas, Adrik across from him, and her next to Franko.

"Oh, by the universe, is it really that bad?" Franko sighed.

"Couldn't be worse," Adrik responded.

"That's an overstatement," Neir said, handing Franko the ice bag and the mirror. The first thing that Franko did was look at himself.

"My beautiful face." He whined. "It is absolutely the worst." He shook his head and sighed again.

"I've been through worse," Neir said. "It'll fully go away in about two weeks."

Franko looked at Adrik. "You could have told the guy not to punch that hard."

"I said you had to draw blood. Never did I say *who's*," Adrik responded. "It had to be believable."

"It was believable, all right." Neir half-smiled at Franko.

"Not funny," Franko shook his head. "You know how hard it was for the creator of the universe to create this *masterpiece*." He pointed at his face only for a second, his expression somber.

"Probably a second," Neir teased. "I'm *kind of* joking." She added when Franko shook his head at her. Adrik only stared at them like he was watching a comical show.

"Are you resting?" Neir said to him. Adrik shook his head.

"He is never resting," Franko added. "Only thinking."

"Strategizing," said Adrik.

"*Scheming.*"

"Do you have enough for tomorrow afternoon?" he asked Neir.

She nodded, knowing what he meant, and got up. "More than enough. I can show you." Adrik made a single nod, getting up in sync with Franko, and followed Neir to the gray hall behind them. Her room stood to the left, while the restroom and another room stood to the right. She grabbed the three keys: one she always carried in her jacket pocket, another she kept in a kitchen drawer, and the last stood in the air vent just beside her. She unlocked the three vertical locks on the metal door first, then typed in the number code on the screen beside it.

Fresh air greeted them the moment they entered the secret room. The lights turned on as soon as the door swung halfway. Neir could hear the air vents blowing air into the room. Each room held its own thermostat, she'd set this one automatically to cold. Yet it was more than usual now with the winter weather outside. They all headed inside and stood around the metal table. The door closed by itself slowly behind Franko without a creak, as it was designed that way. Adrik and Franko looked around at the shelves and shelves of items. Mostly jars and weapons.

"*Allium* jars, Illuminator and light-blood jars," Neir informed. "Stakes, knives, two bows, normal arrows. With the minor hunts, stakes last for about two months." The blood of Illuminators and light-bloods on the wooden stakes was the ultimate recipe for vampire killings—or cutting their heads off.

"Where did you get the blood?" Adrik asked, nodding at the two huge red jars labeled in black marker, *Gold* and *Silver*, for Illuminator and light-blood.

"Stolen from the HSS. They have volunteers who hate vampires as much as us. Some are family members or friends."

"Do you have any supernatural friends?" asked Franko.

"No." Neir slightly shook her head. "Just normal allies." She looked at Adrik, who was already looking at her, focused on her eyes.

"Get everything ready for tomorrow," Adrik ordered. "Franko, you take care of all the bombs, work all night if you need to. Neir, you are in charge of the weapons." He started to turn around.

"What about you?" Neir said. "What will you do?" Adrik turned to look at them, his left leg straighter. Before they had gotten into the taxi, she had seen him quietly getting out a covered sword without the driver looking. Then put it back after getting out, walking normally as if there was no silver blade under his black suit jacket and trousers. *Nice sword.* Neir had said before getting into the taxi. He'd only look at her with that slight, judgy-analyzing look he always gave.

"Delete any tracks," he responded, walking out of the hidden room.

Franko shrugged. "You'll get used to it." He winked at Neir, who proceeded to grab a wooden box from one of the corners of the room.

"Should we?" she said towards Franko, opening up the box and revealing different metal items, bow and arrow steel items, and bullets.

CHAPTER 43
ADRIK

T HREE VERTICAL LOCKS for a hidden room could be easily opened. Adrik could have opened them in less than five minutes or taken off the metal bolts. Someone else with a similar or lesser intellect would last ten to twenty minutes.

Light shone under the cloudy city. It had started to get humid as the Moon replaced the Sun. With the night traffic, it took the driver to arrive at Adrik's hotel in thirty minutes. The old man no longer sat at the reception desk, replaced by a young lady whom Adrik figured was his daughter. He had seen her a few times around and had heard her speak English as well.

"I would like to check out in an hour," he said to her.

"In an hour?" she asked, glancing back and forth.

"Yes."

She nodded. "The paperwork will be ready then, Mr. Baudelaire."

Adrik turned to leave and headed up the stairs. Before getting inside, he could hear movement in his hotel room. He turned the key at once. Duran, the historian witch, sat in the chair by the desk, staring around the room.

"Any difficulties in Kosmos?" Adrik asked, opening up the suitcase that sat on the bed. His other suitcases containing clothing, maps, and a few personal items stood in the corner.

"No, sir. With the protection spell around the shop, everything has been under control."

Adrik nodded at the cases. "They are ready for transfer." Duran nodded, headed to the corner, and created a red portal. He disappeared through it, taking in two suitcases first. Adrik headed to Franko's room through the shared door and picked up the two brown suitcases in the corner. One, which Franko said, contained his personal items, the other a few metal gadgets. They were easily distinguishable as his gadget bag felt heavier than the other. Adrik turned around as the room door opened.

"Good. You're here."

"Of course, boss. Message was received." Franko walked over to him, picking up his extra clothing bag that stood at the foot of his bed. "You could have told me to come with you earlier."

"Change of plans," Adrik stated. "Neir?"

"Getting a few things ready," Franko said, passing the shared door to Adrik's room. "I told her to wait for me before she packed the items."

Adrik nodded, putting the suitcase with the gadgets by the room entrance door. Duran appeared back through the portal.

"Oh hello," Franko greeted.

Duran nodded. "Mr. Sezin." And disappeared through the portal again, taking with him the last suitcase to the first floor of Franko's tech shop. They sat back in the same place they had been a few days ago when the duo had just arrived at the hotel, and Duran began portaling the cases through.

"He knew it was me..." Franko slightly nodded, probably happy about his appearance. "By the way... change of plans? What do you mean change? Besides, carrying the cases. Why am I here?"

Adrik had been waiting for that question and knew Franko's answer. "You are going back to Kosmos."

Franko tilted his head. "No."

"For thirty minutes, Franko. There's a message I need you to send."

The red portal opened back up as Adrik held out some envelopes to Franko. "To remind Arkadia and their so-called bosses who their leader *and* enemy is."

The tool suitcases were placed in the taxi's trunk after Adrik signed the check-out papers under the name of *Lorenzo Baudelaire*. He held the sword next to him under his coat and the driver's view, as he drove back to the 9th arrondissement. It had finally started to slightly rain, and around every five minutes, it would stop. Adrik could smell the humidity in the air. He expected Franko to deliver the messages at a considerable time in Arkadia. After all, the night would be a busy one.

He walked down the street to Neir's apartment, water puddles hitting the outer sole of his black dress shoes. There was no actual chaotic noise in the street except for water dripping and the sound of party music from an apartment a street away. He looked up at Neir's closed balcony windows from her living room. No light shone. It wasn't until he got up to Neir's floor that he swung the unlocked door open and entered. Items had been thrown to the floor. A first aid kit that was on her counter, kitchen dishes, and photograph frames. The center table and sofa were tilted to the side. The door to the hidden room, however, was locked, and her bedroom door was wide open. Her fairly clean room was messy. Everything, including pieces of clothing and items from open drawers, was scattered around the room.

Adrik looked out the window, wondering who had taken Neir. The doors to the living room balcony were closed but not the ones from her dark green room. Forest green curtains flew open with the wind. Signs of struggle and restraint showed around the complex. *Unlocked door. Recent watermarked shoe prints at the entrance. And Neir's room key necklace on the floor of the balcony.*

He picked it up, looking around the roofs of every street. Neir was a parkour expert and could have gone far beyond the visible rooftops. But not far enough to not be seen from where he stood and maybe get assistance.

From the balcony, Adrik climbed up the building's roof. He looked toward the right, hearing voices coming from that direction. Two buildings away, down the next street, stood six people, including Neir. Her hair shone bright in the slight moonlight. Adrik started walking ahead, running within the shadows until he was close enough to hear behind one of the neighborhood's building walls.

"Like I said, *little brother*, I am not leaving Paris," Neir stood her ground, her arms crossed.

"It's not a choice, Neir. It's an order." A young man with blonde hair like hers stood ten feet away, while four others surrounded her, same black uniforms intact. "And I have the power to remove you." He took a step closer towards her. "Neir De Van, you are under HSS apprehension for the charges of exile, rebellious activity in the city, and refusal to depart. It is best if you don't struggle." Neir stood her ground, without moving. Adrik couldn't see her face, but he knew the ruthless expression she held by memory. Still, it wasn't enough. He felt the electricity move through him, wanting to help her.

"How about I do?" she responded, heading towards the woman and man standing to the right of her. She started fighting both, but the two others behind her tried to stop her. Their movements almost matched her speed and force. The hunters together were as fast as her and clearly strong. Neir tried her tricks, but the numbers opposed her. They held her arms behind her.

"I'm sorry, sister," Carden started. "But I can't let you bring down the Society with you." He nodded at his colleagues. "Do it."

"Sir, are you sure?" one of the dark-haired young men asked.

"Positive, Marco. *Do it.*"

They started pushing Neir to the edge of the building.

"It is a crime for an HSS hunter to kill *another* hunter without trial," Neir said towards the group that held her.

"*Former* HSS hunter, Neir. Get it right, sister. You are no longer a hunter or a De Van." Carden smiled. "You are no one. And after this, it'll be like you never even existed."

He nodded at the hunters, leading Neir right over the edge. Neir tried to push back. Her strength against the others wasn't enough to defy physics. She fell right down. And if Adrik hadn't seen Franko walking quickly to the other side of the street earlier, sending Adrik a message, he would've saved her. Carden and the hunters looked over the edge, looking around for the person who was just behind them. Composed on the wall, Neir had turned the corner of the building, swiftly climbing up from the other side. Adrik turned to see Franko down below and nodded at him.

"Looking for me?" Neir asked, metal rod in hand. The hunters looked behind them. "I think you've forgotten, Carden. I am the best hunter in the HSS of my age. *You* are no one. And after this, it'll be like you were never even a hunter."

Carden's grin faded as soon as he turned to see Neir. "Kill her! Now!" The hunters hesitated for a second, then headed straight for Neir.

Adrik walked out of the shadows with his sword in hand. The hunters flinched at his sight yet proceeded toward him while Neir talked Carden to back out. He swung the sword forward, inches away from each of the hunters.

"You can still walk out of this, Carden," Neir advised. "The amateur hunters you have here by your side don't deserve their death after a few weeks at the HSS. Think I wouldn't notice? You don't even want to show your true face to those who've known you for years."

Carden only shook his head, ignoring Neir's words. "I didn't know you made new friends? Who are you?" He looked at Adrik, then at his sword. "Some *theater* performer."

"Do you want to see an act before you leave?" Adrik respon-ded. "With real blood."

"Is he serious?" one of the woman hunters asked.

"*Deadly*," Neir smiled. "So, if you don't want to die now, I'll suggest you leave." The hunters took a step back, away from Neir and Adrik, leaving Carden close to the building's edge. He looked at the hunters and back at the edge.

"Next time I see you, it won't only be me that you'll see. Our father himself will bring HSS guards to take you in," Carden warned.

"Until then, Carden." Neir took a step back next to Adrik, leaving her brother space to walk away. He disappeared between the buildings, following the other hunters and almost falling into a water puddle.

Neir smirked for a second before she looked at Adrik. "Thank you for your support, ally. I'm sure the air would've held me before I fell."

"Franko was on his way," Adrik responded. "He gave you the staff."

"And if he wasn't? If he hadn't?"

"You would've saved yourself." He knew Neir was capable of doing so. She would've found a way if she knew Adrik wasn't around. But he also felt that she wasn't mad about that as she looked out at the sparkling buildings. He showed her the key necklace he'd held in his coat pocket. "You dropped it on the balcony." She looked at him, green eyes fixed on the key, and grabbed it. The anger behind them was still intact. Whether it be him, her brother, the city, or the world itself, Adrik could understand but not feel. He followed known facts and not feelings. And if he did feel anything at all, it was rare for it not to be rage. Now, he felt something else that he couldn't describe. Because for a moment, as he watched her look at the world around them, he could curse, he felt an ounce of peace. She walked away from him, heading to her apartment. Without hesitation, he followed behind.

PART SEVENTEEN

EFFECTS OF TIES

CHAPTER 44
FRANKO

AT LAST, NEIR AND ADRIK entered the apartment through Neir's living room balcony. Franko sat on the black couch, looking at his pocket watch, wondering how he could fix the metal rod. He looked up when he heard a movement on the balcony across him, and they came in. Neir locked the glass doors and closed the white curtains.

"I saw them inside the break room downstairs," Franko started, looking at Adrik. "And took the freedom to bring them up." He nodded at the gadget suitcases on the kitchen floor, remembering he had to quietly steal the keys from the reception office in order to get them, as he knew Adrik had locked the lounge room before heading upstairs. Franko had gotten back from Kosmos faster than expected, requesting Duran to portal him close to Neir's bakery shop. Without a single answer, the witch made the portal and nodded at Franko to leave Metal Tech.

Adrik walked toward the kitchen, placed a suitcase on top of the kitchen island, and opened it.

"What happened?" Franko asked Neir as she passed by him and headed to the secret room. He got up and followed her, entering the room.

Neir started getting a few black arrows and placing them on the metal table, then she looked up. "They were trying to kill me."

"Biliyorum that," Franko nodded. "But why do you seem angry and *upset*?" Neir stared at him, tilting her head to the side. He remembered Adrik had told him Neir had a lot of enemies, including inside the HSS. Her brother being one of them. The blonde young man had stood in front of Neir, surrounding her with HSS hunters.

"Your own brother?"

Neir nodded, throwing Franko the silver cylinder. "Thank you for the rod. And no, I'm not upset about it." Franko grabbed the cylinder. He pushed it open, creating a hollowed metal self-defense rod. After portaling back, he saw Neir standing in front of Lumière du Jour. She stared back at him, not saying anything, but Franko understood the uneasiness in her eyes.

Here. Franko had said, showing her the metal rod he got from Metal Tech during his brief visit. *New invention. Maybe you can try it.* She took the metal staff, closing it to put it in her pocket. *I'll see you at the apartment.* And she walked away, leaving Franko with the thought of where to get lunch nearby. Minutes later, and without any food in his hands, Franko had decided to go back to the apartment, looking at Adrik glancing up at the open balcony doors and entering inside at a fast pace. Franko tilted his head, wondering what made Adrik enter the complex quickly. He looked up and waited, only to notice the green curtains blowing in the air. He'd never seen Neir open those balcony doors, not since they met.

"If you say so," Franko half-smiled, now shaking the cylinder in the air. "This is a work in progress. We are going to need more metal to make an actual rod." Now, he started inspecting the arrows on the table, glancing at Neir and wondering how she could be both emotionally and physically strong. She was a hunter, but she was also human, just like Adrik. And still, both were so similar to each other that they couldn't show their actual emotions.

"We have enough for everything," Neir said, grabbing each arrow and taking off the arrowhead. "If you are trying to appear *normal*, you can't. What is it?"

"Adrik," Franko said, turning around to recheck that the door of the room was actually closed.

"What about him?"

"What *about* him?" Franko looked at her. "You both are more alike than you think. I'm even starting to feel third-wheel effects."

Neir crossed her arms. "We are allies, remember. Limited trust and no friendship. Especially not with Adrik Montova... or his co-workers."

"Ouch. That's *rude*." Franko frowned.

"I told you not to trust me."

"And you ended up trusting *me*," Franko winked at her, putting his hands in the air and showing her the rod. He had seen her body falling earlier, the metal bar stuck in the wall seconds after. If it hadn't been for the rod he'd offered for her to try out, she would've most likely fallen straight to her death.

Neir looked around the room. "Let's get to work. We have a mission to accomplish."

Franko couldn't read people as much as Adrik could. But he didn't need to read Adrik and Neir's eyes to know the awkwardness between them. He felt the air change when both stepped into a room. Like they knew too little about each other but wanted to know much more. Everyone had hidden secrets within them, even himself. It was only a matter of time before their ties would either fully unite them or tear them all apart.

Sleeping on the couch had been better than his old bed in the tech store but worse than the hotel bed he used to sleep in. Franko had heard footsteps early in the morning. He guessed that just like Adrik, Neir couldn't sleep. With the thick white curtains closed, he could pretend it was still night. The entire room was dark until Neir turned on the dim light in the kitchen. Franko slowly sat up.

"Günaydin," he said, still lying down but staring into the white space of the ceiling. "Your ceiling is nice."

"Morning," Neir responded. Franko could hear her moving things in the kitchen, then opening the door of the fridge. "That's how every ceiling looks."

"Not in Arkadia, mostly everything there is made of wood or straight up cement. Dark and depressing ceilings."

"Are you hungry? We can make sandwiches..."

Franko slowly stood, stretching his arms. "Food. The greatest thing ever." He yawned, wishing he had slept more instead of staying up until sunrise. Neir smiled, starting to put the ingredients on the counter.

"Adrik?" she asked, looking at Franko once.

"He was still up when I went to sleep hours ago," Franko said, glancing at the suitcases on the floor. Neir nodded, turning on the stove. "Do you need help?"

"I know how to make normal sandwiches."

"I'm still in search of the best sandwich," Franko half-smiled, looking at the whole wheat grain bread. "Healthy ingredients probably won't help."

"Are you a cook... or a chef?"

"No."

"Right."

"But I know about sandwiches."

"And I know we are wasting time, and you don't know enough French to order takeout." Neir smiled. "I'll make the best sandwiches you've ever tried."

"We'll see." Franko raised his eyebrows, grabbing one of his suitcases and heading to the restroom to get ready.

CHAPTER 45
ADRIK

ADRIK HAD NEVER SEEN a city so bright in the morning even in the snow. He watched as people screamed in French or walked hurriedly to their destination. Cars were honking at the slow traffic. As on most recent days, Adrik couldn't sleep. His body seemed used to it as he was able to stay awake for hours or even sleep while standing, like he felt he'd done an hour ago. Yet his mind stayed thinking, so he wasn't sure if it was actually asleep.

The creaking of the metal roof door reached his ears, he guessed it was Franko. But the second he heard footsteps coming toward him, he smelled the sweet fragrance of Neir's perfume. Sweetness mixed with rose and lemon. She'd only worn it sometimes, like she did when they met.

"I didn't think you liked watching the sun rise." She stood next to him, wearing a black leather jacket with green on the sleeves, and her golden hair was placed in a ponytail.

"That's not what I'm watching," Adrik responded, looking at her for a few seconds.

"I know." She looked down below, watching the people walk the streets. She half-smiled. "It's almost unreal that we exist to save the human race from the supernatural. But look at them, who is saving them from themselves?"

"No one'" Adrik looked back down. "Only you can save yourself. There's no luck, no saints, no prayers that can do as much as one can."

"You don't believe in anything."

"I only believe in myself."

"So do I. In myself." She responded, but Adrik could tell that some of those words were a lie. Maybe she did believe in herself, but the possibility that something beyond could be on their side was a belief everyone had. Even Adrik, at some point between his old Italy home and Arkadia, thought so. In the middle of the sea, he tried to believe it was all a dream. That his prayers would turn time around, sink the boat in which they took him to Kosmos. And it wasn't enough. The deep scars in his palms and the one on his cheek showed him so. Nothing would be enough unless he acted upon himself. Only his rise and downfall would be built by him.

"I came to say time is ticking," Neir continued. "Breakfast is ready. *Sandwiches*."

Franko. Adrik thought, glancing at Neir walking back into the building without turning around.

CHAPTER 46
NEIR

THEY WERE READY WITHIN AN HOUR, wearing all black—except for Franko, who decided dark-brown would fit him better. Maps stood all over the kitchen counter while Adrik re-explained all the steps they needed to take. It wasn't long until the Sun had set in its very high position in the sky.

Neir was used to hunting in the dark. The concealment of the weapons she held had been useful. She had no choice but to hide only a knife and a stake under her black coat as she walked inside the museum again. Like every other day, people headed in and out. After the smoke incident, it seemed they had just gotten a bit more attention. More tourists and humans for vampires to prey on. Just like last time, she walked around the museum on the very top floor, hiding between the people. She had seen the cameras being turned off two minutes ago. Adrik and Franko had gone to the surveillance room with the paid janitors, planning to spike the camera operator's drink again and delete any tracks. Neir suggested Franko should learn more modern tech, other than just creating it. He agreed, looking motivated to learn much more.

"*Ms. De Van.*" She heard a whisper coming from the hallway. Duran, the witch Adrik had hired, walked to her. He wore a gray uniform and pushed a metal cart covered with a black cloth.

"Were there any problems?" she asked.

The man shook his head. "No. They thought it was material to fix the vents. One of the janitors did a good job and appeared at my need when they started asking more questions." Neir nodded, waiting. Adrik and Franko appeared from the end of the hall. *Finally.* She crossed her arms.

"I expect there weren't any problems," Adrik started.

"No, sir. Everything you need is here." The man shook his head again.

"How many?" Neir asked.

"Ninety-six and counting," responded Franko, the number of people he'd seen inside and around the building. "Probably a bit more considering the news."

"Everyone will be busy today," Adrik said. "Even those who oversight underground will try to keep control." Neir knew he meant the HSS. The more chaos, the better. *As long as everything goes according to plan.* "Go back to the warehouse below. Wait for the signal," Adrik commanded the witch, who nodded and walked back to the basement of the museum. Most workers there were in charge of organization and artifact checks.

"Because of the incident, most of the guards are standing on the ground floor," Neir said. "Some of them are vampires, and the human guards are being controlled by them."

"Everything is set," Franko assured, looking at his pocket watch. At this time, the janitors would have stopped any passage to the upcoming third floor for an 'air vent check'. They only needed a maximum of ten minutes for Duran to arrive and leave to the underground warehouse, warning the workers to depart from the museum.

"Then, let us begin with the smoke," Adrik said, pulling off the black cloth and revealing crates filled with weapons on the cart.

"And end with fire," Neir responded, grabbing her green-black bow and colored arrows. Then the crates opened with blood-stained stakes. Franko chose a selection of bombs, placing them inside his coat. Adrik grabbed his sword from inside a special suitcase, sliding it through the scabbard on his waist. Together, they headed to the *No Visitors Allowed* door that led them to the fifth floor.

"The vampire hunter first," Franko said, allowing Neir to open the doors to hell itself.

"With pleasure." She opened the double doors. Adrenaline slowly rushed in as she stepped foot in the hallway. Like Adrik had said, the hall was filled with rooms in which vampires resided. She felt her blood boil. An automatic radar telling her that vampires were around. She walked down the hall, people walked in and out of the rooms. No, not people. *Vampires.* How easy it was for them to fool the weak. Most of them wouldn't know who Neir was. But they saw the weapons and immediately flustered, their eyes turned red as blood.

"Kill them all," Neir said, loud enough for the entire hallway.

Some vampires started to move forward. Franko quickly threw a gas bomb. *Allium* gas spread inside the hall. Some of the vampires lunged at Neir. Arrow by arrow, she shot, eyes fixed on where the heart should be. The victims fell to the floor, their bodies disintegrating. *Wooden-blood* arrows that Neir and Franko had invented. They had stayed up creating a variety of tech. Adrik stood next to her, lunging at vampires with his sword, then staking them with a wooden stake or cutting their heads off. Franko quickly entered each room, checking for the hidden ones.

A crowd of vampires stood at the end of the hall, wondering and waiting for the commotion that was about to happen. Neir could finally see the large room. People stood around, standing over tables, drinking in red-filled glasses with music playing in the background. The entire floor looked almost like a maze with hallways in every direction and old paintings hanging on its red walls. Slight smoke built up as each vampire looked in the direction of her, Adrik, and Franko. The music had lowered.

"Party is over," Adrik shot, signaling to Franko, who threw bombs in every direction he could. "Actual death has come." The *allium* gas bombs exploded, causing shrieks around the room. No one down below would be able to hear. The guests in the museum were already being escorted out due to smoke coming from the air vents. Franko had sent a message to Duran before entering the deadly hall to activate the grenades inside the vents and wait for further instructions.

Most vampires were now on the ground, weak from the *allium* intoxicating their lungs, others dead from the stakes or the wooden-blooded arrows. Since most were night vampires, they weren't strong enough to withstand the pain. The light ones, however, stood up, heading against them. Neir shot out another arrow at them before they could use their Illuminator power. *Net Arrow*: green-coded arrow meant to seize or catch with a net. It wrapped itself around the vampires, making them stumble.

"What about them?" Franko nodded at the people hiding behind the curtains of the stage at the front of the room.

"They are human," Neir answered. "Most likely compelled to forget everything and go back home once they set foot outside this floor."

Adrik tilted his head, looking at one of the women in uniform whom he glanced at when they entered the room. "Get out of here and don't turn back," he said to them. They nodded, running fast towards the exit. Neir walked ahead of Adrik. She had memorized the path to the red double doors. Even so, the maze wouldn't have been able to hide it. Only those doors stood out among them all. She was ready, certain of her actions, until she stumbled. The red halls became blurry, interchangeable in her view.

"Neir?" She heard Adrik ask.

"I can't—" she started. "See clearly." She looked around at the illusions, glancing at the hazy view of one of the lighted vampires. "The vampire. An illusionist." Adrik nodded, understanding what she meant as he was no longer by her side but headed straight for the vampire, using his sword to cut through his neck.

The blurred vision left her, becoming replaced by the smoke of another *allium* gas bomb. "Better?" Franko asked behind Neir. She nodded, looking for Adrik through the smoke. He looked disoriented as he walked towards her. She wanted to ask if he was okay or what was wrong, but he stared into her eyes, focusing on her, and his chest became steady. Neir held her bow high once again, putting a red-coded arrow within it. *Explosive Arrow.* They stood opposite the crimson doors, at the entrance of the long corridor. Neir shot her arrow, it flew straight into the metal doors, the bomb attached to it exploding at once. They ran quickly into the office room with multiple doors around it. Two of the Clan vampires stood in the middle of the room, in front of the black desk.

"Where is he?" Neir clenched her jaw, glancing at the vampire and the desk covered with files.

"Long gone." One of the vampires said as they both lunged forward, grabbing a sword from the stand beside the desk. Adrik, being closer to Neir, jabbed him with his sword while she fought the other one. The vampire tried to force her to look straight into his eyes. *Compulsion.* That was what he was trying to do. Vampires could compel any supernatural, except one of their kind. Without *allium*, hunters weren't strong enough to fight it. But Neir's blood was filled with it. She never missed the three-daily drinking requirement. Her eyes never felt glazed.

"I recommend a better sword." Adrik gritted through his teeth, pushing back the weak vampire. "Or better skills for the matter." Neir's ally moved fast, almost as quickly as the hunter, but not as strongly as his opponent. He was a night vampire; all of the Clan were. Only their leader was allowed to turn into a lighter before everyone else.

Neir fought the other vampire, grabbed a stake from her boot, and plunged it straight through his heart, falling to the floor. The one Adrik had stabbed and sedated with *allium* tried to stand up. He winced from the pain. Adrik was about to stake him.

"Wait," she said, looking at Adrik. She felt he understood her only with one look. Adrik made a nod, giving her the stake.

"*He* will kill you," the vampire shot.

She glared at him. "I would say *we'll see about that*. But *you* won't." Without any other words, she staked him, his body falling.

"This way. To the roof," Franko said. He stood behind the desk, where a door was slightly ajar, and swung it open.

The dark hallway felt like they were underground, but the stairs led up to the roof of the museum. Adrik opened the single door at the landing. A gust of wind hit Neir's hair the moment they stepped foot on the roof.

"Well, *look* who we have here." Nikolas Mondragon stood in the middle, feet away from them. He had been waiting along with his last two Clan vampires, who stood beside him. Slight Sun rays hit all over the city, but the light hid behind the clouds from where they stood, not touching their skin. It would rain at any moment.

"Can't tell if you plan to commit suicide or run away, *Nikolas*?" Neir asked, furrowing her brows.

"Not until I see your death, hunter," he sneered, glancing at her to Adrik and Franko. "You. I remember you, *businessman*." He shook his head, speaking to his vampires. "I knew there was something. But I wouldn't worry. Who are you to go against me and my Clan?" He half-smiled. Neir was ready to shoot an arrow at him if it wasn't Adrik who took a step forward, his face emotionless.

"My name won't mean anything to you," Adrik started. "My

actions, however, will. You may be a dangerous vampire, Nicholas Mondragon. I, on the other hand, am lethal."

Franko nodded slightly. "He's right. I was there."

Nikolas smiled, his white teeth showing. "Did you lose your words, Neir De Van?"

"No," Neir grinned. "I'm just enjoying hearing your last." She held her bow and arrow tightly in her hand to the point where it was starting to hurt. But instead of holding it high enough to shoot, she put the arrow back in the quiver on her back and the bow over her head, across her chest. The vampires slightly moved at her movement, but Nikolas stood still.

"A fair fight," Nikolas said. "I was being cordial in letting you use your arrow. But I can work with this. You'll die easily enough."

Neir smiled, feeling the adrenaline coursing through her. "You'll die in pain. Even being supernatural can't escape you from that." She lunged forward as the vampires started to move all around them, and the air turned gray. Another *allium* gas bomb Franko had thrown. Neir focused on Nikolas. He moved at her pace, then faster. Some of the vampires encircled them, but Adrik was at her side, sword in hand. From the corner of her eye, she saw Franko holding the gun with wooden-blooded bullets. He'd been practicing in the secret room, imagining shooting and hitting imaginary targets.

The Clan leader looked at her straight in the eye, sneering. He charged toward her, first fighting with fits, then trying to bite her. She punched him as hard as she could in the face.

"Nice. Vampires do sweat blood," she said, lunging at him again. He touched his bloody lip and looked madder than before, trying to hold Neir's wrist. But she moved quickly. She heard shots here and there and moved with the sound around her. Vampires fell to the floor now and then. Through the smoke, she caught a glimpse of the vampires trying to bite both Adrik and Franko. She stumbled back, giving Nikolas the advantage to grab hold of her neck. She checked her jacket pocket for an *allium-concentrated* sedative. *Only One. Use it wisely*. She tried to plunge it into his neck but failed. The Clan vampire, being years old and stronger than new vampires, wouldn't last long staying unconscious. She'd only needed a few seconds to help her allies. He quickly saw her motive, grabbed the sedative, and plunged it into her neck instead. In a matter of seconds, she started to feel weak. The *allium-concentrated* sedative not only contained *allium* like the original sedative. It was her idea to boost it by adding sleep-inducing chemicals to make the sedative stronger. She fell to the floor, hearing snippets of the vampire's words as he stood before her. "You'll watch them *die* before you."

In blurs, she watched Adrik and Franko trying to fight the vampires. *Don't fall asleep.* She thought. As long as it was her goal to kill vampires, the hunter blood in her veins would keep her awake like special antibodies against drugs. Adrik ran his sword through one of the vampires but missed the second he glanced at Neir on the floor, and the vampire punched him. Another shot was heard in the chaos. For a second, she was convinced Franko had finally gotten at being a pro with guns. Until she saw Franko's body falling to the floor and the Clan leader holding the gun.

Something started exploding, not only in Neir's head, but down the museum building. *The bombs on the third floor.* Adrik held an annoyed look on his face as he stood up from the bloody ground. Franko lay on the floor unconscious and unmoving. The smoke in the air was no longer visible, and Adrik's straight posture became clearer. Sweat trickled down her forehead.

Her eyes slowly failed her, but the sounds around her rang in echoes.

"Stop." She heard Nikolas say, looking at the two vampires, composed and intact. They walked behind their leader. Blood dripped from their faces, but they looked wide awake. Nicholas had saved his best members for last. Neir felt the cold sedative through her veins.

"Three against one, Mr. Montova," Nikolas said.

"That's *unfortunate*," Adrik responded. Neir could hear the metallic sound of his sword scraping the concrete floor. "But I'll be more concerned for the living than the dead."

"We could've worked together. You could get wealthy and live a quiet life."

"Quiet isn't my expertise."

Nikolas shook his head, stepping over Neir's bloodied arm. "Instead, you made a deal with Neir De Van. The former HSS hunter." She winced, trying to keep her breath steady.

"No," Adrik sneered. "I made a deal with the *Huntress*." Neir heard him take a step forward. "And that makes you my enemy. *Dead or alive*." She saw shadows moving quickly. Adrik was fighting them, including Nikolas. Neir counted two minutes until Adrik slashed his sword through the last of the two Clan vampires.

"Neir." She heard Adrik's voice far away from her say, and Nikolas' words in between it all. Then she heard Briz and Erin's voices in her head. Their bad jokes and happy laughs. She heard her parents' judgments and Carden's mocking laughs. She heard it all. Her eyes saw it all. The truth of her end.

Briz and Erin can't stay alone.
Fran can't die.
Adrik can't be let down.
And I can't fall.

She tried to stand up. Nikolas stood closer, not allowing Adrik to get close to her or Franko. She saw Adrik standing by the edge of the roof, Nikolas trying to lure him into falling. Yet he stayed unmoving, glancing at Neir only for a fraction of a second. It was then that she understood her part. She grabbed her bow and arrow. The weak feeling from the sedative finally left her body with every movement she made.

"See you in Hell, whoever you are, but not in a very long time," Nikolas said. A normal black-coded arrow stood within the bow until the bowstring loosened at Neir's pull. Without hesitating, she shot once at the vampire's leg and slowly stood up as he fell. Nikolas turned around to look at her, scowling. His face filled with rage from the chaos down below.

"You have no one. No allies. No friends. Everyone is painfully burning below, just as you will." She held a wooden stake in her hand. "See you in Hell, Nikolas Mondragon." She was ready to stake him and end his life. Ready to bring peace and justice to the people of Paris. Until a different fire broke out. Gunfire shots in the air flew in their direction. Neir looked around quickly, just as

Adrik did. The distraction allowed Nikolas to take the arrow out of his leg. Before Neir could stake him, he pushed her with force towards the edge, making her stumble off the building. This time, with no rod available, she held onto the cornice of the museum roof. She looked below as gravity tried to push her down. There was nowhere she could balance her feet. Only feet away was a window. She tried to hold on with all the strength she had left.

"Neir," Adrik knelt, holding out his fair-light hand to her. His actual hand. No gloves on. The one without the three silver rings. She looked at it. Scars that might have been due to knife strikes were widely visible, unlike the scar on his cheek. Unless you were at least two or three feet away from his face, no one could see it.

She took his hand. He pushed her up until they were both back up on the roof. There were no shots anymore. They had been gone by the time Nikolas escaped.

"The other side of the museum is collapsing. We should go before witnesses appear," Adrik said, putting his bloody leather glove back on. Neir nodded, heading straight to Franko.

"Franko. *Fran.*" She shook his body, opening his coat to look between his Kevlar vest, the metal sheet, and his brown shirt. The metal vest he suggested wearing below the Kevlar earlier was still intact, with a bullet traversing it by only two or three millimeters.

"I'm never wearing one of these creations ever again." Franko winced, slowly opening his eyes and trying to sit up. "What happened?"

"We'll tell you later. We are in a hurry. Can you stand up?" Neir asked, offering her hand to help him up. He nodded, grabbing her hand to stand up. He winced again, looking around.

"You're alive." Franko looked at Neir, then Adrik.

"So are you," Adrik responded, his face expressionless. "Let's go."

"I could've died, and that's all he had to say," Franko said to Neir.

She half-smiled. "That's Adrik Montova. I'm *kind of* glad you are alive."

Franko smiled back at her. "Thank you, *ally*."

"Shut up."

They walked around the roof, looking for a safe place to climb down. Neir descended first, followed by Franko, then Adrik. She landed in the museum's garden and waited for Franko to head down as she gave him tips on where to hold himself. Adrik looked around, making sure no one saw them once they were out of the garden and back into the streets of Paris. They approached a white van at the end of the street, got on, and drove out of the fiery chaos.

PART EIGHTEEN

CATACOMBS

CHAPTER 47
FRANKO

"YOU BOUGHT A TRUCK?" Franko asked, looking out the window and then at Adrik.

"White van *and* with tinted windows?" Neir frowned.

"And the driver is Duran?"

"He is driving..."

Adrik looked back and forth from Franko to Neir as they furrowed their brows at him. He stared out the window, watching Duran sigh and shake his head at the afternoon traffic every minute or so. "How long?" Adrik asked him.

Duran looked at the phone in the mount holder. "About twenty minutes with traffic." Adrik made a slight nod.

"No one is following us," Neir said, looking out the window from every direction.

"Is there any food?" Franko whispered to Neir.

"I don't know," Neir responded out loud. "Ask Duran?"

"Mr. Duran doesn't like me."

"I never said that," the French witch replied, shaking his head. "And no, we don't have food."

"Adrik," Franko started. "Is there any food in the bags?"

"No," Adrik responded. "Much less sandwiches."

Franko shrugged, sitting back in his seat. Neir looked at Adrik. He made a slight grin, then looked away.

"Fran," Neir began, nodding at a bag. "There are sandwiches in the bag. I ordered about ten for all of us... including dessert this morning before you woke up." Franko got up quickly, forgetting he was still a bit injured. He grimaced, getting the blue bag placed on top of all the filled black bags and brown suitcases. He opened it, getting out a sandwich in aluminum foil, and began to eat.

"Neir." He pointed at the sandwich. "You are a great friend." She raised her eyebrows at him as she grabbed the bag and started handing sandwiches to both Adrik and Duran.

Franko felt his eyes slowly drifting after eating two sandwiches and a cup of sweet coffee. He was surprised he was still able to hear the movement of the van and the noises of the streets.

"Franko. Wake up," Adrik said, his voice loud and clear. He woke up at once and was surprised at how energized he felt all of a sudden.

"What did you do to the coffee?" he asked Neir. She shrugged.

"Added a chemical that acts like caffeine... to wake you up."

"You mean it has *twice* the caffeine."

"Yes."

"Do you not trust me that I could stay awake?"

"You fell asleep."

"Well, now I'm fully awake."

Adrik turned to look at them. "We are close by, and I'm considering dropping you two here."

Neir glared at him but didn't say anything. Duran also stayed quiet, focused on the road, and parked in front of a restaurant.

Neir got off first, then Franko followed as soon as the van stopped. Adrik and Duran stayed behind to get the black bags. *Ansarte.* The sign on top of the restaurant read. Even though Franko had just eaten, the smell of the food ran straight through his nose and stomach. He walked close to Neir, looking around the cafe.

"Follow my lead," Neir whispered to him. He nodded as if he wasn't planning on making small talk. "I'm looking for Zachary," she spoke to the bartender, looking at his badge. "*Michael.*"

"May I know who is looking for him?"

"Someone who doesn't give answers," Neir responded. Michael only nodded, peaking into the door that led to the kitchen area. "Zachary, *someone who doesn't give answers* is looking for you."

Michael turned back out. "He is coming." And headed out to a table to assist incoming customers.

Seconds later, a man with black hair and six feet tall, like Franko and Adrik, came out of the door. Unlike Franko or almost anyone from Arkadia, the man wore a loose black silky robe. He walked without care, almost oblivious to the world around him. Franko wondered how much money he would need to buy a whole modern wardrobe. He had enough money, just not enough to buy the entire building itself. And thousands of sandwiches. Tech and bombs. Or an entire zoo like he had seen in a brochure.

"Person who doesn't give answers," the man smiled at Neir, fixing his blonde strand of hair. "And who *hunts*. It has been a while, hasn't it?"

"I see you haven't lost your sarcasm, *Z*."

"As you haven't lost your *black* and *green*. Still active?"

"You should know *that* answer. And that's why I'm here."

The man held his phone in the air. "I received your message earlier... something about valiant schemes?"

"Which is why we need your help."

"In that case..." He smiled at Neir and Franko. "You can tell your two friends to head to the black door." He nodded at Adrik and Duran, who stood looking around the street. Neir half-smiled and headed to Adrik and Duran. Franko stood still, looking around, and admiring the Victorian painted ceilings.

"Would you like anything to eat or drink?" Zachary asked. "Coffee, maybe."

"If I could get the whole menu," Franko smiled. "That would be great."

Zachary grinned back. "Coming right up."

"We have other things to do, Fran." Neir appeared from behind them. "Time is ticking."

Franko tilted his head. "Did you trade souls with Adrik?"

"No one should trade souls with a demon."

Zachary shook his head. "No one alive has really seen a demon or been one. Not even the darkest of souls," he half-smiled, taking a sip of a yellow liquid, which Franko guessed was wine, from a glass cup. "Come on. Before the restaurant gets filled quickly." He nodded at them to follow.

Neir and Franko walked around the black counter, passing through the kitchen door. Employees worked on cooking, making different extravagant dishes, and smiling at Zachary as he passed by. They walked through a small hall at the end of the kitchen, taking a turn, then entering another door. Two rocky brown halls greeted them, one going downward and another going left, both with a black door at the end. Zachary opened the door at the bottom of the stairs, the keys dangling in his hands. They entered the dark-colored apartment with five stories. Franko gasped at the sight. Here and there were light and dark areas with plants everywhere. A doorbell rang around the entire apartment. Zachary headed to the black entrance door, opening it. Adrik and Duran entered, bags and cases in hand.

"Duran." Zachary smiled, opening his arms. "My old friend. Has been a while, hasn't it?"

"Zachary." Duran held out his hand to shake Zachary's.

He raised his eyebrows. "Still the same, I see." He shook Duran's hand, looking at Adrik.

"Is the whole building yours?" Adrik asked, putting the cases down on the marble white floor.

"Half of it. The other half is my wife's. She has her antique store and storage next door," Zachary responded, holding out his hand. "I'm Zachary."

"Adrik Montova," Adrik greeted with a shake.

"Nice name," Zachary said. "Fits you very well."

Neir turned to Zachary. "How is your wife, by the way?"

"Currently traveling around." Zachary walked to the mini bar across the entrance door. "You know she likes peace. Forests and everything within." Neir nodded.

Zachary smiled widely. "Well! Make yourselves at home!"

"We won't be here long," Adrik informed.

"I'm aware."

Adrik nodded, heading upstairs with Duran behind him. Franko started to take his coat off, the Kevlar, and the metal armor around his stomach. His brown shirt was stained red.

"That doesn't look good." Zachary shook his head. "I'll look for a first aid kit." He walked into another room.

Neir turned around to look at Franko, tilting her head. "Are you ok?"

Franko opened his arms. "Of course, I am. It's just a scratch. The universe couldn't get rid of this body that easily." Neir shook his head, taking a step toward Franko. "Wait." She tilted her head, looking at Franko's shirt. "How did the bullet not go straight through?"

"Thick steel." Franko shrugged, taking a breath. Neir was about to say something else, until Zachary came back with a kit in his hand.

"Here you go. This should help." Franko nodded at him, heading straight to a room for privacy.

"So, you know Duran?" He heard Neir say as he ascended the stairs.

Zachary chuckled. "It's a small world. Who do you think taught him how to portal and send messages..."

Franko couldn't decide whether he was dreaming the moment he entered a room on the second floor. He felt *deja vu* once again, remembering when he first arrived in Paris. He'd learned so much since then, from modern items to a whole different civilization and a larger desire for money. *One day*. He hoped as he sat down on a brown sofa in the corner of the room. In minutes, he took a shower, disinfected the small wound with antibacterial cream, and got ready with new clean clothes. Once he was finished, he left his suitcase at the foot of the bed and headed downstairs.

CHAPTER 48
NEIR

BLACK JACKETS RULED over fifty percent of Neir's wardrobe. Being a hunter almost every day, she'd gotten used to them. Now, being in a simple black dress gave her flashbacks to the times her life had been more peaceful. When she was still in the HSS and going out to the city was an enjoyment. She held her hair back in a half ponytail with a hair clip that looked like an arrow knife. She could hear Adrik and Duran's voices downstairs talking with Zach about the HSS. After Franko had left upstairs, Neir had explained to Zach about the break-in. There were two entrances to the HSS, one of them being by the Catacombs. She had met Zach about five years ago when Neir happened to finally go to Ansarte and try hazelnut iced coffee. She'd gotten into an argument with her parents about her solo hunts. Carden was nowhere to be found, so she walked out of the Catacombs and into the closest hiding place. Zach had been one of her trusted friends ever since, who later revealed he had made an entrance for the Catacombs himself.

"Why? What do you have to do with the HSS?" She had asked. He shook his head. "Not much *yet*. But I know *you*, on the other hand, do. I have a place nearby and happen to go to the Catacombs in the middle of the night. Helps me think and pray for the dead."

"You believe in a higher power?"

"If not a higher power? What else?"

Neir half-smiled. "HSS guards *guard* the entrance to the Catacombs. The Square is filled with cameras that could easily make hunters identifiable."

"You'll be able to get in and out without using the second *secret* entrance."

"You know about that one, too?"

Zach nodded. "As a witch, I dealt with the Society's council before and did my research, too."

"What was your deal about?" Neir asked.

"I'm someone who doesn't like giving answers... at least until it's important to do so." Till then, Neir never knew Zach's dealings with the HSS, nor could she find any archives about him in the files. But she had met her wife before and had never seen a couple so happy. They had been more like family than her own.

Neir walked out of her room all patched up, boots in hand in case her heels broke off in any fighting or unexpected situation. She could run in heels well enough; boots gave her an upgrade. Just as she headed downstairs, she heard Franko's door open. She turned around. He wore a dark blue coat and trousers.

"Wow." He looked at her, brows slightly raised. "You look

great!"

"You don't look bad yourself," Neir smiled as Franko showed off the inside of his coat filled with devices and tools.

"I was planning to wear purple or green, but blue blends into the crowd."

"*Illuminator* colors," Neir said. "They fit you, too."

"Not as much as red does," Franko smiled. "Ready?" They both descended the stairs. Neir could feel Adrik's stare the second they stepped onto the first floor.

"How do we look?" Franko said, his hands wide open. Adrik glanced at them but didn't pay much attention to their clothing. His eyes looked at Neir's, making her wonder what he was now thinking, planning, or scheming.

"Like you are ready for a dance," Zach responded. Duran nodded with a slight smile.

Adrik took a step back. "Let's go over the plan again." He walked over to the large dining table to the right.

"Are you sure?" Neir asked, looking at Zach and feeling confused about Adrik's sudden trust in him. Adrik held up a set of blueprints in his hand. "The HSS blueprints. That's all we needed." She raised her eyebrows at Zach.

"I did say you would need them one day." Zach turned to Neir. "And here we are. Your drawings might have been good, but not as good as the original."

Neir glared at him. "They were decent."

"You don't have artist hands like me," Zach boasted. Neir rolled her eyes at him.

She looked at Adrik, who opened up the maps and laid them

on the table. "You have a new plan, don't you?"

"Still the same," he responded, looking at the blueprints marked with colored dots. "Only clearer." Every place Neir had described and explained to him about the HSS structure was marked. She remembered the Society like the palm of her hand—except for some of the hidden rooms, which she knew they must have. The HSS had been her entire life since she was a child.

"Adrik," Franko frowned. "You did mention using bombs earlier."

Neir crossed her arms. "You want to put bombs in the underground chamber like you did inside the vents of the museum?"

"*Gas* bombs or grenades," Adrik responded. "Completely unharmful."

"You really love explosives."

"We seem to do," added Franko. "Who can blame us? One second and *kaboom*."

"Gas bombs can work as a distraction. All we need is to get in and *show* the truth."

"We will get in," motivated Adrik.

"So it will be." Zach smiled at them as he handed each of them a masquerade mask.

Adrik repeated the steps to Zach, who offered his help instead of relying on Duran's magic. Seeing as Z had already known the layout of the HSS during his unknown deals, made it easier for him to use his magic.

"Fits your eyes," Franko said to Neir, nodding at her mask. He held out his blue one, inspecting it over his suit. His face was less bruised. Zach had offered to fix everyone's wounded faces before the grand entrance. Only Franko agreed without hesitation, Zach's magic turned his face a bit better.

They followed Zach to the end of the second hallway between Ansarte and his apartment. Besides explaining the plan, Adrik hadn't spoken. He only turned around once Zach spoke.

"This is it," Zach said, standing by the rock wall. "You'll be entering a part of the Catacombs that is strictly off limits to visitors. The map will show you the way to the HSS entrance."

"Thank you, Z."

"My pleasure." He smiled at Neir, then looked at Adrik. Zach stood in front of the door, putting his hands up inches away from the middle of the wall. He made a random pattern, his hands flashing a blue color as he did. The rocks started moving to the side by themselves, creating an entrance to the Catacombs. "May we see each other again." He looked at Adrik, who nodded back.

"For a deal. Someday." Adrik put out his hand, shaking Zach's once, and entered the rocky hallway of the Catacombs.

"*Someday*," Zach responded, then looked at Franko. "I'm sure we'll meet again someday—under better circumstances, I hope."

"Of course, I'm not forgetting about that menu," Franko said, entering after Adrik. Neir was up next.

"See you, Z."

"See you." He winked at her. The warlock still appeared the same—tall and lean, late twenties, sharp light-brown eyes that matched his skin tone—except for the color change in the streak of his hair.

"By the way, can you tell me what connection you had with

the Society now? The truth?"

"Alright, just because you asked for it now," Zach replied. "I offered to install the anti-magic alarms for extra protection."

"Why?"

"In case, one day *this*," he shook his hands in the air, "happened. In case one day someone like you needed my help. Life is as precious as time... and you should know that the dampeners won't work if there's no energy below." Neir nodded, recalling how the dampeners activated themselves if the alarms sounded throughout the institute. She wasn't sure about Zach's reasoning for the offer, but now she knew why the HSS was well protected. Because of him, no magic could be used inside, even vampires wouldn't feel their strength. And only Z was in control of the protection. She was about to pass the wall when she felt a slight pain in her left arm between her wrist and elbow. She winced, rubbing her arm faintly.

"Are you alright?" Zach asked, frowning at her arm.

Neir nodded. "Must be from all the action."

"Must be," Zach agreed. "Now go. Time is ticking."

"As Adrik would say, *it always is*." She passed the wall, glancing at Zach one last time before the wall closed.

Adrik and Franko waited for her at the end of the underground hall, holding a lit torch. The entire tunnel was made of limestone and human bones. In the hallways above them, human skulls and femurs were arranged in intricate patterns. Down below, where fewer people happened to walk through, were random stones and debris. Neir walked ahead of them first, following the map Zach had drawn for her up until they were at the other end of the rocky hall. She touched each individual rock, following the pattern in the map by creating an *HSS* letter movement, beginning with the rock that was colored blue. In seconds, the wall opened at a certain time when no one on the other side of it passed by, just as Zack had explained.

"Did it work?" Franko asked, hanging the torch in the sconce on the opposite wall of Adrik's.

"Don't doubt Zach's magic," Neir replied. They waited a few seconds before it opened and entered. The hall on the other side was lit with enough torches to see the HSS symbol of two crossed stakes on the roof. It slowly started as a sketch until they walked further and turned into black ink spray paint. Further ahead, they could hear footsteps.

"Other hunters," Neir whispered, turning the corner, then another. The Catacombs were built like a maze that only the Society could figure out. From stairs to dead ends, they passed, following the footsteps in front of them. It wasn't until the end of the last hall that Neir could see a woman and a man walking toward the vine-filled wall. Except it was no vine wall, but a fake one that appeared like a dead end. Neir put her mask on, as did the allies beside her. They followed them, entering the vines and revealing another small hall, this time with a large metal door. The two hunters turned around at once.

"Oh, hello," the woman began, fixing her light-blue mask. "See, Mark. I told you we wouldn't be the only ones at the masquerade." The young man, Mark, turned around, getting out a key card. One that all HSS hunters had.

"Hey," Mark greeted them. "Yeah, yeah, you were right—

again. But I still don't like to dance. You forced me to come." He smiled at the young woman.

"Dancing isn't my thing either," Neir said, trying to distract them.

"I like dancing," added Franko.

"What about you?" Mark nodded at Adrik.

"Rather be hunting than dancing," Adrik said. "Yet here I am, waiting."

It took Mark a second to realize what Adrik meant. "Right. Sorry. Easily distracted." He swiped the HSS card on the datareader device next to the door. The metal door opened, and it would stay open for only ten seconds. Mark and his date went inside. Neir nodded for Adrik and Franko to head in.

"I thought hunters should not be distracted," Franko whispered to Neir while he passed. "At least we won't have to manage the system." Catacomb halls turned from metal and torches to fluorescent lights. They walked straight into the metal hall with vents on the roof. *Allium* gas precaution in case vampires managed to enter, or sedatives for other beings, including unwanted humans. The automatic doors in the end opened at the time the metal door behind them closed. They were greeted by a vast space with metallic halls and lights in every direction. Nothing had changed. The lobby, chairs, and offices on the first floor remained the same. *Lobby. Maps. Security. Rest Area.* She always thought the large place looked like an airport without windows. Yet the space was a sugar-coated section of the five-floor HSS underground institute. There were more security rooms, more maps, and more areas of rest. It was like a maze that even the directions written on the walls wouldn't help. The *Technical Room* could've meant a hundred different things.

"Thank you," Neir said to the couple in front of them.

"See you guys on the dancefloor," the young woman smiled at them, walking away with Mark.

"Should I give you a quick tour?" Neir asked Adrik, who made a slight nod. "We will be in the auditorium soon anyway." She headed straight for one of the two left halls. With her mask on, no one would truly recognize her as long as she didn't walk into any of her family. Neir De Van hadn't stepped into the HSS in three years, and it would stay that way for a few more hours. Guards stood in the hall as they approached.

"Excuse me, miss," one of the guards in a gray uniform said. "You can't enter the left side of the institute. All routes this way are closed."

"May I know the reason?" Neir asked.

"Orders from the Director," the guard responded. "Everybody had been informed a few hours ago. The right halls are available."

"Right." Neir nodded. "Must have been *distracted*." They walked back to the lobby.

Adrik looked around, his eyes moving at a pace that no one would think he hadn't been there before. It was Franko's eyes that almost sparkled with shock. He wouldn't be the only one. People were standing around the lobby, resting from the ball, or going back to their rooms.

"They blocked all the routes to the important rooms. Conference rooms. Armory. *Archives*," Adrik said, without looking at the public map behind him.

Franko glanced at the map quickly. "The right halls are mostly guest rooms and public spaces."

"That means they are keeping what happened at the museum a secret," Neir guessed. "It was that shocking to them, they are keeping it hidden."

"We knew they were using the masquerade ball as a distraction," continued Adrik.

"They would've had it at some point in the week anyway. But we came with the intention that they would give the news an hour later, as they always do. They might've changed their plans."

"The plan still works whether or not the dance takes place."

Neir nodded. "Then get ready to act. Tonight, you are both HSS hunters." She walked ahead of them, clearly remembering her way to the Ballroom. They passed hallways and rooms, some named and some unknown. *Classrooms. Library. Restrooms.* The ballroom was next to the auditorium. After that were the training rooms. A total of about three hundred people spent most of their time in the HSS, including kids.

She recalled the first time she felt her hunter senses heightened. The video that changed each young trainer's perspective on the darkness of the world. A footage of a vampire turning one of their fellow hunters: Forcing him to drink their blood on him, saying 'I turn you' in Latin, and killing him, all at once. The hunter, whose name was forgotten amid all the shame, became a symbol and a motivation for their mantra.

Hunt with purpose, fall with honor.
Better the grave than cursed hunger.
Steel my soul, let blood not bind;
In death or life, I stay humankind.

Either die as a hunter or be killed honorably by a vampire, but by all means, never become one. So, all hunters trained in those rooms with the daily reminder in their minds, just as Neir had when she was a kid. When the HSS agents seemed like complete heroes. She was ready to be a hunter. Yet no one told her how hard it was going to be to lose family and friends for it.

They turned into another hall. Neir could hear the modern pop instrumental music playing more clearly and green-blue lights coming out from the automatic doors. People were already heading inside.

"This is unbelievable," Franko whispered, then looked at Adrik, probably feeling his stare. "Of course, Adrik. No detouring."

"Fifteen minutes maximum," Adrik reminded. Neir nodded at him, entering the ballroom. Pictures of Neir's last New Year's ball in the HSS raced through her mind. They always changed the theme colors, but green was always a part of it. Her last time had been purple and green. Now, she stood among crowds of green and blue, making her feel like she was ironically underwater. Adrik and Franko dispersed around the room. Some people stood around the cocktail tables, at the edges of the room, while others danced on the dance floor. Due to the news about the museum, there was a chance that not all agents were at the ball. And if they were, Neir was sure they weren't dancing on the dance floor, unlike most of the young adults. Most of the actual adults in the HSS were agents, ranking higher than normal hunters. It would be harder to find people with masks on. But the advantage was that after three years, no one had remembered her eyes. She looked around, concentrating on each table that came into her eyesight one by one. *Chaperones.* They usually stood at one of the tables closest to the dance floor, but she didn't think Tim, as an introvert, would stay in plain sight. Every now and then, she felt stares as she walked around the room, staying away from the people that she'd met before. She passed the food stands, watching Franko looking at the sugary pastries and smiling at people walking by. She shook her head, wondering how someone with such social skills had no actual friends.

From across the room, she could see the silhouette of Adrik. It was impossible not to notice him with his full black suit, silver mask, and gloves on. He always stood straight, hands to the side or back. But now he was blending into the crowd, watching people with his hands on the table. He was good at that. Adapting when he needed to and acting like he didn't care about anyone or anything except revenge. But she couldn't believe it. Neir had tried not to care about family, Briz, or Erin, yet there would always be a scar of emotion no matter what. Even the most evil creatures, including vampires, cared for power or something; nonetheless, as long as it meant survival. And Adrik, just like her, was trying to survive at the cost of all truths.

CHAPTER 49
ADRIK

S HE LOOKED LIKE THE NIGHT SKY on a rainy day. *Lovely*. More so, surrounded by a sea of dark green and blue. Her eyes matched every corner of the room. It wasn't only the way she looked that made Adrik feel like he could feel *something*. But it was the way her eyes watched with a certain emotion, the way he could start to read her. The bravery and fearlessness in the way she walked matched his pace. Her crossed stakes tattoo on her back shoulder matched the black ink of the five gang tattoos on his arm. She looked around at him for a few seconds, only to continue the mission. He could stay all night standing there if he could, but the pocket watch ticking and the young lady approaching him wouldn't allow him.

"Hello, there?" the girl started, her eyes watching him slowly. "I'm Alicia. What is your name?" Adrik only nodded at her.

"My name is of no importance," he responded, still watching

Neir.

"Mystery guy, huh? Or are you a *bad* guy?" She grinned. "Tell me more."

"There's nothing to tell." Adrik glared. "And if I were, why do you even think I would tell you?" The girl stood straight, finally taking a hint at Adrik's annoyance.

"Didn't have to be rude." She walked away without looking back. Once she was out of sight, Adrik looked for Neir again. She was now standing at a table, next to a woman and two men. *She found him*. It was a matter of seconds until the actual disorder began.

CHAPTER 50
NEIR

BLUE EYES. GLASSES. Around the same five feet and five inches tall as Neir. Almost bald. It was Tim, all right. His round glasses below his thin black mask were what helped Neir recognize him better. As far as she remembered, he couldn't see farther than five feet without them. He always had them on when she passed the middle-aged man in the second tech and surveillance room. In exchange for bringing him food during break hours from the cafeteria, Neir would ask him for access to the chemistry file room in hopes of learning more about chemicals and poisons. He agreed every time, allowing the door to the Chem Offices to open during his break and giving Neir a warning if someone was about to enter. Thankfully, no one really entered the file room unless it was the end of the day, and scientists were leaving their reports for the next day.

Neir was actually surprised to see him at the ball. With him being introverted, no one would suspect him to be there out of all places. But there he was, and Neir was ready to make chaos happen. She headed straight for the table. He stood next to another man and two other women she didn't recognize. They seemed to be talking in a low voice, but Tim only nodded.

"I thought chaperones were supposed to walk around stopping chaos," Neir said, her hands crossed. Everyone looked at her, furrowing their brows.

The woman in lime green stood straighter. "What's with your comment, young lady?"

"Is there something we are supposed to know?" added the man in gray next to her.

"Someone is planning to spike the refreshments in thirty minutes," Neir shrugged.

"We have *strict* orders. Are you positive?" The other woman in dark blue next to Tim asked.

"That's what I heard. I wouldn't want to ruin New Year's either." They looked at her serious expression and then around the room as if deciding what to believe or do. Yet, based on previous HSS parties, some of the young immature teenagers would lose control for the sole purpose of *fun*.

As a twenty-year-old now, Neir missed most of the drama. In a year, she would be at the stage where adults decided whether or not they would go hunting abroad, train further to become an esteemed HSS agent, or determine another specific future. Neir would have liked to go back to the United States. Her five-year-old self barely remembered any memories from her place of birth.

"We will inform the other chaperones to stay wide awake for

any inconveniences," the woman in lime green said, starting to walk away. The man next to her followed her to the other side of the dance floor.

Neir stood still, looking from Tim to the dark, blue-dressed woman.

"Like your dress." Neir forced a smile. "I know you are a chaperone, but I wouldn't let the dress go to waste."

"Thank you." The woman smiled back. "I don't really dance, and even if I did, no one would ask."

"What about you, sir?" Neir looked at Tim, who quickly glanced at her.

"I'm not a dancer," he responded, making a lopsided smile.

"I do like dancing... somewhat," Neir admitted. "Just not in front of people." She lied, getting Tim's attention. She did like dancing, yet being a hunter, she didn't have enough free time to do so or anyone to dance with her. "I think it is time to get out of my comfort zone, though. Time is always ticking."

The woman nodded. "Yes. You are absolutely right."

"Give me luck." Neir smiled. "I'm going to find a dancing partner myself." And with that, she walked away, looking at Adrik from the other side. She nodded at him, letting him know the plan was in motion.

Except, she was stopped. For a second, she thought someone recognized her. But it had been three years, and though everybody kind of knew her, she hadn't been so congenial.

"Hey, there," the young man in front of her grinned, his brown eyes looking at her over his green-blue mask. "Are you new here? I haven't seen someone with such great golden hair around."

He tried to touch her hair, but she took a step back.

"You'll die of pain before touching me," Neir warned, trying to move past him. But he moved in front of her in a wobbly way, not letting her pass. *Must be drunk. Or stupid.*

"Playing hard to get. I see."

"I don't have time for your crap." She still tried to walk by him, not wanting to attract attention with the current circumstances. Yet he wouldn't move.

"Time is expensive. You wouldn't want to waste it..." Adrik said, appearing next to the man. "I was waiting for you."

The young man's smile faded. "Sorry, man. I thought she was single." He walked away fast, disappearing into the crowd.

"I would hurt him if I could," Neir sneered, looking at Adrik. "I was coming to you."

"But I came to you. *Time*," Adrik said, showing her the pocket watch under his coat. "And the technician is now heading for a dance."

Neir turned around to see Tim about to dance with the woman in dark blue. The mental trick had worked, just as Adrik had said it would.

"Then, we would have to dance," Neir suggested, already knowing Adrik's answer.

"I don't dance."

"I think it is *time* for you to dance at least once in your life. Time is always ticking." She half-smiled, repeating the same words that she had said to Tim. "Also, it is an easier distraction."

Adrik looked at her without saying anything yet put out his hand. Neir wasn't sure what went through his head. Like most times, she saw his emotions in his face, and other times, like this one, he was unreadable. Mostly detached from the world and in his mind. Always orchestrating. As if everything he ever did was on purpose. And Neir understood. Yet for a second, she hoped that dancing a waltz with him was not on purpose, but because he actually wanted to.

She felt his gloved hand over hers, and the other barely touching her waist.

They danced in silence, slowly getting closer to Tim and his partner. The plan had been for her to stumble among them one way or another. However, the waiter passing by them made it easy. She stumbled close to him, causing the glasses he held in the tray to fall like dominoes.

"Shoot. I'm sorry," she said as the drinks had fallen to cover Tim, the woman, and other guests nearby. Adrik moved towards Tim, holding a handkerchief to him.

"Can someone bring towels? Or napkins?" Neir moved towards them, waiting until Adrik nodded at her. Another waiter walked towards the crowd with towels in his hand and started passing them out. Adrik and Neir moved away, disappearing into the blue sea and heading to the refreshment tables where Franko stood.

"*That* was some distraction," Franko said, eating a chocolate chip cookie. "Glad your dress isn't ruined." He smiled at Neir. She shook her head at him.

"Here," Adrik said, holding Tim's HSS identification to him. "I'll be right behind you." Franko took his last bite, nodded, and walked toward the ballroom doors.

"Go," Neir said. "I'll be great, here." Adrik walked away, glancing at Neir one last time before following Franko.

CHAPTER 51
FRANKO

I'M PROBABLY GOING TO GET LOST was Franko's first thought as he headed out of the ballroom. Of course, he had studied the map, now and then, but looking at the actual institute was another completely different situation. He only memorized certain pathways... the ones he would take the most. The entire HSS was made out of metal, silver, and glass. Walking to one of the elevators in the next hall made him remember the golden tower of Ether. Five seconds later, Adrik appeared next to him. They would go together to the second floor, feet away from each other, to avoid any suspicion.

"Let's go through here," Franko said, nodding at the elevator instead of the stairs.

Adrik looked around. "Through the elevator?"

"Yes... the elevator," Franko said, and let out a small breath. "Of course, you know about elevators..." He pressed the button for the elevator to descend.

"I know how I know about elevators," Adrik said. "But how do you know?"

"Books and the golden tower at Ether have them."

"Without a doubt, they do." Adrik nodded, glaring at the elevator doors like he could burn the metal with his eyes. "I'll go up the stairs." He walked away, toward the stairwell, and disappeared upstairs. Franko shook his head. As far as he knew, Adrik never entered small spaces if he could avoid them. He was sure it was a fear of his that he wouldn't admit. The elevator rang as sounds of metal clashed into each other, and the doors swung open. People in black masks got out, not paying much attention to Franko entering. He only smiled at them but didn't say anything and got inside the wide metal box. Thankfully, no one else was inside with him. He pressed the number *2* on the button panel, waiting for the doors to close until a guy's voice screamed *Wait* from the other side, stopping the door with his hand. *That was close.*

"Sorry. I didn't see you," Franko said.

"No worries," the young man said. He had no mask, gasped, and was putting his blonde hair back.

"Are you alright?" Franko asked the moment the elevator started moving.

"Just fine. Merci."

Franko nodded. For a moment, he had forgotten he was still in France. He had been hearing a lot of English for a very long time and wondered how many HSS institutes actually existed around the world.

The elevator stopped on the second floor. In a hurry, the young man got out, standing still for a while, trying to catch his breath.

"There's a party in some of the rooms," the young man informed. "If you would like to come."

"I have a few things to do," Franko said. "But Merci." He turned around, heading for the right hall as the guy headed to the opposite side. Franko looked back, seeing Adrik appearing from the stairwell. Franko continued his way, knowing Adrik would be cautious behind him. He turned to another hall, looking for the technical room until he saw it. *Tech Room*. He waited only for a few seconds before entering, making sure that no one else, except Adrik and he, stood in the hall. Franko swiped Tim's identification into the card swiper. The door unlocked by itself, revealing a medium-sized room. Wires stood all around the monitors and a desk in the middle, where a man in gray sat.

"Done with the party, Tim?" he asked without turning around. When Franko didn't respond, the man looked at the reflection on the computer. He turned around, looking at him. His face filled with confusion, and his body froze like a statue.

"He's not done, mate," Franko said, taking a syringe out of his pocket. "But you are." He sedated him in the neck. The syringe slowly reduced of clear liquid. "Sorry... not really." The man slowly drifted into sleep without putting up a fight. Adrik entered the room, closing the door behind him. He moved the chair in which the tech man sat to the corner. Franko watched all the cameras. From the ballroom to the chamber halls of the fourth floor, he was able to see the entire right side of the institute. Neir had told him that there were two technical stations with cameras, the first on the left side. The first and official server room could see and control the entire institute. The second was extra precaution and technical aid to uphold half of the underground tunnels. *Which means we could be watched right now.* Franko turned around, looking at the only camera that hung from the entrance of the room. He had no time to waste. Looking at the controls, most of it was labeled. *Zoom In, Zoom out, Deactivate air panels, Deactivate elevators, Turn on alarms, etc.* A lot of buttons and pointers for all computer monitors. *Temporary HSS shutdown.*

"Should be this one," Franko said to himself, pressing down the red button at the corner of the table. The computers shut down to a blue wallpaper and a written message of instructions. *Password.* Franko began to type *HSShunters300* just as Neir had said.

"What an easy password," Franko said. Another message appeared just as one of the electrical panels shone red from the inside. *Press the green handle on the panel.* Franko did what the monitor instructed him. Everything shut off. There were no lights in the room, just as the monitors had also turned off.

"Now we wait," Adrik said, turning on the light in his pocket watch. Franko did the same and sat down, hoping Neir would get there soon.

CHAPTER 52
NEIR

NEIR HADN'T LIED ABOUT the drinks getting spiked. They were indeed, just not from any of the teenagers at the ball, but by her. She contaminated them with diluted drops of Gamma-hydroxybutyrate, a minute after Adrik had left, and waited in the entrance doors. She was glad there were no kids at the masquerade. They usually held different parties for the younger hunters in training.

Seconds before the lights turned off, she headed out of the ballroom. The automatic doors closed behind her, powered down in sync with the lights and everything using electricity. Most of the HSS was filled with technology. One small interruption, and even the AC or access to oxygen would slowly shut down. That's why two tech rooms were created, one for extra control. And only the people in the Server Room would be able to start up the second tech room with their devices after ten minutes.

Neir had gotten used to the dark, as if she could even see through it. She headed toward the stairwell, touching the metal walls with one hand, just in case. Once on the second floor, she walked faster until finally knocking on the tech room door.

"Who is it?" She heard Franko's voice ask.

"Who else, Fran?" she responded. Franko opened the door from inside the room. Some of the doors worked that way, and some didn't. Neir entered the dark room, closing the door behind her, and heading for the electrical control panel. She was about to stumble as she passed by a dark figure. By the wooden scent, she knew it was Adrik.

"Watch it," she whispered, releasing her hand from his arm and continuing towards the panel. She now turned on her phone, flashing light into the panel. *Where is it?* There were a lot of wires everywhere. *Blue. Blue.* There it was. She needed to connect the blue wire with the USB-C end to her phone in order to access the HSS network. Same password as she had told Franko earlier in the afternoon. One press of a button on her phone and she was finally able to talk to Zach.

"Zach. It's time," she said, taking her mask off. "We are in the second tech room. You can portal the items now, and no anti-magic alarm will sound."

"Good luck to you three," Zach said through the phone and hung up. They waited a few seconds until they heard a sudden movement in the storage room closest to the unconscious man, who slept soundly. A slight blue light illuminated the tech room from the storage metal door margins. Adrik opened it quickly, revealing two large cases sitting in the middle of cardboard boxes and wires. He opened one of the boxes, getting a rope to tie the man up. Franko helped him while Neir put the boxes outside and grabbed her clothes to change inside the confined room.

Three minutes have passed. She looked at the time on her phone. *Only fifteen minutes max.*

"I'm ready," she said the moment she got out of the storage room, her comfort intact. The black-green cape matched her green mask.

"Let's go," Adrik said, opening the door back to the pitch-black halls. Neir walked ahead, hearing Franko and Adrik's footsteps behind her. They turned the corner to another hall when they bumped into two men in gray uniforms with flashlights.

"Where are you heading?" one of the men asked. "We need everyone we can get to the first floor quickly. Turn around and walk."

"That won't be possible," Adrik said, moving quickly and punching the man's face. "Go. I'll catch up." Neir nodded, moving ahead with Franko. Adrik fought and sedated the two guards. She could hear one of the men trying to call for help just as she turned the corner, then there was silence.

They reached the end of the hall, where a glass walkway was attached to the other half of the lighted institute. More than a dozen walkways oversaw the entire lobby area from above and crossed to different hallways on the other side.

"Think you can shoot?" Neir asked Franko.

"After all the practice you've taught me," Franko grinned, taking out two tranquilizer guns from his belt. "It would be an honor." He held the gun in his hands, targeting the men ahead. The air crackled from the shots, and the guards crumpled, hitting the floor with dull thuds. Neir and Franko walked across the walkway at a normal pace. Moving the guards into another storage room, this one filled with cleaning supplies. Guards ranked lower than normal hunters and agents. She wondered why anyone would spend more time in the HSS to be a simple guard.

"This way," Neir said as Adrik approached them. She led them down a hallway, turning left and right until she got to a door similar to the second tech room. The only difference was that there was no actual metal sign stating *Server Room* for safety purposes. She swiped the card she had grabbed from the guards; unlike Tim, they had access to almost every room in the institute. Blue light turned to green seconds after the panel scanned the front of the card. She then swiped the side of the card within the panel. The metal door opened at once. She let Adrik and Franko enter first, closing the door behind her.

A room, double the size of the second tech room, stood before them. It was similar in arrangement yet different in size, with more wires and large monitors on the farthest wall. Franko looked around in shock but stayed silent as he and Adrik walked towards the two men sitting down behind the large desk.

"I know, sir," one of the men said out loud, typing a few codes on the computer screen. "We are still trying to fix the power supply on the other side. A few more minutes."

"Appreciate the professionalism," Adrik began, his voice stern. "But make no mistake. I am not a *Sir*." Franko didn't waste any time sedating the man in front of him. The man who'd spoken turned around, eyes wide as he watched his tech partner fall unconscious.

"Who are you people?" he asked, his voice shaking. He looked around, trying to look for a way out, but he was surrounded by Adrik and Franko. Their expressions were visible without their masks.

"Do you really think we are answering that question?" Franko said, shaking his head.

"Who are you?" he repeated, looking at Franko.

"A lot of things," Adrik responded, glaring at him. "Vengeance for the most part."

The man flinched. "What do you want?"

"That is the least of your problems, Fletcher." Neir took a step forward. "Tim sends your regards. Don't you think it's time to pay for your betrayal of your ex-best friend?"

"Did he send you?"

"No. But I know you betrayed him, only to simply move up in ranks while he stood in the same position." Fletcher shook his head. "Am I wrong? Or are you a selfish coward?"

"What do you want?" Fletcher asked, unmoving in his chair.

"Did you betray him? Why?" Adrik said, raising his voice and holding up a knife he'd gotten from inside his coat. "Speak. Or you can give me a reason to cut your tongue."

"Ye—" he quivered. "Yes… I betrayed Tim by copying his evaluation codes. I wanted everyone to stop looking down on me…"

"Good," Neir said, showing Fletcher a recording device. "That's all I needed." She put the voice recorder in her pocket. "*Now*. You will do what we say, and maybe your golden son, who is probably out partying, will not be harmed."

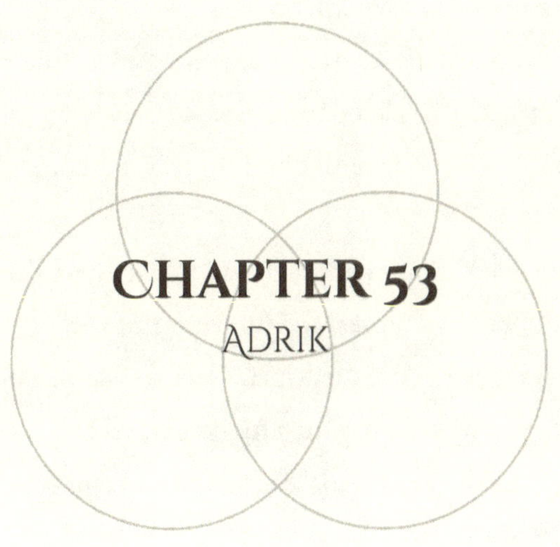

CHAPTER 53
ADRIK

*L*OVE WAS A WEAKNESS. *Caring* was a weakness. Adrik knew that for sure. Family and friends were that weakness. To care was to lose. But to lose was to care. Just as Adrik needed revenge for his family after losing them. And exactly how Fletcher decided to help them for the sake of his son. Whom neither Adrik, Neir, nor Franko cared about. Neir had mentioned him, but as far as they knew, he was somewhere around the HSS, unaware of the current situation and free of danger.

"The archives are on the third floor. The council and director still remain in the meeting room," Fletcher informed Adrik and Neir from the earpiece. They stood at the end of the hall, looking out for potential threats.

"Have fun," Neir said before separating ways. "And good luck."

"Luck is only an excuse for our failures," Adrik said. "Everything is up to us now. We will not fail."

Neir nodded. He knew she understood what he meant, but her eyes softened at his opinion. *I don't believe in luck, Neir. I believe in you.* He thought, but he didn't say. He couldn't say. Not now. Maybe not ever.

Adrik didn't look back as he and Neir went their separate ways, both heading to reveal and find out the truth.

"Good luck to you, too, chief," Franko said through the earpiece. "Do you need help getting to the archives?"

"No," Adrik responded. "See you soon, Franko."

"What do you mean? Hayir. Adrik, don't you dare turn—"

Adrik turned off his earpiece at once. He had memorized the map for this reason. No distractions and only plotting. And to irritate Franko to some extent.

He had to admit that the institute was a maze. *Right.* He'd only had about one to two hours to look at the original print itself, but he remembered enough not to get lost. *Left. Lunch room. Rest room.* To every map, there was a pattern. *Right. Left. Foundry room.* He had looked at the map in Zach's apartment, trying to memorize the drawing and closing his eyes to repeat the way, just as he did now. He led himself to the stairwell. *At the end of the hall.* Neir explained that the elevators and stairwells deeper into the halls of the HSS were scarcely used. Only the ones in the lobby room were more common. However, desperate times called for desperate measures. Agents and hunters, the best fighters of the HSS, were scattered around the left side of the institute.

The distraction on the right side had worked. Some of the hunters had headed that side to aid the rooms and most of the unconscious people in the ballroom. With Neir feeding them a lie, they all believed that some students had spiked the refreshments with a strong drug. The same sedative he was going to use for the three men ahead of him, blocking his way to the stairwell.

"Bonjour. Où allez-vous?" one of the men asked him. As much as Adrik liked metal and silver, he was getting tired of seeing it around him and especially in people's clothing. He stayed quiet, letting the man speak. "Bonjour. New recruiter, who prefers English, I'm guessing."

"Everyone is required to study both French and English. Are you from America?" the man asked, tilting his head, analyzing Adrik up and down.

"Oui," Adrik responded, after all, it wasn't a lie. He was born in America and moved to Italy. "Y a-t-il un problème avec ça?"

"No. No problem. Just curious, that's all."

"In that case. I have somewhere to be." Adrik walked between them, heading to the stairwell.

"However," another man began. "I am curious. Where is your identification?"

Adrik turned around, already planning a tactic to fight them off. "I don't need one."

Three out of ten sedatives were used and stayed nicely placed inside his black coat. The third floor had been emptier. By far, he'd only seen one man glaring at him as he walked by. At the corner of the institute was the Archives, a glass wall protected the large room filled with piles of boxes and file cabinets. Adrik entered the room and started looking around. Everything was labeled and organized. It may have seemed like an easy exploration. *Too easy*. He walked towards the two computers in the corner of the room. With the password, he moved the clicker to turn the monitor on. *Way too simple.* A tab opened up automatically with the words *Search Archives* written at the top. Adrik began to write keyboards. *Italian Village Fires 2000s.* A list of results showed up. Adrik read them as he scrolled down.

1900s Italy Village Fire (Deaths caused by vampires).
Hidden Vampires in European Villages: A Diary.
The Venice Massacre File (2000s)

Adrik pressed the last file. It was only two pages long, and only a slight preview of the first page appeared.

The Venice Massacre File

Written by Anonymous

Our Italian villages were quiet and united until the day of the massacre. There were a total of three villages together, houses closer to the sea and somewhat far from the city itself. At midnight was when the screams started and fire unraveled. I saw everything unfold from the building I resided in, closest to the villages, and on top of a hill. Rumors spread quickly that night that witches had raided the villages in search of hidden vampires. As a light-blood human myself, I had been friends with most of the residents. Truth be told, there were no hidden vampires in those villages, and if they had been, they were long gone. One of my friends, who was a vampire hunter, had stayed a few days ago and had no actual report. Innocent blood was spilled... (to read more, find files in cabinet 378).

Adrik exited the tab quickly, glancing at his silver rings. He started walking around the room, searching for cabinet *378*. But he stopped at the sound of the glass doors opening. Four hunters in green uniforms entered the room.

"I got told we got an intruder," one of them smirked. "I was expecting a lowlife person. But wow, look at this, *friends*. He looks like he could be a hunter." The hunter smiled at his companions.

Adrik tilted his head. "I may not hunt vampires. But I do hunt people who pretend to be in control when they are not." The hunter laughed, and the others followed in pursuit until Adrik approached them, sword in hand. "Let us see how good of a hunter you are."

"You will see," the hunter said. Each of them stood straight for a second, mentally getting ready for a fight, then finally making the first strike. They approached Adrik in unison, using their fists and knives to fight him off. The first two that approached were the weakest. Adrik managed to punch them and cause one of them a cut on their face with his sword. They fell back out of the room like cowards, that even their so-called leader shook his head. The third one approached. He fought well, but not the best, until he drew his knife. He pushed Adrik to the floor and tried to cut his face, stopping only to reconsider. Adrik could read his face and his next move as he drew the knife from his leg. The man had decided that would be sufficient. He stabbed him deep in the leg, close to his knee. Adrik drew a breath as the sharp knife went through his skin.

The hunter beamed widely, moving closer to Adrik just for laughs and not expecting his next move.

Adrik grinned, his back against the cold floor. "You may have a knife. But *I* have the sword." He had no space for mercy in his mind. As if he were going for a hug, the businessman's hands encircled the man. Adrik drew the sword into his back, putting weight into the handle and pushing in through the man's chest. The lead hunter who had spoken earlier had tried to stop him. Yet he was late. Adrik pulled out the sword from the body, his face bloody, bruised, and the pain close to stagnant.

The last hunter backed up, shaking his head with cold, angry eyes. Adrik stood up, straight as he could with his wounded leg. "Never underestimate a *lowlife*."

"You son of a—" The hunter walked forward, but Adrik held out his sword inches away from the hunter's face. He took a few steps back, putting distance between himself and Adrik. "You are a murderer."

"And you are a vampire killer. No difference at all."

"Hope you rot in Hell," the hunter said, taking out a lighter from his pocket. "Along with every file you were trying to look for in this room. Maybe you'll see your partner, Neir De Van, there." He threw the lighter over the cardboard boxes and ran, pushing a red button that not only closed the glass doors but activated the pipes above the room. Fire starter fluid spilled around the room, and the spark from the cardboard boxes expanded quickly. Adrik couldn't turn back to the files. He stood motionless, his eyes ice-cold, but his mind in the deepness of the flames.

Adrik, it's too dark. We will save ourselves, right, brother?

Shh, be quiet.

Adrik! Adrik!

Mom? Dad?

Let her go! Let go of her!

The fire will burn the village. It will burn your entire family.

You are coming to Kosmos.

Adrik turned on the earpiece. "Adrik? Adrik! Neir needs your help. They are taking her. Can you hear me? Get out of the Archives room!" Franko screamed through the earphone, waking up Adrik from his mind. "I can see you through the cameras. Your sword! It was made by an Illuminator Physicist. Stronger and durable. Use it. If it is medium-thin glass, enough force from the sword and the heat can make it break." The sword was not magic itself but was connected to his owner by light magic and through blood.

Adrik held the sword straight. He felt the fire behind consuming him with heat. He threw the sword straight into the glass with all the strength his arms could manage. The glass exploded, shattering fractures fell to the floor in sync with Adrik's steel sword.

CHAPTER 54
NEIR

*L*UCK. She didn't believe in it either. Much less, a god that could help them. As the last time she prayed, she'd been stabbed in the back by family. But she couldn't find anything less emotional to say before she stepped away from Adrik. *Stay safe?* Too caring. *See you later.* There were no promises. So, *good luck* was it. No matter how she said it, Adrik was right. Everything was up to them now, and no one else. *I will not fail.* She thought, not turning back to look at him. She passed two hallways to an elevator. Adrik had gone to deeper stairwells that were not commonly used on non-training days. *The Pros of Holidays.*

With her mask on and green-black cape, she was unrecognizable. Two women and one man stood inside the elevator. A number one lit up in red in the panel above the elevator doors as Neir stood next to them, her back against the metal wall. They didn't ask questions, but she could feel their suspicion the moment they looked at each other. Yet Neir didn't speak, getting out of the elevator on the first floor. She turned left and walked straight, hearing footsteps behind her. She moved aside, letting the two women pass by and enter the office where the Main Meeting room was. Seconds later, she followed them. The receptionist quickly stood up, brows furrowing.

"Excuse me. You can't enter," she began worriedly. "What are you doing?"

"Don't worry, Ms. Adeline LeBlanc," Neir smiled. "I'm a ghost of the past collecting her debts."

"Neir?" Adeline tilted her head. Neir made a slight nod, continuing her way through the white wallpaper walls that were supposed to make every new recruiter feel welcomed. She entered the frosted glass office; the squeaky door made the sixteen chairs on the U-shaped desk turn around. Neir remembered every face, including her father's, who sat in the middle with Carden on the right side and their mom on the left. Some of the council members tensed up at the sight of her stealthy figure.

"Excuse me! You can't barge in. We are having a meeting," one of the older men said.

"Be quiet, Earl," the blonde woman beside her said, squinting. To Neir's surprise, it appeared her dad had changed the gender policies. They all sat quietly, even her parents' eyes filled with confusion. Then she looked straight at Carden, and it was the wide-eyed realization in his face that made her nearly laugh.

Neir smirked. "I've been waiting so long for this." She pulled back her hood and took off her mask. Her blond hair matched her mom's, and her green eyes matched her dad's.

"Can everybody give us a moment?" Neir's dad demanded, eyes still on Neir. "This is a family meeting." Everyone except her dad, mom, and Carden stood up.

"No," Neir shot. "What I need to say has to be heard by everyone. So, by all means, *sit* the hell down." The council members looked at Alaric, Neir's father. He nodded slightly, and they started to sit back down. Alaric stood up, his relaxed eyelids looking up at Neir. She didn't even believe it anymore. Her mom, Layla, sat next to him. A soft smile on her face.

"Neir," Alaric started. "I am glad that you have surrendered for your crimes."

"What makes you think I have surrendered?"

"Then why are you here, daughter?"

"Don't call me that," Neir snapped. "I stopped being part of the family since—"

"You became a criminal," Carden said, interrupting her. "I'm glad to give the council a quick memory lane." Her brother stood up. "Let's see. Went on a killing rampage at fifteen years old, almost causing trouble in human sight. At sixteen, you sneak out during the temporal prohibition. And worse, when you were seventeen. You lied in *court* about your kills and tried to shun me for it."

"You can't take a trip down memory lane. If your own memory is tangled in complete lies," Neir said. "You also missed the most important events."

Carden half-laughed. "Really? What is more important than being an HSS criminal, Neir?"

"At *sixteen*, Carden, you were a coward. Scared little boy, afraid of everyone's opinions, always following me around, and lying at the expense of my accomplishments," Neir revealed. Carden held an expressionless face, but under his eyes, Neir could see his rage.

She turned to her dad, faking a smile. "So no, *Alaric*. I am not here to apologize for being one of the best hunters of my age. And I am definitely not sorry that your dear son is both a liar and still a coward."

"Where's your proof?" One of the council members asked.

"Your purpose for this meeting," Neir smirked, taking her hand from under the coat. A few members shuffled, thinking she would try something dangerous on them. She unzipped the zipper on her black jacket sleeve. It was only for that design that she had worn that specific jacket under her coat. Making sure her arm was visible; she held it out. Some members gasped. Carden looked angrier than he had been before.

"Make sure the Vampire Massacre on the museum goes on the files too," Neir smiled, looking down at her new line of tattoos. Each line for three dead vampires. "And that's not including the ones my partners killed, by the way."

"You killed an average of seventy vampires," Alaric stated. "That's impossible."

"You're lying." Carden shook his head.

"There were others before this generation that managed to do so," Neir said. "I assure you. I am not lying. My marks are as real as the fake ones you have on your arm." He had those tattoos the day after she made her previously greatest vampire kill, just after he betrayed her. Funny, given that no hunter ink could surface on skin steeped in cowardice.

"Bring in the guards," one of the council members said. "You almost exposed us and are a current danger to the Society."

Another member nodded. "Did *you* stop the ball?"

Neir made a slight laugh but didn't speak.

"A lover of chemistry," Layla smiled, not exactly helping the situation. "You always loved chaos."

"So, Alaric? What is your overall decision as the leader of the Society?" Neir asked, unsure of her father's actions. After all, her parents were now close to strangers to her after years of hostility and three years of isolation.

Alaric pressed the red button next to the speaker on the desk. "Send in the guards. *Quickly*. Secure all the left side exits with a few of the best hunters... agents too if available." Yet, Alaric's words and desperation hadn't exactly been expected from her. She felt a sudden wave of rage and sadness that not even the tears in her eyes could drop. The guards in gray entered in less than twenty seconds. "Take her down to the ground floor. She is a criminal." The two guards nodded, starting to grab Neir from her arms to put her in shackles.

"Don't touch me," she shot. "I clearly know the way." Her dad nodded at the guards. She gave him one last look before heading out of the meeting room with four guards, two men and two women, around her. She recognized one of the guards, but she didn't look at her, and neither did Neir.

"So, are you going to do something?" Franko said, interrupting Neir's thoughts. She had forgotten her earpiece microphone was on.

"Wait for it," Neir whispered. The guards looked at her like she was crazy.

"Do it fast. Hunters are heading to Adrik, and long story short, I don't have much time either."

Neir could feel her adrenaline rise as she thought of ways to beat the guards. They still hadn't checked inside her cloak. She made a slight movement, trying to get a few items from inside her clothes, glancing at the guards. They focused their eyesight straight ahead, becoming too comfortable with the guns beside them to notice Neir taking a smoke grenade from the inside of her coat. Until a sudden hissing sound filled their space and the air turned gray. The guards moved quickly through the smoke, but they were not as quick as actual hunters.

Guards were usually family hunter members who had not been trained to be hunters due to personal choice, so they just remained in the HSS for a normal job. Neir grabbed one of the guard's staff, trying to disorient them. Once they were all over the floor, she turned to another hall, trying to head upstairs to help Adrik, until the actual hunters appeared quickly in front of her. *Twelve*. She counted them on her head.

"Neir De Van, give up now," a young woman on the front line said. "You can't take all of the best hunters."

Neir smirked. "This is going to hurt you more than it will hurt me. Trust me." She let her cloak fall, revealing her bow and arrow on her back. And headed right into battle with her former teammates from her class.

CHAPTER 55
FRANKO

T HE COMPUTER SCREENS and buttons on the keybo-ards mocked him. At least that's what Franko felt, even though Neir had taught him the basics of modern technology. From different devices to even the smallest computer symbols. In addition to Ether books, Franko had also picked up a few from Arkadian bookstores—some of which contained secrets of the modern world. Not everyone was interested in those pieces of paper, but Franko was still learning how to read and remembering his days with his old family, he had been inspired. Dreams of modernity haunted him like old memories of him watching TV or holding a phone as a child. Now, it all stood before him doing just the same. The more he saw, the more he could see the patterns of it all. The rush to sit behind a keyboard and begin to type was the same rush he felt when he alternated metal.

"Seems that your friends don't have any luck," Fletcher said as they watched hunters heading towards the Archives room from different cameras. Neir didn't seem to have good luck either with guards heading into the meeting room.

"Some things are meant to happen," Franko responded.

"Can you get me a water bottle from the storage room?" Fletcher asked. Franko tilted his head. "Being around devices isn't a way to cool down." Fletcher continued, and Franko couldn't deny that he could feel the heat of the room. He walked towards the storage room, and just as he had hardly thought, Fletcher had proceeded to run away.

"Oh, this is bad," Franko said to himself. "*Double* bad if I hadn't expected it."

Franko walked to the door, closing and locking it behind him, grabbing the tablet attached to the computer that showed the same cameras on its screen. He guessed every surveillance worker had one since it spelled *Fletcher Tablet 3* on a white sticker. He walked to the storage room, closed the door, and took a deep breath.

"I love animals. But by the universe, I hope there's no spiders," he sighed, entering the air vent behind the carton boxes in the corner. *There are a few spiders*. Franko crawled through the vents, pushing the tablet in front of him with every crawl. Thanks to Zach's blueprints, Adrik had changed the plans for Franko to hide in them while he and Neir were out, in case things went sideways.

"Vents. I didn't mention them because we didn't have the blueprints," Neir had explained at Zach's house a few hours before heading to the Catacombs.

"Now you do." Zach smiled at her.

"Are you expecting me to remember all of this in two hours?"

Franko asked Adrik, who just glared at him. "Of course, boss. Learning it right away."

And indeed, he had… because he had no choice. He turned on his mic, trying to hear Adrik's side, but he still didn't turn it on. Then he tried Neir. He could see through the cameras that some guards were already taking her. *Do it fast.* Franko had said, and was surprised as to how quickly, like Adrik, she could cause and delete chaos. He tried Adrik again as he saw him trying to get out of the Archives room. He finally answered. *Neir needs your help. They are taking her. Can you hear me?* Franko quickly suggested his advice as if Adrik didn't know that already. *Fire* and *glass* weren't really friends with each other. Franko watched Adrik heading out of the Archives room.

Cold air flew through the vents as he waited for a few seconds to catch his breath. Then he continued to crawl. *Left. Right. Down the end.* Until he was at the air vent that led him up and was close to the stairwell. He stood up, managing to crawl up to the other vent, leading him up to the stairwell. He opened the door vent, trying to make no noise, but he could hear footsteps. Taking a peek, he saw Adrik heading down slowly and sweat trickling down his forehead.

"Boss. There are definitely a few *spiders* in there." Franko gasped, getting out of the vent, then looking down at Adrik's bloody bandaged leg.

"The plan continues," Adrik said, not even paying much attention to Franko's worries.

"That looks deep, Adrik." Franko looked at the white cloth turning redder.

"Where's Neir?"

Franko shook his head, looking down at the screen of the tablet in his hand. "Still distracting."

"Good," Adrik said, continuing his way downstairs to the first floor. Franko headed in the same direction, looking down and watching Adrik limp every five seconds. He knew it wasn't the first time he had been beaten up, yet that didn't mean Franko didn't somewhat worry about it. Even watching Neir through the cameras made him feel uneasy. They were all strong, of course, but Franko couldn't help but wonder if they would always be able to escape death.

CHAPTER 56
NEIR

*H*ER LEGS POUNDED WITH ACHE *as her shoe hit the puddle on the concrete floor. Neir had seen a few vampires entering the dark alley earlier. Unlike the stagnant clock in the HSS, the watch on her wrist ticked faster. Her heart raced when she turned the corner. There they were. The vampires didn't say a word, only hissed at the craving for her blood. Neir quickly glanced behind her, checking for her brother. He had stayed behind to stake the last vampire in the past alley. They only needed to finish five more. The ones standing in front of her.*

So, Neir didn't hesitate. She lunged forward and so did the vampires. One by one, she fought. Punching them in the face. Staking the first. One down. They took turns trying to disorient her. Two down. Until she walked back and grabbed her arrow, letting it fly straight to the vampire's heart. Three down.

"Neir," Carden's voice said. He stood next to her at once. Two versus

two. But she grinned at Carden, and he nodded at her. They moved forward against the remaining vampires. Fourth vampire down for Neir in less than a minute. Behind her, Carden struggled. The last vampire choked him against the wall, not letting him reach the stake he'd dropped. Neir grabbed her own, inside her coat, sinking it on the back of the monster, the wood reached his non-beating heart.

"Finally," Neir said, grabbing the dead vampire by the collar to pull him away from Carden. "Are you okay?" She looked at Carden. He made a slight smile before Neir turned away from him, dragging the body to the middle of the alley. "We did a good job, right?"

"We? But sister, I did all the work?" he replied.

"What are you—" She dropped the body but didn't finish her question. Sharp, intense pain expanded through her back between her shoulder and spine. She turned, looking straight a Craven. And he grinned. A wide grin.

Neir tried to speak. Her eyes were frowning at her brother. Surely, she was dreaming. She tried to take a breath. It wasn't real. God, it isn't real. But warmth trickled down her back as she fell. She tried moving sideways so that the knife didn't touch the ground. So that the pain wouldn't deepen. Craven didn't speak. His blurry silhouette approached her with a lighter in his hands. Then the ache was no longer in her back or on her burnt wrist. It was right on her heart.

Weakness rushed through Neir's body as she fought the sedative going through her skin. She wasn't dead yet. Neither when she woke up in the HSS medical center with her back and wrist bandaged up. When she found out her brother had lied to everyone. *He killed all the hunters. One of them stabbed her, and the last one burned her hunter marks. Carden is a savior and a hero. He saved his sister.*

The raging memory was like yesterday. When she found out the truth, she tried to confront him. And he denied, gaslighting her, that she was confused about the events. She wasn't. So, she started a report for the HSS court. They didn't believe her. And she had no concrete proof. The knife had been touched by other medics, and her marks were gone.

The Huntress breathed in and out. She had tried to fight the hunters, using net arrows at the ones that kept coming into the hall. But she wasn't expecting to be sedated right after. Or for two of the hunters who held her up to lead her to an unknown room, and up through a large set of stairs. To make it worse, they had taken away every weapon she had, including the microphone in her ear.

Neir tried to stay awake as they took her through a close hallway she hadn't seen before.

"Where are you taking me?" she asked, her rough voice close to a whisper. "Where are we?" She saw silhouettes standing in front of them. *Carden.* They threw her onto the floor. Metal touched her ears the moment she hit the cold ground.

"Don't worry, sister, you won't be here for long." Carden's voice echoed. "You'll be dead long before our parents can change their minds."

The sedative, Neir could feel, wasn't strong enough. She felt tired, weak, yet was able to wake up minutes later.

"Neir? Neir. Can you hear me?" A familiar voice spoke. "Neir. Wake up!" *One I hadn't heard in a while.* Neir opened her eyes, blinking at the fluorescent lights above. She looked straight at the person who'd spoken. Someone whom she'd almost thought of not seeing again.

"Briz?" Neir exclaimed, crawling to the iron bars to reach Briz's arms, hugging her. "Hey."

"Hey," Briz greeted her with a half-smile on her face. "You don't seem too bad." She nodded at Neir's wounds on her face.

"Nothing I can't handle," Neir responded.

"Have you seen Erin?" Briz asked anxiously. "Is he ok?"

"Yes. I sent him to the police station to make your disappearance report. An adult is watching him. I went to check on the process a few days ago."

"Thank you, Neir. Thank you so much," Briz reached out for her hand. "And you? Are you ok? You know your brother is a maniac, right?"

"Yes." Neir nodded. "And that sounds like something Erin would say." Briz smiled. Neir had been waiting to find her. Little did she know that Carden would lead her straight to her. "We need to try and get out of here." Neir adjusted her eyes to the surroundings. Eight cells divided by steel poles stood in a straight line around them, Neir on the third one and Briz on the fourth. Only two doors were on both ends of the slim hall in front of them. There were no cameras in sight. No bed or items inside the cells that would help them get out. And even if they tried, three locks with different types of keys for Neir weren't easy to unlock.

"You aren't asking any questions..." Neir said as she concentrated.

"I did. A lot, but the guards and your brother wouldn't answer. He only repeated that he was going to take revenge against you. But I have *so* many questions for you."

"Ask me."

"Did you know I was here?"

"Yes."

"How?"

Neir sat back on the poles, giving up on the metal around her. She recalled Mondragon's contract with Carden on his desk, moments before his escape. Adrik was sure it was Carden who helped the Clan vampire escape. "I saw some files on the people who kidnapped you—in their old home, to be specific. Erin described how they looked, and after seeing my brother's name on the files, I knew he was probably the one who held you captive." Neir should've been surprised at Carden's alliance, but he'd done so many horrible deeds. She looked down at the marked right arm, the bright new hunter marks overshadowing the burnt scars underneath. They had been worse before and had faded after a while, but they were still visible three inches away. And Neir could still hear Carden's mocking laughs as he burned her arm, wanting her victories unseen.

Neir watched Briz narrow her eyes, still thinking. "Neir? Who are you? Who are these people?"

Neir let out a small breath, looking at Briz with seriousness. "The people who kidnapped you were vampires. This place is a Hunter Secret Society." It was no use hiding it anymore. "And... I am a vampire hunter."

CHAPTER 57
FRANKO

A SUBTLE SMELL of sewer water reached Franko's nose a few twenty steps into the ground floor and the intersection of two hallways. He took a right and walked down the narrow hallway, leading him to a wide room filled with vaults. An old weary man sat at the table in the corner, a monitor in front of him. He sat back, sleeping and snoring. Franko let out a breath, taking small steps to the desk.

"Hello..." Franko said, swinging his hand in front of him. "Deep sleeper. Can't blame you, mate." He moved the mouse on the computer, turning it on, and trying to find a file that would inform him of the vaults' owners. *52—Carden De Van.* "52. Got it." Franko exited the screen and took another look at the man once again. His name tag read *Roger*: *Vault Keeper*. He looked back at Roger, tilting his head while he snored.

There were a total of a hundred vaults, some as large as rooms and others as small as normal safes. *52.52. 52.* 52. Franko looked at the vault before him. Just like every other secure room, there was nothing for it to open except a built-in junction box. He raised the little metal door. Now, he understood why they had Roger as the keeper of the vaults. The bomb timer started ticking, counting down a minute. Franko looked at the four wires attached to it, looking inside his coat for the pliers.

"Red, blue, black, and green," Franko whispered. "Which of you will not *kaboom*?" Between all the colors, he could tell neither red nor blue would cause harm. The HSS was surrounded by black and green. Someone could easily tell the irony of those two colors. "What if that's what they want thieves to think?" Franko murmured to himself. The timer kept ticking, he had thirty seconds. He tried to remember anything that could give him a clue, looking around for ideas. Then he saw Roger still sleeping and the computer. The vault numbers on the computer screen had been highlighted in different colors. 52 had been green. Franko held the pliers close to the green wire. He closed his eyes. *By the universe, may it be green.* He cut the wire, and the timer stopped ticking as the sound of metal inside the vault door creaked, opening the door automatically. Franko let out a gasp, looking up. "Thank you. I knew you couldn't let me go yet."

He took one last look at Roger before entering the vault.

"By the universe..." Metal boxes, paper currency with differrent designs, and gold stood right in the middle of the cylinder-shaped room. Franko could stand there staring at it if he wanted. Yet he went straight away to the boxes. Neir needed his help. After minutes, he searched for files and USB drives inside the scattered boxes. *One USB flash drive.* Yet there was nothing to be found in the boxes or around the room. Franko couldn't leave without evidence. He couldn't leave his job unfinished. *Think.* He looked around the room once again. *A USB drive.* Neir had said Carden saved all his camera and important files on drives. *A weird habit of his to do so.* Franko thought. But then again, tech was tech, and *modern* tech was astonishing.

Most of the boxes in the vault were scattered. The ones in the middle he found were tilted to the side. Everything was random, disorganized. Everything except the pile of gold. The golden coins and bars fell to the floor, making echoes around the vault as Franko pushed them aside. A black USB drive sat right in the middle of the metal floor. He grabbed it, backing away from the now messy vault, then looked back to see the gold. All the money he wanted sat just a few inches away. He could have it all. He could take it, and no one but him would know. Well, probably Adrik would. But he didn't need it at the moment to survive. He knew he would earn what Adrik would pay him for his talents. Just as Adrik earned it during his gang operations in Arkadia—most of it, anyway, if he didn't need to steal to survive. Franko himself had to admit he had stolen a few times as well, for food or resold items, before meeting Adrik. And even though he could steal right now. Even if the gold looked so beautiful and bright, he turned around, closing the vault door behind him. Whether the universe would give him riches or not, he knew the only way to feel prouder was to earn it.

Roger's snores increased the closer Franko approached the table, taking the drive out of his pocket and into the USB port on the computer. Three unknown folders popped up on the screen.

Roger shifted to the side in his seat, and Franko froze, maintaining the usual silence for a few seconds. He moved closer to the screen, pressing the first folder. He skimmed through it quickly till the last and fifth page, where the leader of the vampire Clan had written his name. *The Contract with Nicholas Mondragon.* On it were written their deals in bullet points.

- *Carden and members of the HSS, listed below, will not hunt the Clan and swear protection (likewise from both groups).*
- *Neir's friend, Briz, will be kidnapped from the Clan on orders of Carden De Van.*
- *Neir will be eliminated by Nicholas Mondragon.*

Franko moved on to the next files, not surprised at the contract Neir had managed to get from Mondragon's office before heading to the museum's rooftop. Twenty-eight pages was how long the second file was. Each of the pages with different hand signatures, Carden's and HSS members. And each with the same written words in bold. Quid pro quos and exchanges of money. Contracts that Carden had made to get more allies within the HSS. Most of them wrote that they would fight with him against Neir if it came to that point. Franko shook his head, feeling distressed at how Neir's own family could be her enemy. He hadn't known her for long and didn't need to tell that Neir had fought her own battles, both physical and emotional, all by herself. Pain from and for family was what Franko understood from her. Not the same way, but it was there regardless. Only Adrik's pain stayed secret.

Finally, the last and third folder. *How can it be worse?* Franko thought, clicking twice to open it. He felt as if he had stepped into a crime scene the moment he looked at it. "I've changed my mind. *This* is bad. This is really bad."

CHAPTER 58
ADRIK

"THE DRIVE?" Adrik asked Franko the moment he entered the vault hall. Franko walked back and forth quietly with his hands on his hips and tapping his finger every counting second. He looked up at Adrik, eyes wide and confused.

"Right here," Franko said, holding Carden's USB drive in his hand. "You?" Adrik showed him the gray USB drive he had been holding since the Advanced Archives room on the first floor. The HSS had been transferring paper files to drives for five years and arranging them in a new room. The archive scene on the fourth floor had been a mere distraction, a way to get the *original* file. He nodded at the old man in the chair, who snored like he hadn't slept in days.

"Really *deep* sleeper," Franko informed, putting the drive into his pocket. Adrik walked towards the table, putting the drive into the USB port. He hadn't had the time to view the file on the first floor. Guards and HSS members had started to look for Neir's allies minutes ago.

On the computer, the same files that he had seen in *Italy Vampire Massacre* showed up as a list. He pressed the last one he wanted to continue reading. The one that would contain information about the murders of the village.

The Venice Massacre File

Written by Anonymous

Our villages were quiet and united until the day of the massacre. There were a total of three villages together, houses closer to the sea and somewhat far from the city itself. At midnight was when the screams started and fire unraveled. I saw everything unfold from the building I resided in, closest to the villages, and on top of a hill. Rumors spread quickly that night that witches had raided the villages in search of hidden vampires. As a light-blood human myself, I had been friends with most of the residents. Truth be told, there were no hidden vampires in those villages, and if they had been, they were long gone. One of my friends, who was a vampire hunter, had stayed a few days ago and had no actual report. Innocent blood was spilled under the hands of witches.

I have seen magic on my own, and based on the rumors, I could hypothesize that witches were involved. However, from my scientific research and information from hunters, there was no proof as to who is to blame for these immoral acts. Some other humans believe the fire had been caused by a gas leak that later expanded to the houses near-

by. The cause of all the deaths was pronounced as unknown. May they rest in peace.

"*No.*" Adrik stared at the screen, re-reading the written words. *Witches. No proof.* He shook his head, stepping back from the table.

There was nothing. No evidence. No names. No new information. Nothing to help him find the truth. *Nothing* to get revenge for.

"Adrik?" Franko started. "Boss, it's time to go." Adrik closed his eyes for a second, controlling his breathing. He couldn't fail yet. He never failed at anything, much less his own operations. He nodded, eyes wide awake and burning. He took the USB drive from the computer and back inside his coat pocket. "Let's go find Neir."

CHAPTER 59
NEIR

N EIR WAITED FOR Franko and Adrik to find her. She checked the inside of her boot again to see the microchip locator attached to the collar padding; it blinked bright red every second that passed. An idea of Zach.

Briz sat in her cell quietly, back resting against the metal wall. It was then that Neir noticed the bags under her eyes. She usually wore makeup to hide them, but now they were clearly visible and darker. There was a plate next to her that seemed to have been filled and used before. Carden had kept her alive for a reason. Neir guessed that it was maybe to keep her in fear, but she couldn't help but think that Carden was just incapable of killing someone. Her brother might be a maniac, but he couldn't be a killer. After all, he had sent Mondragon to kill her instead of doing it himself. At least it seemed he had a broken piece of heart inside.

The entrance door flew open at once to the sound of a small

bomb exploding by the door. Neir moved back, following in sync with Briz. Smoke half-filled the entire room as footsteps approached the cell doors.

"Neir?" Franko's voice echoed, appearing in front of her cell with Adrik behind him.

"Took you look enough," Neir said, looking from Franko to Adrik, who seemed more expressionless than ever. He walked to her door.

"Wait." She nodded at Briz's door instead. "Get her out first." Adrik headed to Briz's door and worked on his thieving talents. Within seconds, the metal door to Briz's cell was opened. He approached her door next. It was at that second that she looked down at the bloody bandage on his left leg. He'd been hurt, yet the look in his eyes said the opposite. He was in pain from something else.

"Adrik…" Neir started while he unlocked her door.

"We don't have time, Neir," he said, looking at her only a second before her door opened. Neir stepped out, hugging Briz first, who raised her brows at her, then at Franko.

"You're not a—" Franko began, the moment Neir hugged him, "—hugger?"

"Shut up." Neir half-smiled at him. "This is the only hug you'll receive from me, *Fran*." Franko smiled at her.

"Hunters are on the way," Adrik said. He walked out of the hall at once.

"What happened?" Neir asked.

"The files held no information about his mission. He couldn't find anything," Franko explained in a whisper.

"Whatever it is, it seems he won't give up trying to find it."

Neir wasn't sure what else to say.

"But," Franko continued. "This truth belongs to you." He held out a black flash drive in his hand and plugged it into a wire attached to the tablet. "All the files Carden saved. It contains all the information to set you free." Neir grabbed it. She remembered telling Franko about it. A mere guess. Even with Mondragon's contract copy, they wouldn't have believed her. They would have probably accused her of forgery. *Carden has used USB drives to transfer every important document, especially his video camera files, after the SD memory card would get full*. She had told Franko. *It is a habit of his to have everything saved. Must be there.* And he had found it.

"We should walk ahead, though," Franko suggested as he let Briz walk forward first.

"Hello, I'm Franko," he greeted Briz.

"I'm Briz. Neir didn't tell me she had other friends." Neir proceeded behind them, trying to view the files as the voices of Franko and Briz's conversation faded in the background.

)) ◗ ● ● ◖ ((

There were no words in Neir's mind while she walked into the office of the HSS. Hunters and guards tried to stand in her way.

"I'm not here to fight you. I need to see Alaric! Where is he?" She screamed down the hall, pushing the people in her way. "Where is he?" She entered the office, guards reaching out for her.

"Adeline," Neir started. "Where are they?" Adeline's face lit up at the sight of Neir. She had been one of the only people who knew her since she was a child. Since then, Neir has always trusted her.

"In the lobby, making a speech, honey," Adeline replied. Neir nodded, turning around to head out to the hall. The hunters still stood in her way, weapons in their hands and their stances ready for a fight.

"Don't move," one of them said. "I'll shoot you, criminal."

"You will not shoot anybody, Wright." Adeline moved in front of Neir. "Now, make a way to let *her* pass and see her parents." Adeline waited, looking straight at each hunter without flinching. She knew almost every one of them. She held the key to all their personal files. "Don't you forget she is the daughter of your current director. One day she might even be yours."

Wright hesitated, his bulky stature standing in front of the group. "Alright," Wright demanded to the group around him. "Let's clear a path."

"Hey!" one of the other hunters, who Neir guessed was a student, said. "What are you doing? She is a criminal."

"You heard me. Make a way!"

The hunters moved aside, clearing the hall to the path towards the lobby. Adeline walked next to Neir.

"Thank you, Addie," Neir said, as they headed out of the hall. "This is my last chance to show the truth."

"Always, dear," Adeline smiled. "Don't you think I ever forgot you always baked me lunchbox cakes for my birthday."

"I am three years behind now. I didn't forget either," Neir smiled, looking at Adeline.

The entire lobby area was crowded. Neir's parents stood on

the middle platform, fluorescent lights flashed and reflected everywhere from the glass all around them. Craven was nowhere to be seen. Talking and whispers surfaced around the room while Alaric tried to start his speech.

"I won't get there in time," Neir murmured, remembering that Adrik, Franko, and Briz were heading out through one of the emergency exits close by the old Archives room. If the HSS still tried to lock her up, she hoped the bomb Franko had been waiting to use wouldn't cause much damage.

"Give it to me," Adeline said. "I'll make sure it gets to him."

Neir looked at the drive in her hand and nodded, handing Adeline the USB drive. "Please make sure the video in folder three gets played on all televisions around the HSS. They have to see it." Adeline nodded, grabbing the drive and starting to turn to the crowd. "Adeline," Neir said. "Find Lumière du Jour in the 9th arrondissement. Your three cakes will be there waiting." Adeline beamed, glancing at Neir only for a second before heading straight into the mass.

Neir hesitated as she turned around to leave, her arm suddenly pulsing with pain. But she couldn't leave just yet. She had to make sure that the drive got into his father's hands. After all, everything she had done was for her parents to realize the person they were missing. She couldn't leave yet. She wouldn't leave. So she waited to see Adeline hand Alaric the drive, then instructed him to look at the last file. Neir could see Adeline shaking her hands, probably explaining the importance of it. She had been a trusting member of the family for years, there was less than ten percent of likelihood that her parents wouldn't try to listen to her.

Neir waited for a few seconds, watching Alaric attach the USB drive to a computer with Adeline's help. Layla talked to some members of the council down below the stage. The projector and television in the room and hallways were turned on. Voices lowered down to zero. The last video file started playing on the screen. *Everyone will know.*

Carden stood in his room, recording the video with a camera Neir had given him when he turned thirteen. She could tell because he used to always record everything with it. He never let go of that damn camera, he tried to fix it every time if something went wrong.

"Hello, I'm Carden De Van." He smiled, his blue eyes and golden blond hair shining against the light. He must've been sixteen. Weeks before, Neir had been shunned out of the HSS. "I am here recording this video for my family, especially my *hero* of a sister, Neir. This is the day your life will start to go downhill, sister. No one will know. Not even after your death, when I become director of the HSS. But besides you, *sister*, there's someone else standing in my way." Carden walked out of his room. The lights in the HSS flickered in the video. It must've been night when he did it because most of the lights turned off after one in the morning. He also must have at least two accomplices. Signals, stares beyond the camera, and footsteps made Neir believe so.

Surely, Carden couldn't have done it alone. He walked with the camera into Atticus' room, ex-director of the HSS and her dad's best friend. He showed Atticus deep asleep and a glass cup with probably bourbon, on his nightstand. Carden placed the camera right in the stand, close enough to see Atticus' chest expand from his breathing. Then Carden walked to the other side of the bed, grabbed the extra pillow, and moved back to the ex-director's side. Carden's eyes became cold. He didn't even hesitate. He didn't hold back from suffocating Atticus with the pillow. Atticus had been drinking, maybe had gotten weak from it, to push back Carden. But it was no use. Atticus struggled to get hold of himself, his alcoholism, and his breathing. His hand hit the nightstand, shaking and making the camera fall to the floor. Carden's boots still showed him against the bed until he stopped moving, grabbing the camera to show his face one last time. "It's done. But don't you worry, Neir. *You're next.*"

The entire crowd had gotten immensely quiet. Neir turned to look at her parents. Her mom stood there speechless. Her dad had frozen in place. He shook his head as his eyes fell to the floor for a few seconds, then looked up the moment whispers resurfaced. He looked into the crowd, taking his time to finally look at Neir. She looked back at him only for a second. But now, it was time for her to leave.

Neir pushed herself out of the crowd, feeling people's stares surrounding and following her. She disappeared into the left side hallways of the HSS. Everybody who cared at least a fraction of her, she hoped, waited at an exit on the corner of the fourth floor. *Not behind me.*

"Neir!" She could hear Alaric screaming down the hall.

"Neir. Please stop!" Her mother pleaded. *Now* they called for her.

Neir stopped, turning around. Not for them, but for what she had to say. "*Now* you believe. Can you now see that the truth is as real as the marks on my arm?"

"Neir—" Alaric started.

"No. I did everything I had to do to be a good hunter. I did everything, even after Carden burnt the *hunter marks* from my arm that night before I was shunned out. I did everything for my sake. *To survive.*"

Alaric slightly shook his head. Her parents were feet away from her. Was it due to shame? Or was it because they still didn't know her at all?

"You still broke the law, *knowing* the law," Alaric continued. Neir clenched her jaw, not believing that they were still trying to speak against her.

"And you broke *our* trust. What is the *difference*?"

"We believe you now, Neir. We believe you, and we don't hold anything against you. Your wrongs... they don't compare to a fragment of what Carden did."

Neir laughed. "What great timing. Don't you think so?"

"We are so sorry, Neir," Layla said, wiping a tear from her cheek.

Alaric nodded. "I am sorry. I am truly sorry."

"No!" Neir shook her head. "You didn't need proof to believe me. You needed to trust me. You both were my parents, too. But you wanted a great, controlled, responsible child, and you couldn't have it. Carden *failed* you! And you don't get to pretend you didn't *fail* me!" Neir turned, walking a few more steps away from them.

"Neir, please don't leave," her mom pleaded.

"You can stay, Neir," Alaric stated. "You can stay and become a great agent, director if you want to."

"Let's get one thing straight. I will not follow your footsteps." Neir stopped, turning to look at them one last time. "I was here for the truth. Not to make a bond that was never there in the first place."

She walked ahead, about to turn left to the next hallway. But she could still hear her parents' unmoving stance and the sound of Alaric's radio turning on.

"All HSS members, agents, hunters, and guards," Alaric said. The echoes of his voice from each person with a radio sounded around the nearby halls. "By my orders, Neir De Van was not and is no longer a criminal. Her charges have dropped. No one will stop her or look for her. She did nothing wrong. Regarding Carden De Van... he is a dangerous felon. Our main priority is him. Find him and anyone who works with him. My son will be condemned so that my daughter can be free."

The radio and noises had stopped. Only for a microsecond, everything, including Neir's heartbeat, had stopped. But even she knew, it was too late for her footsteps to do so.

PART NINETEEN

SILVER LINING

CHAPTER 60
THE MIND

TRUST, TIME, AND TRUTH were what mattered most to Adrik. He glanced at Franko, then checked over the edge of the wall for Neir until he saw her coming down the hall.

"Are you finished?" he asked Franko, who stood behind him with Briz, trying to open the emergency door. Franko looked back at him.

"Nearly." He raised his brows. "This tablet isn't really helping me get the password."

"Did you try *metal*?" Briz suggested. "Anything that Neir had said before?"

"Tried that already."

Adrik looked at Franko. "Try again."

"That won't be necessary," Neir said, approaching them. She looked tired, her wavy, crimped hair becoming messier. Adrik had been too distracted to fully look at her. The scars on her face and bruises on her hands. Behind him, the panel by the door turned green. The emergency door slowly swung open in sync with the one at the end of the white secured hall, similar to the actual HSS entrance. "Alaric, let us go. I am free."

"That is good news. Congrats!" Franko said.

"Thank you, but not yet. Not until we are out of here."

"No need to say less." Franko smiled, entering the hall quickly. Briz walked behind him. Neir looked at them, turning one last time to look at the metal halls behind her.

Adrik bent down, getting the items that stood behind him. "This belongs to you." He held out Neir's green bow and arrows. "I got them on my way down from the Advanced Archives."

Neir half-smiled at him, looking at the weapons like a treasure. She took them, rubbing her left arm for a second and putting her bow back where it belonged. "I can't believe I'm saying this, and if you tell anyone I'll kill you... But thank you, Adrik. For *everything*."

"Not yet, Neir. Not until we are out of here," he said. "And that's what allies do." He headed out to the white hall and back to the Catacombs of Paris.

The air felt fresher out in the catacombs. Adrik felt himself breathe more easily than before. There were times he had forgotten he was underground instead of above, where the oxygen was held stagnant. He walked in front of Neir as she walked Franko through the maze tunnels.

Minutes passed by while they tried to get close to the exit of Pont d'Iéna, a rocky door underneath a bridge over the River Seine and across the Eiffel Tower.

"Are we almost there yet?" Franko coughed, seeming suddenly out of breath. He stumbled, holding himself from the rocky wall and composing himself before anybody else noticed.

"Almost..." Neir responded, continuing to walk straight. "One more left and right, then down that hall you'll see a white colored panel."

"Stop," Adrik said, stopping in his tracks the moment he heard a water stream and footsteps moving that were not theirs. Neir looked around as well, ready to grab her bow. "Go ahead. We will be right behind you." He murmured to Franko, signaling him and Briz to get to the end of the tunnel. Franko nodded, letting Briz go ahead first, disappearing around the corner of the hall.

"The Society let us go. It can't be them." Neir shook her head. "But I know damn well Carden won't give up on revenge."

"Neither do we," Adrik said, looking behind Neir just as she looked behind him.

"Or his accomplices."

One last fight. Adrik wanted to say. But there was never one last fight in his plan. Never a timer that stopped. Always a never-ending scheme. And he had to admit the chances of ever freezing in time were less than negative infinity itself. He felt the blood rushing to his face as he passed Neir and fought the hunter behind her. His sword in hand felt weightless but his leg did not. So he put more pressure on making sure his hand drove the sword close to his opponent's leg, causing him to fall in pain. Behind him, Neir used her bow. She hit the hunter a few times until he fell too.

Adrik could hear more footsteps running through the hidden halls. Neir stood before the hunter; her eyes filled with anger and rage. Maybe for herself, maybe for her family, or her father's best friend.

"We don't have the time, Neir," Adrik said. "Let's go." She nodded.

They ran quickly to the end of the hall, where Franko and Briz waited. More hunters headed their way, and Franko's tapping leg wasn't helping. Neir placed her hand over the panel. It glowed green to identify her as an official HSS hunter.

"Any time now," Franko said. The door would only open if no one from the outside was watching or in view of the hidden door, which defeated the purpose of an emergency door. Five seconds passed by when the door swung open. They ran outside as quickly as possible. Two seconds later, the hunters would've grabbed hold of them.

"To the Eiffel Tower," Neir instructed. "Hurry. They can still be looking for us."

Still past midnight, and people walked around the bridge and the parks of the Eiffel Tower. Adrik inspected around, making sure that no one fell out of place or that they didn't attract attention as they headed into the closed construction site under the tower. It sparkled yellow and blue all over the city, making Neir's hair visible golden, Briz's eye bags darker, and Franko's tired smile disturbing. Yet none of them spoke, not after walking up the stairs to the second floor or taking the elevator up to the top. Adrik held his breath for most of the ride, concentrating on the city before him. A city that, just like Arkadia, was surrounded by the secrets of a country. He felt the fresh air relieving the second the elevator door opened.

"How did it go?" Zach greeted them, eyebrows raised with his arms up, then flopping at seeing everybody coming out in a sour mood.

"We have plenty of time to talk about it, Z," Neir responded. "But right now, can you please take Briz to the police station?"

Adrik walked past them, heading to the front of the tower. Franko walked around, looking in every direction with a set of *This is great* or *This is amazing*. His voice faded in the light of Adrik's eyes. Over the city he couldn't control, he felt the darkness hit, the rage, the anger, the slight sadness, and the pain. He felt it all and let it stay inside his head. And it would stay there until it drove him insane. Until he released his vengeance. Until he found the truth.

Franko now stood next to him, quietly watching the blinding lights. Neir walked over to his other side, the rose smell of her hair in the air.

"So much for plan A," she said.

"If you think I can't do worse, you haven't seen anything yet," Adrik responded. "This is not the way we go down. Not yet."

"What is Plan Z, then, boss?" Franko asked.

There was only one way Adrik could've found it all. An easy way out that he had known since the beginning, he stepped into Lunar Castle as a guard. He didn't want to ask for it. He wanted to do it himself. But now he had no choice. No trust. No time. And no truth.

"Finding *Clara De Rose*."

Only someone could properly hold the answers to Adrik's

mission. The eidetic holder of memories. Only her ability to look at others' memories would set the truth free. Because what is not real other than people's unaltered memories? They held history, feeling, and the truth of life. Whether she wanted to be found or not. Adrik had to be the one to do so.

TO BE CONTINUED...

ACKNOWLEDGEMENTS

When I began the Illumiverse, my plan was to only write a trilogy with The Illuminators. However, this story idea expanded the Illuminator world and the series. This spin-off completely changes the plot of what happens to the main characters. I wanted to make three points of view to briefly show each character and their story, considering that we get to know people from Clara's memory in The Illuminators.

I truly hope that you enjoy Adrik's story and the people he gets close to for his deals and plans. Writing in third person was different for me, but I enjoyed it. I realized that my writing becomes better and better with each project, therefore, I am excited for everyone to see what changes in my writing and the characters.

Not a lot of people read this story, but I do want to say thank you to my friend, Jesi, for her continuous support. I would like to thank my siblings, especially my younger sister, who watched me format and write this book. My older brother, who was somewhat an inspiration for Adrik with his crazy quotes, and my younger brother, who read a few chapters with me for editing motivation.

Thank you to all of you, and I hope you enjoy this spin-off!

FREQUENTLY ASKED QUESTIONS

1. What inspired me to be a writer?

Like I'm sure every other writer has said, I began to write because I loved reading. I loved going to the school library to check out books because my parents wouldn't let me buy actual copies at the time. Until I managed to persuade them that reading was a valuable habit. I started reading more and writing diaries. Till then writing almost daily became a habit.

2. When did my writing journey start?

My writing journey started when I wrote in my diary every day. To be more specific I liked movies and shows like Twilight and The Vampire Diaries. I might've begun writing in diaries, either due to TVD or after watching The Adventures of Sharkboy and Lavagirl. The mix between supernaturals, magic, and dreams were topics that interested me.

3. How did Three Silver Rings come to be?

The idea of writing this book did not spark until I finished editing The Illuminators. I wanted to have another plot and characters in Clara's life that actually changed it for good. I wrote this story with more action compared to TI, which is one of the reasons I enjoyed re-reading it. Small spoilers... this series will continue to become better and better. There's going to be so many plot twists and shocking events.

4. Any other hobbies besides writing?

Other hobbies that I do are playing piano, photography, editing, and making videos. Playing piano interested me since I was younger, but I didn't fully play songs or actually bought a keyboard until I listened to the Twilight soundtrack by Carter Burwell.

5.   What makes this story unique?

Dichotomy makes this story unique. This series is a battle between good and bad or light and darkness. I believe readers will be able to connect with the experiences of these characters and find their own path to light. Unlike other stories, I want the Illumiverse series to send a message to all the people that anything in the universe is possible. That everything can be accomplished with the mind, heart, and soul. If you search the light, you will find it.

THREE SILVER RINGS PLAYLIST

Enemy - Imagine Dragons, JID

Bones - Imagine Dragons

Trained to Kill - Andrew Britton, Andrew Skeet, David Goldsmith

Hit The Road Jack - 2WEI, Jon, Lady Bri

Blood // Water - grandson

Everything Black - Unlike Pluto, Mike Taylor

Dead to Me - Lox Chatterbox

Play with Fire - Sam Tinnesz, Yacht Money

Trail of Revenge - Andrew Britton, Andrew Skeet, David Goldsmith

Rebel - OTR, LOWES

Big Bad City - Evalyn

Twisted - MISSIO

Warriors - 2WEI, Edda Hayes

Sociopath - StayLoose, Bryce Fox

Gasoline - Halsey

All the Lines - Fleurie

I Don't Believe in Satan - Aron Wright

Dangerous Game - Klergy, BEGINNERS

Where Your Secrets Hide - Klergy, Katie Garfield

World on Fire - Klergy

Redemption - David O'Dowda

Nightcrawler (instrumental) - Travis Scott

Intro (Infected) - Sickick

No Time to Die - Billie Eilish

Walk Through Fire - Zayde Wolf, Ruelle

Okay - Chase Atlantic

Beggin' - Maneskin

Way Down We Go - KALEO

Silver Lining - Hurts

Guadalupe Gonzalez is a Texas-based author of YA fantasy and fiction novels. She graduated in 2022 with an Associate's of Life Sciences and in 2025 with a Bachelor of Science in Forensic Chemistry (including a minor in Forensic Science). After graduation, the goal is to publish more books and pursue a forensic chemistry career. She doesn't plan to stop writing and publishing stories anytime soon.

STAY CONNECTED WITH LU ON:

Website: www.illumiverse.store

Instagram: instagram.com/lugonzalezauthor

Youtube: www.youtube.com/@lu.theauthor

www.ingramcontent.com/pod-product-compliance
Lightning Source LLC
Chambersburg PA
CBHW050612110726
47899CB00001B/85